KERI ARTHUR

Deadly Vows

A LIZZIE GRACE NOVEL

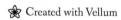

With thanks to:

The Lulus
Indigo Chick Designs
Hot Tree Editing
Debbie from DP+
Robyn E.
The lovely ladies from Central Vic Writers
Lori from Cover Reveal Designs for the amazing cover

CHAPTER ONE

"The point of a muting spell is to actually mute your output, not amplify it."

Monty's voice was dry, and I scowled at him. He was the resident witch for the Faelan Reservation—a position that theoretically meant he was the government's mouthpiece and enforcer, but in reality he did little more than provide magical assistance to the reservation's rangers, if and when needed. He was also my cousin, and the only relative I had any contact with, let alone actually liked.

"I *am* trying—"

"Then try harder." Amusement creased the corners of his silvery eyes. "Right now, blind Freddy could see the ebb and flow of your magic."

"It's not like I have a lot of the goddamn stuff—"

"If we were just talking about personal magic, that might be true. But we're not, are we?"

No, we weren't, thanks to the presence of wild magic. My mother had unknowingly been pregnant with me when she'd been sent to restrain an emerging wellspring, and the energy that had almost killed her should certainly have destroyed me. Instead, it had somehow fused to my DNA, giving me a deep connection to the wilder forces of this world—though it was a connection no one, least of all me, had been aware of until I'd come into this reservation less than a year ago.

I sucked in a frustrated breath and tried to envision the shield Monty was attempting to teach me. Like any witch, I'd been taught the basics of controlling magical output at school, but Belle—who wasn't only my best friend and a fellow witch, but also my familiar—and I had never gone beyond that. We'd run from Canberra, my parents, and my husband when we were barely sixteen, and had generally avoided witches ever since.

But basic wasn't going to cut it now. Not when Clayton Marlowe—the bastard I'd been forced to marry—was on his way here to claim his errant bride and no doubt take what he'd been denied on our wedding night. We had no idea when or how he'd arrive; we only knew the looming confrontation would *not* be pleasant. And not only because our escape had made an utter fool of him, but because Belle had placed an anti-erection spell on him, thereby emasculating him.

"Start again," Monty added. "And this time, say the spell out loud so I can check your sequencing."

I did so. The air shimmered as power rose in response, and the glittering threads of magic quickly formed a shield that I then attempted to draw back inside.

This time, the damn thing failed the instant it touched my skin.

I growled in frustration. "What the *hell* am I doing wrong?"

"I honestly don't know."

He picked up his coffee and took a contemplative sip.

We were sitting on the floor in the middle of his sparsely furnished living room. The orange menace that was his cat —and familiar—watched from the sofa, a mix of disdain and amusement on his furry features. Eamon and I had something of a love/hate relationship—I hated him, and he loved attacking me. I daresay the only reason he hadn't launched his deadly little claws my way today was because Monty was in the room.

Outside, the wind howled and rain drummed across the tin roof, a sound I normally found comforting. This afternoon, it set my teeth on edge, if only because it held echoes of the personal storm I sensed coming my way.

I took another of those deep breaths that did absolutely nothing to control the uneasy churning in my gut, and then picked up my coffee. It needed a shot or two of whiskey to make it more palatable, and while I had no doubt Monty would provide it if asked, I did have to drive home. I might be dating the reservation's head ranger, but he wasn't the type to look the other way if he caught me doing the wrong thing.

I took a sip and then said, "Do you think the wild magic is the problem here?"

He hesitated. "It's not entwining itself through the actual spell threads, but it may well be that it's somehow disrupting your ability to draw the spell into your body. It shouldn't, but—"

"The wild magic does a lot of things it shouldn't in this reservation."

"And that's problematic in this particular case."

Because the one thing we desperately needed to do was conceal my connection to that magic. Clayton had to believe I was still the underpowered, inconsequential witch who had escaped his clutches nearly thirteen years ago. If he believed me to be anything else—if he saw the wild magic within me—there would be absolutely no escape from him.

While he was powerful enough in his own right, our marriage had given him a direct connection to my parents, who were arguably the most powerful couple currently working within the hallowed halls of Canberra's High Witch Council. Any child conceived between us would—even with my lower-class magical status—naturally be treated with greater deference.

But if he saw the wild magic?

Not only would I be placed under a microscope in order to understand how it had happened, I'd be treated as nothing more than a baby-making machine in the hope that at least one child would be similarly gifted. I didn't want that outcome for *me,* let alone any daughter of mine.

Odd that you mention a daughter rather than a son. Belle's thought whispered into my mind, her mental tone sleepy enough to suggest she'd been taking an afternoon nap. While she was telepathic, I actually wasn't. The ability to share thoughts as easily as speaking out loud was one of the many benefits that came with her being my familiar. *It's not like he'd be treated as any less of a science experiment.*

Yes, but I've just got an inner feeling my firstborn will be a daughter. It certainly wasn't the first time the certainty of a daughter had risen, though usually it rose in conjunction with the desire for a more permanent relationship with Aiden, and was swiftly followed by the acknowledgement that *that* would never happen. When it came to witches and werewolves, we were a fun time, not a long time. The fact that my relationship with Aiden had lasted over five months now was something of a miracle.

I hope my frustration wasn't responsible for waking you.

No, I had the alarm set. Kash and I are heading down to some fancy new restaurant his mate is opening in Argyle tonight.

I thought you'd stopped dating Kash because you were getting bad vibes about his interest in your grans books?

I did, but he's no longer working on the books and he keeps flinging interesting enticements my way. Her amusement echoed down the mental lines. *Besides, the man is good in bed, and it's not like I'm getting a lot of action elsewhere at the moment.*

Only because she wasn't trying all that hard. Hell, she was just over six feet tall, with ebony skin, long black hair, eyes as bright as polished silver, and a build that was Amazonian. To say she attracted adoring male gazes wherever she went was something of an understatement.

"I get the feeling," Monty said, "that your attention is elsewhere."

I blinked and refocused on him. "Sorry, Belle was chatting to me."

"I don't suppose she came up with a solution to our current problem, did she?"

"No—"

"Then tell her to shut the hell up, because we need to pin this spell down." He paused. "Be polite, of course. I don't want my future wife getting annoyed with me."

Belle's snort echoed so loudly down the mental lines that I winced. *He is persistent, isn't he?*

You've only yourself to blame. You did go to that premiere with him.

And I have absolutely no regrets—it was a brilliant night, and he was, for once, most charming company. Shame he reverted to his usual annoying self the next day.

"Do I want to know what she's currently saying?" he asked, amusement twitching his lips.

Say anything, and you die, Belle said.

I grinned and risked death. "She called you extremely annoying, but I reckon if you were to get premiere tickets for the latest incarnation of *Evita*, she'll get over that opinion real quick."

I'd normally threaten to kill you right now, but you speak nothing but the truth.

Of course I did. I was privy to her thoughts, after all, and knew she liked Monty far more than she was willing to admit.

"I expect dinner to be included in the deal, given how hard those tickets are to get," Monty said.

If he gets tickets to the premiere, dinner will be on me. Fair's fair, even when it comes to Monty.

I passed this on and he grinned. "Challenge accepted. Now, can we get back to the business at hand? Because, seriously, we have no idea how long we actually have before Clayton appears, and if it's tomorrow, you're in trouble."

I was in trouble anyway, and we all knew it—especially if my father decided to accompany Clayton. We'd had no word that he'd left Canberra, but that didn't mean anything. Not when he had the means and the power to stop any unwanted attention.

I tried the spell again. The result was exactly the same.

Perhaps, Belle said, *the problem is the teaching method.*

Meaning Monty?

Her laugh echoed through my thoughts. *No. I meant the formality of the spell. What you're both forgetting is that we've spent the last twelve years reorganizing various spells to suit ourselves. Why would this be any different?*

I repeated her comment for Monty's sake, and his

eyebrows rose. "You know, that's a possibility I hadn't considered. And while I don't usually condone stuffing about with the semantics of spells, it's definitely worth trying in this case."

Any other suggestions, Belle?

She hesitated. *What you're trying to do is cloak the wild magic's output by putting an internal barrier between it, your own natural magic, and the world in general. So perhaps imagine that from the get-go rather than trying to drag the shield inside after formation.*

I took another useless deep breath and then began the spell yet again; this time, rather than imagining a shield, I created a wispy, silvery curtain that filtered down through the inner me, forming a barrier that covered me from the top of my head to the very bottom of my feet, and through which only my natural magic was visible. I tied off the end of the spell very carefully, using the wild magic deep within as a power source so that it didn't draw too much on my own strength, and then activated it.

Monty sucked in a deep breath. "Whatever the fuck you just did, it totally worked."

Relief surged so fiercely that it left me shaking. I licked my lips, trying to keep calm, and then said, "Is there any magical output at all?"

"There's a faint bleed of your natural magic, but that's it. How long do you think you'll be able to sustain it?"

"I don't know." I wrinkled my nose. "What's the usual time span for these sorts of spells?"

"Generally, twelve to fifteen hours, depending on the strength of the practitioner and how long they've been shielding. It gets easier the longer you do it."

"Yours isn't on full time, though."

"It's always partially on—I generally only fully mute

when I'm in the presence of unknown witches. I also disconnect when I'm sleeping."

You can't risk partial coverage, Belle commented. *Not when we haven't a clue how or when the bastard will make his grand appearance.*

Agreed. I pushed upright and walked around the room. Eamon took a half-hearted swipe at me as I passed his sofa. "Is the spell covering movement? Is there any accidental leakage?"

"None. It's bloody brilliant." He took another sip of coffee, his eyes slightly narrowed as he continued to study me. "I guess the next question is, how easy will it be to drop if you do need to use the wild magic? Or did you weave in an exception to allow that?"

"I didn't, but I could easily enough. I might just see how long this spell lasts first, though."

He nodded. "Once you're used to its presence, you can start honing the technique and adding exceptions."

And then pray like hell that it works in the presence of someone as powerful as Clayton, Belle said.

If it doesn't, then the game is over before it starts. And *that* was something I certainly didn't want to think about right now. *Hadn't you better go get glammed up for your date?*

Just about to. Oh, and don't forget to stop at the bottle shop on the way home.

That's the one thing I won't forget. Not when we'd used the last of the Glenfiddich in the Irish coffees we'd made last night—a fact that had horrified Ashworth, the Regional Witch Association representative who'd come here to investigate a murder and had not only decided to stay, but was now the closest thing to a grandfather I had. His horror over the 'waste' of such fine whiskey didn't stop him and Eli—his husband, and a retired RWA witch—from partaking in quite a few, however.

I picked up my cup and drank the remainder of the coffee. "Are you going out tonight?"

Monty nodded. "Got an invite to that new restaurant that's opening in Argyle."

I gave him a long look. "Why do I suspect it isn't a coincidence that you and Belle are going to the same event?"

"Because you're always reading a devious intent behind any action I might take when it comes to her. And while it generally *is* the case, this time I was actually invited out by a rather lovely young woman."

I raised my eyebrows. "And do I know this paragon?"

"Probably not, as she's only new in town. I literally ran into her just over a week ago at the supermarket."

"And as a thank-you, she invited you to an exclusive evening?"

My disbelief was evident, and he grinned. "I think it safe to say she was bowled over by my charm."

I snorted. "I take it you've already been out with her?"

He nodded. "Her brother is the restaurant's owner, and she came up from Melbourne for a few weeks to help out."

"So, what was she doing in Castle Rock?"

"She wasn't. I was down there." He grimaced. "I'd been investigating the wedding reception murder at the Lake House and—"

"Murder?" I cut in. "I thought the groom had had a heart attack?"

"That's what his poor bride initially thought, but the ambulance crew discovered otherwise and called Aiden."

"I take it an autopsy has been performed?"

He nodded. "It revealed he'd lost all his blood and his heart was missing."

I blinked. "How?"

"Via a cut under his ribs, apparently."

"How big was the damn cut?"

"Tiny."

"Then how—"

"We have no idea," he cut in. "If it happens again, I've suggested they bring you in. You might be able to pull something useful from the poor sod's memories."

"Only if his death is fresh."

The brain didn't die the minute the heart stopped—generally, there was up to a six-minute window of brain viability in which memories could be read. After that, deterioration began. But even within that window there were some levels of memory that could be affected, particularly short term. In the past, reading the minds of the dead had provided vital clues about the killer, though it wasn't without cost or dangers. There were plenty of stories around about psychics being ensnared by death while psychically connected to the mind of another, and it wasn't something I wanted to risk too often.

"Fresh or not," Monty said, "your other psychic senses might pick up something Aiden and I missed."

I couldn't help smiling. "Once upon a time, you would never have admitted my psi skills were useful."

"Yeah, but I was young and dumb back then."

My smile grew. "So, do you think we're dealing with some sort of vampire?"

He hesitated. "The typical vampire bite mark was absent, but the whole 'no blood' thing does tend to indicate a bloodsucker of some kind."

"The kind that apparently also has a liking for hearts." I shuddered at the thought. "At least that should narrow down the search parameters."

"One would think so, but my research has so far revealed a surprising number of supernatural beasties that like their blood with a bit of human heart on the side."

"Then let's hope it's nothing more than a top-up feeding and the creature behind it has long gone."

Monty snorted as he climbed to his feet. He was tall and well-built, with bright silver eyes and short crimson hair that gleamed like dark fire. "In this reservation? Unlikely."

Which was a sad but true statement, thanks to the fact the reservation's largest wellspring had been left unguarded for entirely too long. While wellsprings—and the wild magic that emanated from them—were neither good nor bad, an unprotected one would always draw evil. The larger wellspring might now be fully protected, but the waves of its power would still be echoing through the darker places of this world. It could be years before the reservation stopped being the spirit world's number-one vacation spot.

I followed Monty into the kitchen and dumped my cup in the sink. "I'd better get going so you can get spruced up for your date."

"You're not going?" he said, surprise evident in his voice. "I thought Aiden, as head ranger, would be invited for sure. Most of the local dignitaries are going to be there."

"He was, but he's working the late shift tonight."

Monty grinned. "In other words, he didn't want to go hobnobbing. He just wanted alone time with his girl."

"A truth I cannot deny." I rose on my tiptoes and kissed his cheek. "I'll see you tomorrow."

He nodded. "I might even bring Bree with me—she has yet to taste the delights that are your cakes."

I raised my eyebrows. "This wouldn't be another ploy, would it?"

He slapped a hand against his chest. "I am once again mortified that you think me capable of such deviousness."

"This from the man who readily admitted to such deviousness only a few minutes ago."

"Ah, damn, so I did." Amusement danced through his expression. "Belle might be my foretold future wife, but I can't see the point of moping about until she comes around. A man has wants and needs, you know."

"And *I* do not want or need to know about them, thank you very much."

I spun around and headed down the hall to grab my coat. It hadn't been raining when I'd left the café, so I'd grabbed the shorter, less waterproof one, meaning I'd no doubt be soaked by the time I got to our new SUV—a replacement for the one an Empusae had blown up, which itself had been a replacement for the wagon destroyed by a soucouyant. Demons seemed to have something of a vendetta against our vehicles.

Monty opened the front door and peered out into the stormy afternoon. "I'd offer the use of an umbrella, but it'd be pretty useless against that wind. I do have a Driza-Bone, if you want to borrow that."

I hesitated, and then shook my head. "You'll need it for tonight."

"I do have more than one coat in my wardrobe." His tone was dry. "And if you go out there and catch a cold, Belle would not be pleased with me."

"Fine," I said, amused. "I'll borrow the coat."

He disappeared briefly into the other room to get it. Once I'd put the thing on and rolled up the sleeves, I grabbed my keys, slung my bag over my shoulder, and then dashed out. The wind hit like a sledgehammer, throwing me sideways for several steps before I caught my balance. The rain sheeted down so heavily that it was almost impossible to see the SUV—which, given it was bright orange, was something of a feat. I staggered toward it, one arm raised in a vague effort to stop at least some of the rain hitting my face.

Just for an instant, a shadow moved near the SUV—a shadow that was big and powerful. I stopped, my heart leaping into my throat, and my fear so fierce I had to clench my hands against the instinctive need to create a repelling spell.

It wasn't Clayton. It couldn't be.

He wouldn't be out here in the storm—discomfort was *not* his thing.

For several seconds, neither of us moved. Me because fear had all but frozen me, and the stranger because he was peering into the SUV through the passenger window.

I licked my lips, pushed away the gathering panic, and somehow said, "Oi—what are you doing?"

The stranger's gaze jerked toward me; his features were a little blurred thanks to the sheer force of the rain, but that was enough. The build might be the same, but that blur confirmed it *wasn't* Clayton. The face was too angular, and his nose too long and sharp. It might have been more than twelve years since I'd last seen him, but the overall structure of his face wouldn't have changed *that* much.

The relief that surged was so damn strong that for an instant, my knees went to water. The stranger took advantage of my brief inability to move and bolted down the street.

I took a deep, shuddery breath and forced my feet on. But as I clicked the SUV's remote and the lights flashed in response, unease prickled up my spine. I paused, one hand on the door handle as I studied the rain-swept street. There was nothing to see aside from a few cars parked further down. Lights were on in several of the nearby houses, but there was no one else crazy enough to be out in weather this bad. The air was crisp and cool, and held nothing other than the scent of rain—not that I'd smell anything or anyone else if they were far enough away or downwind of me.

So why did it suddenly feel like I was no longer alone? Why did it feel like I was being watched, and that my watcher was decidedly unfriendly?

Nerves? Or a premonition?

I scanned the street again, then tugged the door open and clambered into the SUV's relatively warm confines. After locking all the doors, I started the vehicle, my hands shaking as I shoved it into gear and spun away from the curb.

The feeling of being watched persisted, but there were no other cars on the road, and no one following me.

It was nerves. Just nerves.

A result of seeing the stranger checking out my car, perhaps.

Or perhaps not, an inner voice whispered.

I shivered and, after picking up our alcohol supplies, drove home. I hung Monty's dripping coat on a hook to dry, then pushed open the door that divided the store and laundry areas from the café and headed upstairs to our flat.

Belle stepped out of the bathroom, a towel wrapped around her hair. "Are you okay? I've been getting the weirdest vibes from you for the last twenty minutes or so."

I grimaced. "I think all the preparations we're taking to combat Clayton are finally getting to me—I saw a stranger checking out the SUV and basically had a panic attack."

She frowned. "Why was he checking out the SUV?"

I shrugged and placed the whiskey on the counter of what passed as the kitchen up here. Like the living area beyond it, it was tiny, holding little more than a microwave, a kettle, and a coffee machine. We didn't really care, given the two bedrooms and the bathroom were large for a flat this size. Besides, if we had more than two guests—all that would fit on the sofa—we simply migrated downstairs to the café.

"I suspect he was looking for sellable items. Aiden did mention a few days ago that there'd been a rash of car break-ins lately."

She crossed her arms and leaned against the doorframe. "And did he break in?"

"He didn't get the chance—and he bolted the minute I called out."

"All of which doesn't really explain the uneasy vibes."

I wrinkled my nose. "As I said, it was just nerves. Nothing to worry about."

She snorted. "Yeah, trusting that statement. You want me to make you a loaded coffee to calm said nerves?"

I smiled. "If I have too many more of those, I'll be well on my way to becoming a lush. What time is Kash picking you up?"

She glanced at her watch. "In twenty minutes."

"Then you'd better get ready. I'll head downstairs and finish the prep for tomorrow."

She nodded and continued on into her bedroom. Once I'd changed out of my wet jeans and shoes, I went down-stairs and spent the next couple of hours baking slices and finishing off the veg and salad prep. By the time I'd finished, it was close to eight and my stomach was rumbling a loud reminder that it hadn't yet been fed. I made myself a steak sandwich, grabbed a piece of the freshly made chocolate-

and-salted-caramel brownie for dessert, and then headed upstairs to catch up on the news.

My phone rang around nine; the tone told me it was Aiden. I hit the answer button and said, "Hey handsome, how's your night going?"

"It was perfectly fine until a few minutes ago."

"What's happened?" I asked, even though it wasn't exactly hard to guess.

"It would appear the vamp with a taste for the newly married has struck again." His voice was heavy. "And this time, he's killed them both."

CHAPTER TWO

"Shit." I rubbed my eyes with my free hand. "Do you want me there to attempt a reading?"

"Yes. I know it takes a toll on you, but it might be the fastest way to track down the thing doing this." He hesitated. "Belle's at that restaurant opening in Argyle—will that be a problem?"

"It wouldn't be the first time we've done a long-distance connection, but there's little point in worrying about it until we know if it's worth trying. Where are you?"

"I'm at the station—the call has only just come in. I'll pick you up in a couple of minutes."

"Okay."

I hung up and ran downstairs to the reading room. The spells protecting the room shimmered briefly as I entered, a visible indication that they were active and working. Though relatively small, this room was probably one of the safest places in Victoria when it came to dealing with any sort of magic or occult entities. While the building as a whole was surrounded by spells that guarded us against all manner of things—from preventing anyone intending us harm entering the café, to protecting us against a wide variety of supernatural nasties—there were a whole range of additional measures *within* this room. No spirit or demon was getting in here, even if it somehow broke through the main spells.

I opened one of the storage compartments hidden behind the bookcase and grabbed the backpack we now held 'at the ready' for situations like this. It not only contained my silver knife—fully sheathed and tied securely into the pack so there was no chance of Aiden or any other werewolf touching it—but also a selection of potions, amulets, and holy water, which gave us basic coverage for all manner of nasties. Combined with the multi-twined copper and leather charm around my neck—which was probably the most powerful item I'd ever created, and one I'd duplicated for both Aiden and Belle—I should be well protected.

I only wished it were that easy to protect myself from Clayton.

I shoved the thought back into its box, grabbed my coat and keys, and then headed out into the rain-swept night, huddling under the overhanging veranda for protection as I waited for Aiden.

Once again, the feeling of being watched stirred.

I clenched my fingers against the repelling spell that pressed against my fingertips, a little alarmed by the automatic nature of it. Though it was personal magic rather than wild, it nevertheless shouldn't have happened. Spells had to be spoken—they didn't just appear as and when needed. But maybe this was another example of the wild magic changing the rules when it came to what I could and couldn't do.

I studied the street warily. While chatter and music

came from Subway down the road, there was no one on the street and few cars driving by. I had no sense of anyone hiding in the shadows, and there was no caress of magic to indicate a witch might be near. Which, if they were shielding, was not unexpected.

And yet...

My gaze rose to the rooftops of the buildings opposite. It wouldn't be the first time a foe had hidden up there, waiting for the right moment to strike. But I still couldn't imagine Clayton doing so—not on a night as hideous as this. Besides, he wasn't the type to stalk his prey. He'd strike fast and hard, as he had with the whole marriage thing—there'd been no more than a week between my father and Clayton agreeing on 'the deal' and the marriage contracts being signed. Aside from the priest who'd performed the ceremony, the only witnesses had been my parents. It was little wonder that few in Canberra even knew about it—the documents had been sealed, and Clayton had apparently been carrying on as any single man would—well, aside from his apparent inability to get an erection, that was.

Lights swept around the corner, and I once again thrust the worry from my mind. There was nothing else I could do until either my watcher showed his or her hand or they got close enough for Belle to raid their minds. Although given how thoroughly she'd stormed into Clayton's, making him utterly incapable of any movement or even thought the night she'd rescued me from his clutches, it's possible my watcher would wearing the latest electronic protection against telepathic intrusion. Clayton certainly would be.

Aiden's blue truck pulled up next to the curb. As I walked over, he leaned across the front seat and opened the door. The cabin's pale light silvered his dark blond hair and deepened the shadows in his blue eyes. While most

Australian wolf packs were amber-eyed and either brown, red, or black in color, the O'Connors were the more rare gray wolves.

I shoved the backpack into the foot well and then climbed in. His warm, musky scent teased the air, and I flared my nostrils, drawing the delightful aroma in as I leaned across and dropped a kiss on his cheek. "Where did the murders happen?"

"At a small B&B on Hunter Street."

Which wasn't a street I knew. I grabbed my seat belt and clipped it on as he accelerated away from the curb. "Who reported them?"

"The owner." There was something in his expression that had wariness rising. "Her name is Lacy Marin, and she's a good friend of my mother's."

I couldn't help my snort. "Meaning I should expect a mix of attitude and frostiness being flung my way."

His mother—Karleen Jayne O'Connor—had certainly made no secret of her disapproval of me, nor her determination to end our relationship. I was both human *and* a witch, and as such would never be a suitable match for her son. The longer Aiden and I were together, the more likely it became she'd do something more concrete to split us up. She'd already threatened to place a wolf embargo on our café, but if she'd been paying any real attention to our business of late, she'd know that wouldn't actually close us. It *would* severely dent our profit margin, however.

"She'll be polite." His voice was flat. "She won't dare be anything else in my presence."

Which was the exact tactic his mother had taken, and oh boy, the minute he'd stepped away, the alpha bitch had come to the fore. Still, in this particular case, it was unlikely

Lacy would throw too much attitude my way; not when there were two dead bodies in her B&B.

It turned out Hunter Street was only six streets away, so it didn't take us long to get there. Aiden cut the siren and stopped in front of a white weatherboard miner's cottage. As the red-and-blue lights swept across the shadows of the night, a small woman wearing a bright red raincoat and matching gumboots came out of the more palatial house on the opposite side of the road and strode toward us.

"Wait here." Aiden climbed out and met Lacy Marin at the front of his truck.

She took a set of keys out of her pocket and handed them to him. "I locked the doors once I'd reported the murders."

Her voice carried easily, despite the heavy drumming of rain on the truck's roof. Either she was shouting or my hearing was, for some weird reason, suddenly sharper.

Aiden nodded. "Jaz should be here in fifteen minutes to get your statement. In the meantime, you'd better get out of this rain."

She nodded and turned around, her gaze briefly meeting mine. Though her expression gave little away, contempt was very evident in the glint of her golden eyes.

My sight, I noted somewhat uneasily, had also sharpened. Either that, or my imagination was running away with me yet again.

As Lacy Marin strode away, Aiden moved around to grab his kit out of the back of his truck, then opened the passenger door and helped me out. Rain blasted into my face and ran down the back of my neck; I shivered, shoved my hands into my pockets in a vague effort to keep them warm, and quickly followed him through the picket gate and down the stone stairs. The old cottage was well-kept and pretty typical in style for its era: a red tin roof, sash windows on either side of the red front door, and a wide veranda that did at least offer some protection from the worst of the weather.

I ran a hand down my face to get rid of the moisture and studied the building with my 'other' senses. There was no immediate sensation of evil and nothing to suggest that souls lingered inside, which meant these deaths were ordained.

"Anything?" Aiden asked softly.

I shook my head. "If we are dealing with some sort of supernatural entity, then they didn't come through this door —there's no resonance."

"It didn't. Lacy said the main bedroom is an extension at the rear, with double doors leading out to the hot tub and patio. They were open when she arrived."

He handed me a set of gloves and shoe protectors; I leaned against the wall to put them on. "They weren't murdered in the tub, were they?"

I'd seen plenty of brutal murders in this reservation, but for some reason, the thought of it occurring in water had my skin crawling.

He shook his head and opened the door. "They're in the bedroom. Lacy said it smelled as if they'd been dead for at least a few hours."

"I wouldn't have thought putrefaction would have started that quickly, given how cold it's been these last few days."

"It depends on the situation. It can start as early as six hours after death, but it's usually somewhere between twenty-four and thirty-six hours. Speaking of which—" He dug back into his kit and then tossed me a small jar. "Use this."

"Vicks VapoRub?" I said, surprised.

"Dab it under your nose. It'll help."

"Meaning you can smell them from out here?"

"Werewolves have a keen sense of smell, remember? But in this case, there appears to have been major bowel leakage after death."

"Great," I muttered, and wondered why *that* seemed so much worse than the many other gruesome things I'd seen over recent months.

I unscrewed the lid, scooped up some of the VapoRub, and dabbed it under each nostril. The menthol scent had me blinking back tears—it seemed ten times stronger than I remembered. I resisted the urge to immediately wipe it off and followed him into the cottage. The small front room held a large-screen TV, a fireplace that held only a few glowing embers, and two generously padded sofas. A couple of mugs sat on the coffee table as well as several take-out containers. There was little to suggest evil had been here.

I walked around the room, skimming the top of the sofas and coffee table with an outstretched hand. While psychometry generally worked better with possessions worn close to the skin—things like necklaces, rings, or watches, rather than items of clothing—it *was* still possible to feel or even track someone through items they may have touched for a few hours. Of course, contact *did* have to be very recent, and that wasn't the case here.

Not that I expected anything else, but still...

I motioned Aiden on. The next room was a combined kitchen and dining area that ran the full width of the house; there were dishes in the sink and two coats slung over the dining chairs. A large glass sliding door led out to a covered patio deck and, to the right of this, was the door that no doubt led into the rear bedroom.

Unsurprisingly, the pulse of evil—and the smell of shit —emanated from it. The Vicks wasn't doing a whole lot to combat it, either.

I did a circuit around the kitchen and living area, just in case, but again, there was nothing. Whoever—whatever— had caused these deaths hadn't entered the rest of the house. And *that* meant the entity responsible knew exactly where his victims were—not hard for a vampire, as they could hear the pulse of life from some distance away.

I took a deep breath to gather courage—a major mistake given the foul scents in the air—and then followed Aiden into the bedroom. It was as bad as I feared it would be, but it wasn't just the smell of shit and urine that had me gasping. It was the emotion—the realization and terror of death that lingered in the air.

At least one of the two people on the bed had been awake when they'd been attacked.

I swallowed heavily and quickly shored up my mental shields. While I'd long ago learned to protect myself against emotions—be they via touch or the ones that lingered in the air after traumatic events such as this—my control had been somewhat spotty recently. Either that, or my ability to sense emotions was getting stronger... which shouldn't be possible, but that seemed to be a recurring theme in this place.

I finally looked at the bed. It was a massive, wrought-iron thing that made the two people lying on it seem diminutive. Both were naked, appeared to be in their mid-twenties and, at first glance, showed no obvious sign of injury or trauma. I hesitated, and then followed Aiden across the spacious room, stopping at the end of the bed while he continued on to the side of it.

I crossed my arms and tried to ignore the thick caress of

fear and evil. "Are we dealing with the same predator who took out the groom last week?"

He nodded and pointed a gloved finger at a small wound just under the man's ribs. "It certainly appears to be the same MO, although we'll need an autopsy to confirm it." He glanced at me. "I didn't think vampires could cross thresholds without invitation."

"They generally can't, although that rule only applies to personal residences rather than commercial, and this would probably qualify as the latter." I rubbed my arms against the pressing weight of emotion. I had no idea which of these two had been awake when evil had preyed on them—fear didn't tend to have an overly male or female feel—and I really didn't want to dip into either of their minds and experience that death firsthand. But what choice did I really have if we wanted to stop this thing before it took more lives? "Do you still want me to attempt the reading?"

His gaze rose to mine, concern evident. "Can you?"

"Their emotions linger, so there's a slight chance I might be able to pull something out. Don't get your hopes up, though."

He nodded and pulled out his phone. "I'll take some photos while you contact Belle and get set up."

I silently reached out. After a couple of moments, Belle said, *What's up?*

I'm about to read the minds of a dead couple. Not sure if I'll actually get anything because they've been dead for a while, but I've got to try.

Is this related to last week's murder?

It seems so.

Hang on then, and I'll go grab Monty. He can keep an eye out for me; it's damn crowded here, and I'd hate anyone to distract me when you're mind diving.

Good idea. Although I daresay his date wouldn't be too happy about him suddenly abandoning her for another woman.

Her mind slipped from mine, and I used the time to study the two victims with my 'other' senses. The thick, dark emotion I was sensing seemed to be hovering over the man more than the woman, suggesting he was the one who'd woken in the midst of the attack. So why hadn't he reacted? Why had he simply lain there? Did the thing behind these murders have a means of immobilizing its victims? Vampires could certainly alter perceptions so that they sometimes appeared to disappear, but that was simply a psychic ability—a type of telepathy that clouded rather than controlled.

But vampires generally left distinct bite marks behind, and there were no such marks here—only that small, half-inch cut just under their ribs.

That very much suggested we were dealing with something other than a vampire, which in some respects, was a shame. At least if it *had* been a vampire, we could have gone to Maelle Defour for help. She was the reservation's resident bloodsucker, although few outside the council actually knew that. The rangers certainly hadn't been told, and I sure as hell wasn't going to be the one to do so. Aside from the fact I'd promised not to, the bitch was scary. She definitely wasn't someone I wanted to be on the wrong side of.

But she *was* someone we should probably talk to, and the sooner the better. If there *was* another vampire lurking, she'd know about it.

Righto, Belle said. *We've been ushered into a private room, and Monty's on door watch.*

I swallowed to ease a suddenly dry throat and then said, "I'm ready when you are, Aiden."

He nodded and stepped away from the bodies. "I'll record events; just remember to state what you're seeing."

"*If* I see anything."

I moved closer to the dead man; his emotions pressed harder against my shields, and my skin crawled. He'd definitely seen their attacker. Whether any memory of it remained was another matter entirely.

I lightly pressed my fingers to either side of his skull, his flesh cool against my skin. Fear surged, though I wasn't entirely sure whether it was his or mine or a combination of both. I tried to ignore it as I closed my eyes and opened the psychic part of me.

For several seconds, nothing happened. His terror and disbelief washed through me, but that was a lingering emotional output rather than actual memory. At a surface level, his mind was utterly dark. Utterly dead.

I frowned and pushed a little deeper; nothing remained except the deepening chill of death.

Our only hope was the rear recesses of his memory, but even if some memories did linger, the likelihood of them being the ones we wanted weren't great.

I sucked in air and dove into the deadness. It gathered around me, pushed into me, making my heart race even as its chill began to invade my body.

"Anything?" Aiden asked softly.

I shook my head and kept pushing. His mind—his memories—were cold... so damn cold.

Lizzie, you need to pull back.

I will... in a second.

Ice gathered within, and I shivered. Death's fingers were now crawling from his flesh to mine, but there was something in the distance, a flicker that was a possible memory. I reached harder, drew closer. It was a fragment and as fragile as fog, but if it gave some clue as to what had done this, then I had to at least try to snare it.

My breathing became a harsh rasp, and the icy numbness crept from fingertips to my wrist and then crawled up my arm.

You need to pull out. Now. Or I'll make you.

Just one second more...

"Lizzie," Aiden said. "Stop. You're starting to look like death warmed up."

I ignored them both and, with a last desperate push, reached the fragment. It wasn't the past—it was a tiny piece of the present... *A face, a veil, half a body floating above us, her entrails slapping warmly against my stomach. A forked tongue, flickering out, cutting flesh—*

The connection severed abruptly, and I fell backwards with a gasp. Aiden caught me before I hit the floor and then swept me into his arms, carrying me over to a nearby chair and placing me down gently.

I was shaking so hard my teeth chattered, and my heart pounded so fast that I couldn't catch my breath. Aiden squatted in front of me and began rubbing my hands. I could barely feel it, my fingers were so damn cold.

Damn it, Lizzie, that was stupid—

Perhaps, but it was still worth it.

Given those fragments don't make sense, the jury is out on that one. Her anger—and fear for me—ripped through her mental tones. *What sort of demon has half a body and their entrails hanging out, for fuck's sake? No living one, for sure.*

Which means we might be dealing with some sort of ghoul.

Maybe, but that still doesn't excuse going as deep as you

did. Fuck it, Liz, you were so close to the edge this time that I had trouble pulling you out. You scared the hell out of me.

I'm sorry—I didn't mean to. I hesitated. *I had to try, though.*

No, you actually didn't. Not if it puts your life in danger. Next time I say stop, damn well stop.

I will.

Her snort echoed loudly. *Say that with a little more conviction, and I might just believe you. I'll leave you to Aiden's tender ministrations. Yell if you need me.*

Thanks, Belle.

Her thoughts left mine, and I became aware of the warmth creeping back into my fingers. It damn well *hurt*. Belle's fear had certainly been justified—if the chill had crept any further up my arm—if it had reached my chest and my heart—I would have died.

I sucked in several deep breaths and then met Aiden's gaze. His expression was grim, and his fear swam around me, a thick scent that filled my nostrils. "Damn it, Liz, you frightened the hell out of me. I could literally see death creeping up on you."

"Belle said the same thing." I kept my voice light, even though I wanted nothing more than to wrap my arms around him and hold on tight. Against the cold that still had its hooks in me. Against the deeper danger that loomed on the not-so-distant horizon. "But I'm fine. Really, I am."

He didn't look convinced, and that wasn't entirely surprising, given I still felt like shit warmed up and no doubt looked like it.

"Can I get you anything? Coffee? Whiskey? Woolen gloves?"

I laughed, as he'd no doubt intended. "If you have the latter two in that kit of yours, I'll love you forever."

Something flared in his eyes. Something so heated, deep, and *real* that it made my heart sing. No matter what this man said, there was at least some part of him that wished we could be so much more than temporary lovers.

"Unfortunately, I don't," he said. "But I can get Jaz to grab them if it'll make you feel better."

I smiled and kissed him. It was light but tender and made me want a whole lot more. But now was neither the time nor the place. "Thanks, but I'll be just fine after I rest. In the meantime, I did see something, though I'm not entirely sure it makes sense." I quickly updated him and then added, "Either the memory was a false one—maybe they'd been watching a horror movie before they went to bed—or we're dealing with some sort of ghoul."

He frowned. "Can a ghoul even interact with the real world?"

"Ghouls fall more on the demonic side of things, rather than ghostly, and tend to have a love for human flesh."

"This one is only taking the blood and the heart, though."

"Which doesn't discount the possibility—demons have their food preferences just as we do." I shrugged. "Do you want me to attempt another—"

"No," he cut in bluntly. "I do not. I want you to rest right there until I can get someone to take you home."

"There are cabs in this town," I said, voice wry. "I'm quite able to grab one."

"Yes, but I'd rather ensure—"

"Aiden, honestly, I'll be fine. But I really need to get out of here—the man's emotions linger, and shielding against them is pulling at my strength."

His gaze swept me for a moment, then he nodded and rose. "Fine. But please go home and rest."

I raised my eyebrows. "What makes you think I won't?"

"Because you've the look of someone who has the scent of prey in her nose, and that generally means trouble."

"I only wish that were true—it'd make tracking down this thing a whole lot easier." I paused and glanced across to the French doors. "Didn't you say they were open when Lacy got here?"

He nodded. "Why?"

"Given the weather, it's doubtful our couple would have left them open, even if they had been using the hot tub. So if our murderer was responsible, she might have left either a fingerprint or some other sort of residue on the handle. Help me up."

He did so; the room spun briefly, and the thick taste of bile hit my throat. I swallowed heavily, then forced my feet to move. Aiden kept a steadying grip on my arm—obviously, I wasn't hiding the weakness as well as I thought.

I raised a hand and ran it just above the door handle. My fingers tingled briefly over the left one but not the right, but it wasn't enough to garner any sort of impression. Nothing other than hate, at any rate.

Why would a ghoul hate?

They're ghouls, came Belle's comment. *I'd have thought hate comes with the territory.*

"Anything?" Aiden asked.

"She touched the handles, but I'm not getting much more than that." To Belle, I added, *Why are you following my thoughts? Shouldn't you be with Kash, enjoying the party?*

Kash has cottoned on to Monty's dare, and we're consoling ourselves at the bar.

Are you sure that wasn't Monty's plan all along?

Even he wouldn't go that far. Not when he was obviously enjoying her company.

It was *very* interesting she'd noticed that, but I had enough sense not to say it. *Enjoy the rest of your night, then.*

The booze and food is free, so how could I not?

Her amusement faded from my mind. Aiden called me a cab, then escorted me back through the house and waited on the front porch with me.

Lights swept around the corner, and the fierce wail of sirens bit through the night; a heartbeat later, the green-striped white SUV pulled up beside Aiden's truck, and Ciara—who wasn't only the coroner, but also his sister—climbed out. After grabbing her gear from the back of the SUV, she dashed through the rain to the front porch.

"What have we got this time?" she said, giving me a quick but friendly nod.

"Two bodies, but similar MO to the groom's murder."

She grunted and looked at me. "You able to get anything?"

"Nothing useful."

"That's inconvenient."

"Yes, it is," I agreed wryly.

"The bodies are in the rear bedroom," Aiden said. "I'll meet you there in a minute."

Ciara nodded and headed in. I crossed my arms and shivered, though it wasn't so much the night's chill but rather the still-fading remnants of death. Aiden wrapped an arm around my shoulders and tugged me closer to his big, warm body. He didn't say anything and neither did I. We didn't really need to.

The cab came a few minutes later. I tugged the coat's hood over my head and, after dropping a kiss on Aiden's cheek, dashed out into the wild night. It didn't take long to get home; once I'd paid the driver, I climbed out and swung my pack over my shoulder.

It was then that I noticed them.

Tiny threads of magic, floating through the air.

Tiny threads that had been torn apart.

My gaze jumped to our café on the other side of the road.

Multiple layers of the magic protecting the building were missing or had been rendered inert.

Someone up to no good had tried to get inside.

CHAPTER THREE

That the attacker hadn't entirely succeeded was no doubt due to the fact that the remaining layers were enhanced by wild magic. Whoever did this—be it Clayton or one of his flunkies—had obviously decided getting into the building wasn't worth the risk of provoking it.

If it *was* Clayton, then he now knew about my affinity with the wild magic, even if he couldn't be aware of the full extent.

Rain poured from my hood and pooled around my feet, but I didn't immediately move. I just studied the building, looking for possible snares or traps. I couldn't see any, but that didn't mean they weren't there. Clayton, like most fully powered blueblood witches, was utterly capable of concealing his spells.

I swiped the rain from my face, then forced my feet into action and quickly crossed the road. Energy pressed at my fingertips in readiness, but no one jumped out at me and nothing magical attacked. The front door hadn't in any way been jimmied, and the windows remained locked. I hesitated and then walked around to the rear of the building.

Our new SUV sat alone in the parking space, and the back door looked untouched. I tested the handle; still locked.

I hesitated again and then walked back to the front door. While I could have gone through the rear entrance easily enough, the hallway beyond was small and had very little in the way of fighting room—something I'd discovered the hard way a few months ago. I shoved the key into the lock and, just for an instant, magic crawled across my fingers. Though it was little more than an echo of the power held by the man behind it, I remembered its feel well enough.

Clayton.

Clayton had been here.

Fuck.

Panic surged, and my gaze darted left and right; there was no one on the street, and absolutely no indication that I was being watched.

It didn't matter.

He'd been here once.

He'd be back.

Fuck, fuck, *fuck.*

I remained in the doorway, dripping water onto the floorboards as I studied the shadows with both my regular senses and my psychic. There was no sign of intrusion. No sense that someone waited inside, ready to pounce. No emotion in the air beyond the echoes of warmth and happiness that lingered after yesterday's trading.

The building remained safe. *I* was safe. For now.

But that would only last until Clayton figured out a way to get past the wild magic.

A chill crawled up my spine, and it wasn't entirely due to my soaked shoes and cold feet. I stepped inside and then closed and locked the door. But I didn't immediately move;

I simply stood there, my forehead resting against the door, sucking in air and trying to control the fear that rampaged through me.

I wasn't sixteen. I wasn't powerless. Not anymore.

And yet the knowledge that Clayton was now in the reservation—that it would only be a matter of time before he confronted us—made me feel like that frightened teenager all over again.

I'm coming home. Belle's thought was sharp and worried.

Don't. Our deeper protections still stand, so I really am safe. He won't dare tackle the wild magic—he saw what it did to my mother.

And what if you're wrong? What if he was just waiting for you to arrive?

Then it's better that you remain at a distance. It allows me to call on either your talents or your strength if necessary, without putting you in his path.

We can't hide forever, Liz, and I for one have no intention of doing so. This is part of his game. This is what he wants—us in a state of panic.

Well, it's damn well working.

Because of what you went through. Because of what he did. But you're not that person anymore.

I know. I sucked in another of those breaths that did little to help the sick churning in my gut and pushed away from the door. *I can't imagine Kash will be happy about leaving the party early.*

Like I really care what he thinks when he's chatting up another woman. Besides, Monty's already volunteered to bring me home.

Despite the seriousness of the situation, I couldn't help smiling. *Of course he did.*

He thinks it would be a good idea if he adds an additional protection layer over ours.

I frowned. *Why? Clayton could bust his magic as easily as he did ours.*

Yes, but he believes it might just make Clayton rethink a second entry attempt.

Again, why? He was never one to worry too much about what those lower in power thought.

I know, but Monty is the resident witch here and, as such, the government's mouthpiece. Even Clayton can't afford to disrespect that.

Maybe. Maybe not. *I guess it really depends on whether his anger is more the "I made a deal and you will honor it" or the "I've gone insane and you will pay" type.*

I suspect it might be the latter—especially if my anti-erection spell really has lasted all these years.

There was no regret in Belle's mental tone, but why would there be? She'd unleashed that spell to save me from rape, and if Clayton had spent the years since in manhood hell, then I for one thought it well deserved.

Though I had no doubt we were both likely to pay a high price for it.

We'll be there in half an hour, she continued. *Have the coffee ready.*

Will do.

I sent Aiden a quick text to explain what had happened and asked him to be careful. His response was immediate and made me smile: *Do you need me there?*

No, I sent back, *Monty and Belle are coming home to help shore up our defenses. We'll be fine.*

And if I said that often enough, I might even start to believe it.

I headed upstairs for a shower, though the heat didn't

really do much to chase the chill from my flesh. Once dressed, I trundled back downstairs to put on the kettle and consoled myself with a thick slab of chocolate cake.

Monty and Belle arrived just over ten minutes later.

"Fuck," I said, as they walked through the door. "You must have broken the land speed record to get here so fast."

Monty's grin flashed. "I figured that if the rangers *did* pull me over, I'd just have to say you were under attack, and I'd probably get a lights-and-sirens escort here."

"I wouldn't bet on that," I replied, amused. "Especially if it was Tala who pulled you over."

Tala was Aiden's second-in-charge, and though she'd come to accept that my abilities were real, and even somewhat useful, she tended to play by the rules even more than Aiden.

"Even Tala would know better than to delay us when your safety is on the line," Monty said.

"Except in this case, it wasn't. And you were well aware of that."

"Yeah, but she wouldn't have been." He pulled out a chair and sat down. "Clayton really did a number on your spells, didn't he?"

"Yes." I finished making our coffees, sliced up more chocolate cake—it was definitely a two-pieces-of-cake night for me—and then carried it all over. "But at least he didn't get in."

"Only thanks to the threads of wild magic," Belle commented. "Which means we'll need to use it to shore up—"

"No," I cut in. "Under no circumstances."

"Why?" Monty accepted his coffee with a nod and helped himself to a piece of cake. "He now knows you can use the wild magic, so why bother pretending otherwise?"

"If my inner wild magic remains concealed, then we might get away with saying the wellspring was still unrestrained when we created those spells and that its presence was unintentional."

Monty snorted. "And how many of the witches who've stepped into this café have actually believed that statement?"

"Not many, but remember, Clayton's memories are of an underpowered sixteen-year-old. He won't be looking for anything more."

"And if you *can* keep shielding as well as you are at the moment," Belle said, "it gives us a slight advantage over the bastard."

"Maybe." I scooped up some chocolate cake and munched on it contemplatively. "Monty, did your dad have any success digging out the marriage certificate?"

He shook his head. "The priest who performed the ceremony died a few years later—"

"Isn't *that* convenient," Belle said, voice dry.

"He was older than Methuselah when he performed the ceremony," I said. "I'm surprised he lasted a few years—I'd have thought a few days would have been stretching it."

"Why is his death a problem?" Belle asked. "The marriage would have been registered with the Witch Registry of Births, Deaths, and Marriages—"

"And, by law, access to such a record is restricted for sixty years," Monty said. "Liz can certainly request a copy of it, as can an attorney on her behalf, but my father can't."

I wrinkled my nose. "Maybe that's what I need to do, though it will out the situation to everyone up there, and that may make things worse."

"I'm not entirely sure they can get worse, especially given it will take time for the request to be processed,"

Monty said. "And even if we do get the certificate, it doesn't actually prove his guilt."

"It proves she was underage when it happened," Belle retorted.

"Which doesn't mean anything if there was parental approval—and there was."

"Yeah, it was just the bride that didn't approve." I scooped up more chocolate cake. "And how in the hell are we supposed to prove that? It'll be my word against that of my parents and him—and we all know who the courts are likely to believe."

"There *is* one way," Monty said. "But it will mean reliving everything that happened."

"And?" I said, as he ate some more cake rather than continuing.

"Well, didn't you say Ashworth had asked the Black Lantern Society to do a little underground investigating?"

"Yes, but the records are locked down magically and they can't access them without alerting either my father or Clayton."

"Which is just another pointer to the influence they have in Canberra," Belle said, voice dry. "And while locking a record in such a manner *is* illegal, it's more a misdemeanor few will quibble about."

"Except for the fact that their actions point to guilt more than innocence," Monty said. "And it gives the Society a legal reason to get involved. They're not just underground purveyors of justice—they also have a history of representing less-fortunate witches against the High Council in court cases. As such, they have both attorneys and truth seekers on their books."

"Truth seekers?" Belle asked. "Is that a psychic or magical talent?"

"It's a bit both, really. They usually work with an auditor, who records the session and ensures everything being done is above board and legal."

"Great, but how's that going to help us?" I asked.

"Simple. We get Ashworth to request a seeker ASAP. They record what happened for posterity, and when Clayton makes a move on you, we threaten to take him and your father to court. They may be powerful, but they aren't above the law."

"I'm not entirely sure of that." My voice was grim. "I'd hazard a guess that my father is on first-name terms with at least half of the presiding judges."

Monty's smile was rather fierce. "And the Black Lantern Society has the pull and the power to request none of them preside over the case."

"If this society is so powerful, how come they're not more well-known?" Belle said. "I can't remember hearing anything about them when we were up there."

"We were teenagers," Monty replied dryly. "It's not like we paid a whole lot of attention to the legal happenings of the world."

"True, I guess."

He reached across the table and grabbed my hands. "Liz, if you want to be free from Clayton, then you have to take the fight to him. What he and your father did was not only wrong, but also illegal. We know that, they know that. That's why they've kept their search for you under the radar; it's why Clayton has made no mention of it in nearly thirteen years. They want you back, but in a manner that will raise few suspicions."

"And Clayton suddenly appearing with a reluctant wife in tow won't raise any suspicions at all now, will it?" Belle said, her tone sarcastic.

"Well, no, because she's no longer sixteen. In fact, I expect most would consider it an advantageous marriage for Liz, considering her lack of magical strength."

I pulled my hands from Monty's and rubbed my forehead wearily. "If there's one thing I'm certain of, it's the fact that he won't play fair, which means we really have no choice but to fight him any way we can. I'll talk to Ashworth tomorrow."

"Good," Monty said. "In the meantime, let's get the protections around this place shored up."

He picked up his coffee and strode toward the reading room without waiting for either of us.

Belle's gaze met mine, her expression one of tolerant amusement. *You can't fault his determination to keep you safe.*

Keeping me safe also keeps his future wife safe. I pushed away from the table with a laugh as she tried to whack me. *You enjoyed his company tonight, and we both know it.*

Well, yes, but please don't tell him that. He'll be unbearable.

"Ladies, stop the secret squirrel business and get your butts in here."

"He's not going to attack again tonight." I picked up my coffee and followed Belle into the reading room. "He'll wait until he thinks we've relaxed a little."

"Expect the unexpected is a motto I think we should all adopt right now." Monty pushed the furniture to one side then sat cross-legged on the floor. "Ready, ladies?"

I nodded, and after a deep breath to center our energy, we began to spell, weaving line after line of protection magic around and through the remaining threads. Monty then ran an alarm thread around the entire lot. While it wouldn't take much to unpick, he assured us we'd all know the minute anyone attacked our spells, no matter where we were in the reservation.

By the time we finished, twenty minutes had slipped by and all three of us were close to exhaustion.

I picked up the empty cups and climbed wearily to my feet. "Are you coming in for breakfast tomorrow?"

He hesitated. "No, as I'll need to check in with Aiden on the murders first. Besides, it's better if we leave the council of war until the afternoon, when you're not as busy. But I'll send Ashworth a text when I get home—the sooner he's updated, the better."

"It's close to midnight—he's not going to be happy."

"I know," he said cheerfully. "That's the whole point."

I snorted and headed out of the room. As I rinsed the cups, Belle followed him to the front door and locked up behind him. Then she walked back and gave me a fierce hug.

"It will, in the end, be all right. I'm positive of that, if nothing else."

I smiled. "Is that wishful thinking or one of those vague premonitions you've started getting?"

She shrugged. "Who can be sure? It's not like I'm used to this whole premonition thing. That's supposed to be your talent, not mine."

And it had been, up until the moment we'd been forced to utterly merge minds in order to thrust out a white witch who'd decided to claim Belle's body as her own.

"Unfortunately," I said, "My premonition skill set is telling me quite the opposite; if we get out of this alive and intact, it'll be something of a miracle."

Belle's gaze swept my face, concern evident. "Clayton might be incandescent with fury, but even he wouldn't resort to murder."

"He doesn't have to—not to make life hell for us." I shivered and rubbed my arms. "But you were right before—we can't let him get to us. We need to continue on as normal—with just a little bit more caution."

"Which means no going anywhere alone." She pointed sternly at me. "Got that?"

I saluted lightly. "Loud and clear, ma'am."

She snorted and pushed me toward the stairs. "Go to bed."

I did. And, rather surprisingly, slept long and deep. But perhaps my body was simply getting as much as it could before the shit hit the fan.

The café was insanely busy from the get-go, so it wasn't until midafternoon that I had a chance to look at my phone and saw that Ashworth had left a message asking me to ring him as soon as possible.

"Hey, what's up?" I said, the moment he answered.

"A hell of a lot from the sound of things, lassie." His Scottish accent was a little more evident this morning, suggesting he hadn't gotten much sleep last night. "Got a text from Monty at midnight and have set a few things in motion."

My stomach twisted. Every step we took toward protecting ourselves was one step closer to confrontation.

"With the Black Lantern Society, I take it?"

"Yes. My sister was none-too-pleased about being woken at such an ungodly hour, but that soon passed once I told her it was about Clayton."

I frowned. "Why? What's changed up there that's made him to go from an eminent and well-respected member of the High Council to someone who has more than a few enemies?"

"Everyone in high power has enemies, lass, but Clayton has done himself no favors over the last few years. Even your father has somewhat distanced himself—"

"Is *he* still in Canberra?"

"He was as of last night."

A tide of relief swept me. It didn't really mean anything, because it really wouldn't take that long for him to jump on a plane and get to the reservation. But, at least for the time being, we only had one autocratic asshole to deal with.

"Sophie agrees that our best shot of bringing both him and your father to court to face questioning, and hopefully disciplinary action, is to employ the services of a reader and auditor immediately. As such, they'll be down within the next thirty-six hours."

I blinked. "That's fast."

"We need to be fast." His voice was grim. "If either man gets word of the Society's uptake of your cause, it could escalate things badly."

I wasn't entirely sure how things could get much worse than what was already coming, but I wasn't about to put that out there, just in case fate was listening and decided to take up the challenge.

"Thanks, Ira. I really do appreciate your help."

"Least I can do for my favorite witch—aside from Eli, of course." The amusement in his tone faded as he added, "In the meantime, use that anti-tracking charm we created for you."

"Will it work against someone like Clayton?"

"Until he gets close enough to sense the magic or he realizes the reason he can't track you means there's a spell at work, yes."

"Hopefully neither will happen anytime soon. We need the breathing space."

"Chin up, lass. You're not alone in this fight. We're all behind you, no matter what happens."

Tears touched my eyes and I blinked them away. "I know."

"Good. Then stop fretting; you'll only make yourself ill."

I smiled. "You're sounding more and more like my grandfather every day."

"This would be the dead grandfather?"

"Well, yes, but you know what I mean."

He chuckled. "I do. Talk soon."

I hung up and accepted the mug of coffee Belle shoved into my hands. "Just got a call from Monty—he's off to meet some friend of his who's an expert in the occult. Apparently he's only in Victoria for the day."

I raised my eyebrows. "Why did he ring you rather than me? And how did he get your phone number?"

"I gave it to him last night—I figured it'd be a good safety precaution if you suddenly went missing."

"If I suddenly went missing, you could contact him telepathically."

"Only if he was in range."

Amusement twitched my lips. "Meaning you've willingly given him the means of contacting you anytime he desires. Are you ill?"

"He's received the usual warnings and has promised not to abuse the situation."

"Of course he has."

She gave me the look—the one that said "shut up now or pay the price."

My smile widened, but I resisted the urge to tease her further. "Have you got any plans for this evening?"

"No—why?"

"I'd like to pop over to Émigré."

She raised her eyebrows. "You're not going to Aiden's?"

"Yes, but he's on late shifts this week, so he's not picking me up until ten."

She leaned a hip against the counter and took a sip of her coffee. "I take it then that this visit isn't for pleasure?"

"No. I want to question Maelle about the murders."

"If there was another vampire in the reservation, she would probably have already dealt with it. She's not the type to share."

"None of them are, but it *is* possible she doesn't know. She doesn't leave her lair very often."

Belle snorted. "That may be true, but I'm betting she knows exactly what's happening, both here in Castle Rock and the reservation in general."

Of that, I had no doubt. Especially given she not only had Roger—her man-ghoul servant—to do her bidding, but an unknown quantity of 'feeders'. "Shall we head over early, before it gets too crowded?"

She nodded and accepted the order Penny—our waitress—handed her with a smile. I finished my coffee and then got back to work.

It was close to seven by the time we arrived at Émigré. Despite the early hour, the venue was obviously already full, given there were over a dozen people lined up outside waiting to get in. I supposed it wasn't unexpected, given it was Saturday night, but Émigré had similar lines on Mondays and Tuesdays, which were traditionally slow for most venues.

But maybe Maelle—who'd admitted to being familiar

with the darker arts—was subtly applying magic to keep the customers and money rolling in. Just because I couldn't feel it, didn't mean it wasn't happening.

The building itself resembled something straight out of a science fiction movie and had become a minor tourist attraction in recent months. Though it had once been an old pub, the entire thing was now painted matte black—even the windows—and the walls were decorated with weird, almost alien-looking biomechanical forms. The front door resembled an airlock and was guarded by two rather sinister-looking security guards wearing black. They opened the door the minute they saw us approaching, ushering us inside against a tide of protests from those standing in the line. We checked our coats, then stepped through the second set of doors; the music that had been barely audible outside hit full-force. It was fierce and joyous, and instantly made me want to dance—and there were a hell of a lot of people here doing just that.

The room itself was split into two sections—one side of the upper tier held a series of 'pods' in which there were seats and small tables, while the other half was dominated by a long bar that was made from twisted metal and glass. The lower tier was entirely devoted to the dance floor.

I lifted my gaze to the vaulted ceiling. The huge room had been painted a battleship gray, rather than black, and the ceiling again had a series of intricate and intriguing biomechanical and alien forms crawling all over each arch. A dark glass and metal room had been built into the point where those arches met. It was right above the dance floor and had a 360-degree view of the entire venue while generally being concealed from casual sight.

Maelle's lair.

I couldn't see her shadow through the glass, but that

didn't mean she wasn't aware of our appearance. There was very little in this place that she missed.

As if to emphasize this point, a tall, thin man with pale skin, paler hair, and eyes that were a weird milky white emerged from the crowded dance floor and bounded up the steps. Technically, Roger was a thrall, which basically meant he had—via a process that involved magic and the consumption of Maelle's flesh—received eternal life in return for eternal servitude.

His gaze swept us both, and something close to disdain touched his expression. And with good reason—jeans, sneakers, and comfy old sweaters were not approved attire in this place. "The state of your dress indicates this visit is an official one."

"Yes. There's been a couple of murders, and I wanted to ask Maelle some questions if she's free."

"For you lovely ladies, she always is." He motioned us to follow him. "I do hope, though, that you're not suggesting she is in any way involved in these murders."

"I wouldn't be so foolish as to come into her lair with such an accusation." Not without spells at the ready and a major arsenal of stakes, silver, and holy water at hand. And even then there was no guarantee of survival, given her age and speed.

"Foolish certainly isn't a word my mistress would use in conjunction with you." Amusement lurked in the cool undertones.

My eyebrows rose. "Then what word *would* she use?"

"Dangerous." He glanced over his shoulder, his pale eyes holding an unholy glint. "*Very* dangerous."

That last part had been said by Maelle rather than her creature. The two were telepathically linked, and she could, if she wished, both see and speak through him.

"I think we both know you have little fear of me, Maelle."

"You are this reservation's guardian, young Elizabeth." Roger's tone was still Maelle's. "That makes you the most dangerous of us all."

I snorted but didn't bother replying—though a tiny part of me couldn't help but wish it was true. There might have been a greater chance of our surviving what was coming if it was.

We made our way up the steps at the far side of the dance floor and walked toward a pod that was closed off by a wrought-iron door. There was an inconspicuous keypad on the right-side wall; Roger tapped in the code and the door slid aside to reveal a circular, black glass staircase.

"Please," he said, and motioned us on.

Our footsteps echoed as we climbed. The metal door at the top was open and the room beyond filled with shadows despite the bright array of lights that constantly swept across the dark windows. A black glass desk dominated the rear portion of the room; a couple of plush-looking chairs sat at the front of this and a third behind it.

Maelle stood near the glass panel with her back to the door but turned as we entered. Tonight she wore a Regency riding habit that was dark blue in color and had gold braid across her chest. Her rich chestnut hair had been plaited and curled around the top of her head and looked rather crown-like. Her porcelain skin was perfect; there were no lines on her face and absolutely no indication that she was, in fact, centuries old—if not older.

Her lips were a stark contrast to her skin, though the deep ruby red was not due to lipstick but was rather an indicator of how recently she'd fed. It was a sight that always had relief surging—I'd already survived one vampire attack and I had no intention of going through that again. And while Maelle had vowed to the council not to drink from the unwilling, she also seemed rather determined to taste the power in my blood.

"What murders do you wish to speak to me about?" Her softly accented voice carried easily over the thumping base of the music coming from below. "The only death the gossips whisper about is that of the groom late last week."

"The person behind that one struck again last night."

"Another groom?"

"It was a newlywed couple this time." I hesitated. "The rangers initially suspected a vampire, but it hasn't the usual hallmarks."

"So you've come to the local expert for advice?" Her expression was amused, thankfully. She motioned toward the chairs in front of the desk, her movement elegant. "Please, sit. Can I get either of you a drink?"

"Thanks, but no." Belle perched on the edge of the chair, her spine stiff.

And with good reason, came Belle's thought. *The bitch might want to taste your blood, but she wants me in her bed.*

Oh, I don't think you'll escape the whole blood thing. I think that's part and parcel of her loving. To Maelle, I added, "A sparkling water will be fine, thanks."

She handed me my drink and then picked up hers and sat down at the desk. The liquid inside the glass was thick and a deep red in color, and I had a suspicion it wasn't tomato juice.

"Give me the details of these murders." She took another sip that left her lips an even richer color.

I thrust down the mild rise of horror and obeyed.

She frowned. "You are right—while there are certainly vampires who prefer to drain, few would eat the flesh of their victims, let alone go to the trouble of extracting the heart in such a manner."

"Why's that?" Belle asked. "Vampires are capable of processing food and liquids, aren't they?"

"Liquids, yes, but we only consume food on rare occasions, when it is necessary for appearances' sake." She shrugged. "The change we undergo to become eternal alters the structure of our digestive system, and leaves us incapable of processing solid food. The result can be... unpleasant."

If the woman who'd rolled around in the bloody remnants of a body that had exploded right here in this room considered the results of eating unpleasant, then it was not something I *ever* wanted to see.

"Do you have any idea what sort of creature might be responsible for these deaths?"

"There are many who would fit the bill, and this reservation has already seen a number of them." She took another sip of her drink. I hadn't thought her lip color could get any deeper, but I was wrong. They were so damn dark now, they were almost black. "But you have suspicions, do you not?"

"We were thinking it might be some sort of ghoul."

"Perhaps, although the fact there was nearly a week between attacks would suggest it is not a standard ghoul." She paused. "If one *has* come into the reservation, however, that is grave news indeed."

Belle frowned. "Why? I mean, they're no worse than some of the other supernatural critters that have hunted here."

"Except many ghouls have insatiable appetites."

"Why am I not surprised," Belle muttered. "This reservation doesn't appear to attract the milder form of evil."

"Indeed it does not." The glint in Maelle's eyes suggested she was including herself in that statement. Her gaze switched to me, and the glint was replaced by something altogether more intent. "Why was your café attacked this evening?"

I blinked even as my stomach twisted. "Who told you that?"

She waved a hand. "Anyone with an ounce of magical knowledge would have seen the dismembered threads carried on the wind."

Meaning one of them had been near our café close to the time it had happened, and *that* was an unsettling possibility. There could be very little reason for either of them to be driving past at that hour, given our end of Mostyn Street was a cul-de-sac. It *was* possible she'd sensed the attack and had decided to investigate, but given she hadn't bothered leaving her lair when her feeders were being killed off, why would she do so to investigate an unusual attack on my place?

Then another possibility hit, and my heart leapt. Had she seen Clayton in her travels last night? Had she met him? Talked to him?

Even worse... had she made a *deal* with him?

CHAPTER FOUR

The little I knew about her said it was unlikely. She was in my debt, and I doubted she would in any way harm me until that debt was paid.

But she was also a vampire, and they had a long history of dark and bloody deeds. Maelle, for all her refinement, had the heart of a monster.

I took a quick drink of water and heartily wished it was something far stronger. "The attacker is a man from my past—"

"The man you have been running from these many years?" she cut in.

The thump of fear got stronger. "You've been checking on me."

"As I have said, I always ensure I am familiar with the power players in whatever town I choose to settle in." Her expression was amused. "But fear not—my enquiries would not have revealed your whereabouts to this man. My sources don't inhabit the world of witches willingly. I think it more likely he's here because of the tracer."

"You don't miss much."

"I cannot afford to, young Elizabeth." She studied me for a moment, her expression giving little away. "Do not forget that I am in your debt—and that is a situation with which I am never comfortable. Not for long. If you desire any help getting this witch out of your life, then I would be more than happy to oblige."

And if that isn't a threat wrapped up in an offer of assistance, I don't know what is, Belle said. *I seriously wish we hadn't helped this bitch.*

Refusing her wasn't really an option. I forced a smile and said, "I appreciate the offer and will certainly enlist your help if necessary... but I can't afford to kill this man."

"I am capable of more than merely death."

The flicker of light—or was it darkness—in her eyes suggested death remained her first and second option. Dark magic, I suspected, was a distant third.

"I know, but this man holds a lot of power—"

"And such power always calls to one such as me."

"I meant in standing and alliances rather than actual magic, though he has plenty of the latter."

"Ah." She shrugged, the movement casual and unconcerned. "The offer nevertheless remains. And please do remember that it sometimes takes one monster to render another impotent."

I nodded, gulped down the rest of my drink, and then rose. "Thank you for seeing us, and for the offer of assistance."

She brushed the comment away with a graceful hand. "I will ask Roger to keep an eye out for a ghoul, if indeed that is what lies behind these murders. He is familiar with their scent, as we have dealt with them in the past."

I frowned. "Ghouls have a scent?"

"It is... acidic. Ashy. It speaks of the cemeteries in which they are often found."

"And the best way to kill them?"

"That would depend on the type of ghoul," she said. "But generally, what works against a vampire will work against a ghoul, though I have a personal preference for decapitation."

Of course she did. And she probably feasted on their blood afterwards. "Thanks, Maelle."

She nodded and turned her chair away from us. Summarily dismissed, we headed back down the stairs and were silently escorted out of the building by Roger.

Belle drew in a deep breath once we were out in the open air. "Well, that was interesting."

"It always is when it comes to Maelle." I grabbed my car keys out of my purse and walked down to where we'd parked the SUV. "But at least we did get some worthwhile information from it."

"Maybe," Belle said. "But I'm thinking we should seriously put some distance between us and her. I'm not liking the vibes she's throwing at the moment."

"I've never liked them, but I believe it's better to keep communications open rather than cut them altogether."

"Oh, on that we agree. I just think we should find a different venue to attend for a while."

"Which would affect you more than me." Aiden definitely wasn't a fan of the place, so I generally only went there with Belle.

She sighed. "I know, and it's a shame, because owner aside, the place rocks. And it's not like we've many other dance venues open in the reservation—and don't you dare suggest those ballroom things Aiden drags you to. They don't count."

I unlocked the SUV and climbed in. "I'm not entirely sure how many more we'll be going to. His feet are constantly in a bruised state."

Belle laughed. "Well, he can't really complain when he was given fair warning of your three left feet. But he's a damn werewolf—why aren't they healing between shifts?"

"He reckons the damage is so constant, his natural healing magic is struggling to keep up." And while he *had* been joking, I also suspected there was a tiny grain of truth in the statement.

Belle snorted. "Then he needs to take the hint before the healing ability throws up its hands in disgust and gives up."

After a quick check of the mirrors, I pulled out and headed home. "It's hardly fair he gives up something he loves because his partner sucks at it. I have suggested less frequency, however."

"A good move for both of you, I think."

It didn't take us long to get home, but as we drove down the lane that led to the parking area behind our building, lights pulled in behind us. My heart leapt, and fear surged... and then I realized it was Aiden's truck. He parked beside us and climbed out, a backpack and what looked to be a sleeping roll slung over his shoulder.

As Belle walked over to unlock the café's back door, I stopped and waited for him. The man moved with predator's grace, and despite the cold, warmth curled through me. "Are you planning on going camping tonight?"

"Yes—here."

"And why would you do that when you've a perfectly good bed—" I stopped as realization hit. That curl of warmth got stronger.

"Until that bastard is tracked down and neutralized,

57

you can't risk staying at my place. I'll do everything in my power to protect you, but my place is an open book when it comes to magical forces. He can gain access far too easily for my liking."

"I *can* place protections around—"

"Why bother when your building has already proven capable of withstanding his assault?"

I wasn't sure that was entirely true, but all I said was, "I appreciate the offer, but in reality—"

"I'm not entering into a discussion about this, Liz." His voice was flat—determined. "He can't attack the magic protecting this place *and* defend himself from physical attack at the same time. No witch can. If he does try to enter, I *will* stop him."

"You can't stay awake all night, Aiden. Not when you're working."

"I'm not tomorrow—it's my day off."

"But you're on the following days, so the argument remains."

"Which is why I have the bedroll. You'll know the minute he attacks, and I'll know the minute you wake in fear."

I wanted to wrap my arms around him and hug him, but we were still in the street, and he tended to avoid overt displays of affection when in public.

"Okay, but I do have a queen bed, so there's no need—"

"It'll be entirely too distracting if we share a bed. Besides, there's the 'no sex with boyfriends in the building' rule you and Belle have going."

And with very good reason—neither of us wanted to remember past partners whenever we walked into our bedrooms. We both knew it took far longer for the heartache of a broken relationship to heal when memories echoed.

But *this* situation was very different to those others.

"I'll accept no arguments on this either," he added. "So can we please take this inside? Otherwise, those goose bumps of yours will turn into mountains."

"Fine." I turned and headed in. "But the sofa pulls out into a bed, so you can use that."

"I'm not entirely sure that old sofa of yours will be more comfortable than the floor."

"Then you'd be wrong."

I locked the door and followed him across the room. Belle had made us all coffee and stacked a selection of brownies onto a plate. Aiden dumped his bag and sleeping roll onto the nearby table and then pulled out a chair. "So, what were you both doing over at Émigré? You're not exactly dressed for a night out."

I raised my eyebrows. "How did you know we were there?"

He reached for a salted caramel brownie, a grin twitching his lips. "Jaz mentioned it. She was driving past when you were going in, and wondered if our plans had changed."

"You discuss your evening plans with Jaz?"

"Well, no, but in this reservation, it's rather hard to keep anything secret. The gossips do like to keep up with current events."

I snorted. The gossip brigade, as they were officially known, was a group of twenty-seven women who met at least a couple of times a week to discuss any and all local events. Some months ago they'd decided the Psychic Café would be their main meeting haunt, and while that was good for business, it wasn't great for keeping secrets.

"We met a friend there." The lie tasted a little bitter on my tongue, but I couldn't admit the truth. He didn't know

Maelle was a vampire, and I'd promised I wouldn't say anything. I'd rather Aiden be upset with me than her, when the truth did eventually come out.

He studied me, his expression suggesting he suspected the lie. But then, he'd always been able to do that—one of the many reasons he was such a good ranger. "Why there? Why not here?"

"Because that's where she wanted to meet." I shrugged. "Anyway, said friend is something of an expert when it comes to vampires and other nasties, and gave us some interesting information."

Once I'd updated him, he frowned and said, "If I send a team to investigate the local cemeteries tonight, is there anything they can do to protect themselves against this ghoul, if that *is* what we're dealing with?"

"Decapitation was mentioned as one method of killing them, so I think shooting their heads off would probably work."

A smile twitched his lips. "And if 'probably' doesn't?"

"Tell them to carry long knives."

"And it might be worthwhile to carry some salt," Belle added. "Most supernatural beasties hate the stuff. If they're attacked, they can either throw it or—better yet—use it to form a circle barrier around themselves."

"And that will protect them?"

"It should, as not many supernatural beings will actually cross it."

"Good." Aiden rose and moved to the other side of the room to make his calls.

Belle sipped her coffee and then said, "I might head over to the storage unit tomorrow and see if I can find anything in the old index books that deals with ghouls."

Belle's grandmother—Nellie—had been the owner of a vast collection of rare and irreplaceable books on magic and the supernatural. Unfortunately, her indexing system was handwritten and tended to be somewhat haphazard, which made it hard to find anything quickly. We were in the process of converting everything over to electronic format, and not just for ease of access or even protection against some sort of disaster. We'd rather belatedly realized that a backup was very necessary in case the High Witch Council ever discovered Belle had inherited Nell's library—which should, for all intents and purposes, have been gifted to the National Library.

I wrinkled my nose and reached for a brownie. "I'm not entirely sure that's a good idea."

She frowned. "Why?"

"Because Clayton is out there, watching us. The last thing we need to do is bring his attention to the storage unit."

She made a frustrated sound. "Good point, but damned inconvenient."

"Better to be inconvenienced than have your gran's books confiscated."

"True." She wrinkled her nose. "I wish there was some damn way to track him."

I raised my eyebrows. "I think tracking him is the *last* thing we need to do."

Especially when any sort of confrontation was something the sixteen-year-old inner me was still desperate to avoid.

"Not us, specifically. I'm thinking more along the lines of Monty, Ashworth, and Eli—"

"I suspect it's gone well beyond the point of talking sense into him, given what Ashworth said about his fall from grace in recent years. Combine *that* with the impotency spell—"

"A spell I will never regret, no matter what he does to us."

Even as she said that, trepidation stirred and my gut began to churn. Not for my safety, but rather Belle's. I put the suddenly tasteless brownie down and said, "Are any of your gran's spell books upstairs?"

"Yes—why?"

"Look through them and see if there's anything that will protect you against magic."

"What's the point? No spell we create will ever stop Clayton's magic. He's just too powerful."

"Maybe, but if I wrap wild magic in it, it'll help."

Her frown deepened. "I thought you wanted to avoid any overt displays when it came to wild magic."

"I do, and it's a risk, but I'd rather that than risk losing you."

Alarm overtook the confusion. "Do you really think he'd go so far as to hurt me?"

"The easiest way to stop me is to hurt you, Belle, and he's well aware of that."

Fear, anger, and determination all flashed through her expression. "Then maybe we need to do more than simply talk to him. Maybe what we really need to do is give him no choice but to walk away."

I snorted. "And how the hell are we supposed to do that?"

"Well, he has to be staying in the reservation somewhere, and he certainly won't be camping out. He's not the type to go without his luxuries."

"True, but—"

"If we can find him, we can confront him. All of us,

together, recording everything that is said and done. Combine that with the truth seeker's report, and we may just be able to force his agreement to an annulment."

"I don't know." My voice was uncertain. "It's a big risk."

"Sitting around waiting for him to show us his cards is an even bigger one," Belle said. "At least this way, we have a fighting chance."

"A fighting chance of what?" Aiden said, as he sat back down at the table.

"We're talking about Clayton," Belle said. "I don't suppose you can abuse your ranger powers and get someone to check if he's staying within the reservation?"

"Already doing it," he said with a smile. "But there's a lot of hotels and B&Bs here, so it will take a few days. I take it you've now got a plan of action for when he *is* found?"

"Confrontation," Belle said. "A pack of us—wolves and witches—with the meeting fully recorded on a number of devices."

He glanced at me. "I like this plan, but I suspect Liz doesn't."

"I don't. I can think of too many things that could go wrong."

He reached out and caught my hand. "So can I. But no matter what evidence we collect, no matter what Ashworth or this Black Lantern Society does to help you out of the marriage, you will have to face him in the end, Liz. It's the only way you'll ever be truly free."

"All of which makes absolute sense. But this is something I've spent a good part of my life running from. It's going to be hard to change that habit."

And hard to ignore the fear and the memories that would rise the minute I saw him. Memories that might well freeze me in place for too many vital seconds.

"We have no choice," Belle said gently. "There's nowhere else to run. Not anymore."

Aiden glanced at her. "Meaning what?"

"We suspect the wild magic will prevent us leaving."

His frown deepened. "But Liz and I leave all the time."

"Not permanently."

"It's wild magic we're talking about here. It's not like it has any sort of cognizance."

"Except that it *has* since your sister became part of it," I said.

Katie's soul—via a spell so powerful it had literally torn her witch husband apart—might have originally inhabited only the younger of the two wellsprings here in the reservation, but her influence had recently started to cross over.

"Remember," Belle added, "Liz is the only means of communication *and* interaction Katie has with the real world. She won't support us leaving, because she'd lose that."

His expression suggested us leaving permanently wasn't something he'd support, either, and that warmed me in so many ways. His gaze returned to mine. "Have you actually discussed this with her?"

"No, but it's not like I really need to. I've used the wild magic—and been in communication with her often enough —to know it's a foregone conclusion."

He grunted. "Well, I admit that I'm not sorry it's happened. I'm not ready to lose you quite yet."

Belle raised an eyebrow, her expression wry. "I take it, then, you will inform us when you *are* ready to lose her? Because I'll need to have vast vats of whiskey and a truckload of chocolate ready."

Something flashed in his eyes, something that was both acknowledgement of the jibe and anger combined. The latter made no sense, given his oft-repeated warning that he wasn't into forevers—not with witches, anyway.

"I'm not the type to simply jump from one partner to another, Belle—even if that partner *is* a wolf."

"Happy to hear that." She picked up her empty cup and rose. "Now, if you'll excuse me, I've got some transcribing work to do."

Aiden watched her leave, then returned his gaze to mine. "I've got the feeling she's a little annoyed at me."

"It comes from her overprotective tendencies when it comes to me." I shrugged. "I have a habit of falling for entirely unsuitable men."

"At least you know better than to fall in love with me."

My lips twisted, though there was little in the way of amusement. "It's not always easy to control the heart, Aiden. At least it isn't for me."

Which was as close to an admission as I dared get.

He didn't immediately reply, but his conflicting emotions were very visible in his eyes. He wanted me in his life, he obviously cared for me deeply—and perhaps even loved me—but he wasn't about to admit any of that. Not to me. Not even to himself.

And for one simple reason.

When he fell in love, he wanted it to be with someone who could give him what I couldn't—full-blooded werewolf children. Apparently, any children born from the union of a wolf and a witch had little chance of survival. Those who weren't stillborn often had such serious defects they died before their first birthday. According to Aiden's mom, very few lived to claim their wolf heritage, let alone make it to adulthood.

And while I had no doubt Karleen would do or say anything to prevent a union between her son and me, there'd been no lie in her words. She obviously witnessed someone go through that very situation, and had no intention of watching her son suffer it.

I picked up my coffee and the remaining brownies and then rose. "Let's head upstairs. It's more comfortable."

We spent the rest of the night snuggling on the sofa, watching Netflix and talking about anything and everything but the elephant in the room that was our feelings.

Belle was right—I was going to be an utter mess when we did eventually break up. But there was no chance in hell I'd change the situation, even if I could.

As that old saying went, it was better to have loved and lost than never to have loved at all.

And I did damn love the man.

Aiden didn't head back to his own place in the morning, instead staying to help us out. Which was just as well, as we were swamped midmorning with customers and Penny was all but run off her feet. Once the café was closed, I sent Belle upstairs to read through her gran's books while he cleaned up and I caught up on the prep. It was close to dusk when his phone rang. He leaned a hip against the counter to answer and, after a slight pause, stiffened. "Have you called Monty?"

"I don't think Monty's back from Melbourne," I murmured.

He glanced at me, one eyebrow raised in question. I nodded and silently added to Belle, *Looks like I'm standing in for Monty again.*

I do like how he calls on you rather than Ashworth in these situations, Belle said. *Ashworth is the more logical choice, given his history working for the Regional Witch Association and the fact he subbed in the position before Monty arrived.*

I think he likes my face better than Ashworth's.

Belle snorted. *That is a certainty.*

I grinned and walked into the reading room to grab my backpack, then followed Aiden outside. The truck's lights flashed as he clicked the remote, and we quickly climbed inside.

"Where are we going?" I asked, as he reversed out and then headed for the street. "Has there been another murder?"

He looked right and left before pulling out onto the street with lights and sirens on. "No, but they were certainly newly married. The creature ran after they defended themselves."

"If we're dealing with a ghoul, I'm surprised."

"The woman threw salt at it."

Wise woman. "So I'm along for the ride because your rangers weren't able to track it via scent?"

"They can, but I told them to wait until we got there."

I frowned. "Why? Salt obviously works, and they're armed besides."

"Except this thing appears to be something other than a ghoul."

My frown deepened. "What makes you say that?"

"Because," he said, his voice flat, "this one had huge, bat-like wings, only half a torso, and intestines that trailed along behind it like streamers."

CHAPTER FIVE

The description matched the fragile memories I'd caught in the last victim's mind. Even so, I had to ask, "Are you sure the couple weren't drunk?"

"According to Jaz, no. And they have pictures of this thing."

"Most people would be a screaming mess after seeing something like that."

"Apparently, she watches a lot of those ghost hunter type shows."

I snorted. "I suspect there wouldn't be many ghost hunting shows highlighting *that* sort of spirit."

A smile briefly flirted with his lips. "Does the description of this thing match anything you've seen or read about?"

"No, but it's not like I had any reason to study the supernatural before I came to this place."

He grunted. "If we manage to track it tonight, will you be able to deal with it?"

I couldn't help a smile. "Unknown, given I have no idea

what we're dealing with. But if you wanted certainty in that regard, you should have called in Ashworth."

"I would have, but he and Eli are off the reservation tonight."

I glanced at him. "How do you know that?"

"Gossip."

I chuckled softly. "Well, if we *do* track it down, I'll do my best to deal with it. But if worse comes to worst and it runs, I'll throw a tracking spell. If it *is* some variation of ghoul, it'll go to ground for the day. That'll give us time to find and kill it."

He nodded and didn't say anything else. Several kilometers out of Castle Rock, he turned onto a dirt road and sped up a slight incline. The building on the top of the hill was another small, whitewashed cottage with a red tin roof and red-painted door. The veranda out the front was large enough to hold a rough-hewn table and two bench seats, and no doubt had a magnificent view over the valley.

All the lights were on inside, and there were three vehicles parked to the right. The first was a black Mercedes SUV that probably belonged to the couple who'd reported the incident, but the others were ranger vehicles.

Mac—a brown-haired wolf who'd transferred into the reservation a few years ago—stepped out onto the veranda as we pulled up.

I slung my pack over my shoulder and followed Aiden.

Mac gave me a nod of greeting and then said, "The creature tried to enter via the rear glass doors."

Aiden motioned him to lead the way. "It seems to be developing a pattern."

"Well, I guess glass doors would be somewhat easier to break into, given the lack of legs." His tone hinted at amusement. "The doors weren't forced open, though."

"That suggests they weren't even locked."

Mac glanced at me over his shoulder. "They weren't, but the creature didn't get far, as the salt was thrown before it could attack. I guess it was lucky they'd been eating dinner and the shaker was already out on the table."

"Timing *is* everything in the survival stakes," I said. "Though it *is* a little odd the ghoul attacked so soon after dusk. They tend to wait until deeper darkness has arrived."

"We're talking about a creature that supposedly has no bottom half, so I think odd is a given." The amusement was clearer in Mac's tone this time.

"Where does the scent trail lead?" Aiden asked. "Into the scrub or down into the valley?"

"Former. I tracked it as far as the boundary but no further." He shot me another look. "Was the creature simply spooked by the couple's actions, or does salt really work against something like this?"

"Salt—pure salt—is a deterrent against most supernatural beings, though it's better used in a protection circle or as a barrier against entry in doorways and windows."

"Huh." Mac's gaze switched to Aiden. "Which means it might make sense for us to add a permanent tub of the stuff to our kits, boss."

"Ask Maggie to get onto it tomorrow."

Other voices were now audible. One was Jaz, another ranger who'd only recently moved into the reservation after marrying into the Marin pack. The other was most likely the woman whose love of ghost-hunting TV shows had probably saved the lives of her partner and her.

We walked around the rear of the building but didn't head toward the still-open French doors. Instead, Mac leapt off the veranda and strode across to a stone path that wound its way up through a garden filled with trimmed roses and deciduous trees.

The rear fence was a weatherworn and hip-height picket; beyond it lay trees and scrub. I drew in a breath and caught a vaguely odorous scent that reminded me of death and decay.

"I'll take the lead," Aiden said. "Mac, rear point. Liz, if anything tweaks your senses, let me know."

I nodded and tried to ignore the tension gathering within. The small gate creaked as Aiden opened it, the sharp sound echoing across the stillness of the night. Which, more than anything, pointed to the presence of evil having slipped past here not that long ago. Night creatures were far more sensitive to all things supernatural than most humans; the fact that even the possums weren't moving about spoke to the foulness of this thing.

The hill soon steepened dramatically, and my legs began to burn. As my breathing became harsher, Aiden caught my hand and tugged me on. I wasn't entirely sure it helped, but at least it meant I wasn't slowing them down too much.

The tree line thinned out as we neared the top of the ridge, and stars gleamed in skies only partially covered by clouds. Aiden paused, his gaze searching the tree-lined valley below us, while I rested my hands on my knees and sucked in air. Fit I was not, even though I'd recently started intermittent jogging—though not in any way to lose weight, as I was perfectly happy just as I was. Of course, my definition of intermittent differed wildly from Aiden's, which was why I tended to do it mostly on the days I stayed home. Belle was a far more patient and understanding jogging partner—mainly because she didn't feel obliged to stay by my side the entire time, which in turn meant I could not only stretch out the running intervals but also shorten the time spent running. Although it had to be said, jogging wasn't as bad as I'd feared. My muscles certainly recovered faster than I'd ever presumed they would.

Mac stopped beside Aiden, his hands on his hips and frustration evident. "The trail's gone cold."

"Yes." Aiden glanced at me. "Are you getting anything on either a psychic or magical level?"

"Not a glimmer." I pushed upright and studied the valley below. "I don't suppose there's an old graveyard down there somewhere, is there?"

"No." He drew in a deep breath and released it slowly. "I guess we've no choice—"

"There *is* Barnett's farm," Mac cut in. "It's on the far side of this valley, I know, but they do have a family burial plot on their land."

I frowned. "I didn't think it was legal to bury people outside a public cemetery? Or does the rule differ in the reservation?"

"Only to some extent," Aiden said. "Every pack has burial grounds within their compounds, but humans still need approval from the appropriate department to bury on private land. Even then, it's usually only granted if there're prior burials on the site."

"In the Barnetts' case, there're five generations buried there," Mac said. "Is that a big enough graveyard to attract something like this?"

I shrugged. "I can't really say for sure, given I have no real idea what we're dealing with."

"Meaning it *is* worth checking," Aiden said. "We'll head back down and drive over."

"Good, because you weren't ever going to get me to walk over."

Aiden chuckled and pressed a hand to my spine, gently ushering me back to the path. Though it was easier going down, it still took nearly half an hour to return to the house.

Aiden motioned me toward his truck and then walked inside to talk to Jaz. I opened the passenger door but didn't immediately climb in, instead studying the surrounding night as awareness prickled across my skin. My watcher was once again out there.

I hesitated, one hand clenched against the need to raise some form of defensive or even tracking spell. If my watcher was Clayton, then nothing I did would matter. If it wasn't, then he'd most likely be protected against any spell I could raise. Or, at least, any spell that didn't involve the wild magic.

That suggests you're not carrying Ashworth's diversion charm on you, Belle said, mental tone annoyed.

No. Totally forgot about it.

Then I'll make sure you shove it in your purse when you get home.

Footsteps approached. I half turned and watched Aiden stride toward me.

"What's wrong?" he immediately said.

"Nothing." I hesitated. "Can you smell anyone nearby?"

He raised an eyebrow but flared his nostrils, drawing in a deep breath. After a moment, he shook his head. "No —why?"

I shrugged. "It's probably just imagination—"

"If there's one thing I've learned over these past few months, it's that when you say it's probably your imagination, it's not. So give."

I grimaced and climbed into the truck. "I keep getting the feeling that I'm being watched."

"Well, if Clayton's here, that's not surprising. He'll be

tracking your movements so he's got a clearer picture of his attack options. Classic hunter action."

"Yeah, but Clayton's no hunter. He generally prefers immediate confrontation over stealth."

"Except when it comes to snatching innocence, apparently." Aiden's voice was flat and yet hinted at fury. For me. For what had been done to me.

"And *that* is what in the end saved me. He didn't expect resistance." Didn't expect Belle to come roaring to the rescue.

Aiden reached across and gently gripped my thigh. Warmth bled into my skin but failed to ease the inner tremors.

"There's a good chance we'll find him before he decides to do anything," he said. "Trust that. Trust *us*."

"I do." I just didn't trust that Clayton would react in any normal manner.

Silence fell, and night closed in. After another twenty minutes, Aiden slowed and pulled into a long, tree-lined driveway. Stones crunched under the tires and, up ahead, a house lay wrapped in darkness. As we pulled up, the external lights came on and, seconds later, so did the internal ones.

"Wait here," Aiden said, and climbed out.

He leapt up the steps and strode toward the front door. It opened, revealing a middle-aged man wearing a T-shirt and boxer shorts. Aiden spoke to him for several minutes, then came back. The owner went back inside and the lights went off.

"He's not coming with us?" I said.

"Better if he doesn't, especially if this thing is there." Aiden started the truck and followed the drive around to the left. The headlights picked out a track that wound past several old sheds.

"What excuse did you give him for us needing to see the family cemetery?"

"I told him we were tracking a burglary suspect, and his current trajectory had him heading this way." He slowed as a gate loomed. "You want to open that?"

I did. It was a process we repeated twice before we reached the top of the long hill. In the glow of the headlights, a peppercorn tree stood guard over a metal fence. Beyond it were a number of headstones.

I climbed out and moved to the front of the truck. The breeze was stronger up here than it had been on the other plateau, no doubt due to the fact that the only tree up here to break its force was the lovely old peppercorn. At least this time the resulting goose bumps were actually due to the chill in the wind, rather than any sense of evil.

"Anything?" Aiden asked, as he stopped next to me.

His body cut the wind and allowed his warm, musky scent to wash over me. I drew it in, somehow finding both comfort and strength in his closeness. And hoping, with all that I had, that Aiden wouldn't be amongst those made to pay for my presence here.

I frowned, wondering if it was a warning of what was to come, or simply fear. I hoped it was the latter. I feared it was the former.

Especially given my watcher had even followed us up here.

"Liz?" Aiden prompted gently.

I swallowed heavily and tried to concentrate on what we were hunting rather than what was hunting me.

"I'm not immediately sensing anything, but we'll need to get closer to be sure."

We walked on. I silently wove a containment spell around my right hand; the threads gleamed silver and gold in the darkness, the former an indication that despite the fact my inner concealment spell remained active, the wild magic within would not be contained. At least not when it came to creating magic—and that was going to be problematic.

Although I guess if it came down to a duel of magic between Clayton and me, the appearance of wild magic within mine would be the least of my problems.

We walked through an open gate into the private cemetery. There were five lines of gravestones, some so old the writing on them had all but been erased by the wind and the weather, and others so new the golden letters gleamed in the pale light of the moon.

There was nothing to indicate a ghoul or some kind of demon was using these graves as a shelter, and relief stirred, even though its absence here only meant it was free to create havoc elsewhere.

"Nothing looks disturbed to me," Aiden said. "And the breeze is free from the foul scent we followed from the cottage."

"I'll still do a full check, just on the off chance it's somehow concealing itself from me."

The result was the same; the ghoul wasn't here. I released the containment spell and flexed my fingers to ease the remaining tingle.

"I guess it was always a remote chance," Aiden said. "Let's get you home—"

"Not before I secure the graveyard. It may never come up here, but it's better to be safe than sorry."

I swung the pack from my shoulder and pulled out the bottles of holy water. There wasn't enough to protect the entire plot, but it was the graves that really mattered. The three I carried should be enough to stop the ghoul or spirit breaking into a coffin to wait out the daylight.

I uncorked the first of them and began the spell. I walked as I spoke, trickling the holy water on the ground, creating an unseen barrier that would allow humans and animals past but keep the monsters out. It was a basic spell, but sometimes that's all that was needed. Besides, anything more complicated would have to be boosted to last any length of time, and I really didn't want to waste that sort of strength right now.

Once the entire area was covered, I activated the spell and studied it through narrowed eyes. Surprisingly, there were no threads of wild magic visible; maybe it only attached itself to the stronger spells.

"All set?" Aiden asked.

I nodded. "The spell will only hold a couple of days at most, but hopefully we'll have caught the ghoul by then."

"Going on past hunts, I wouldn't be betting on it." He lightly guided me back to the car, his fingers pressing warmth into my spine despite the layers of clothing.

"I've got to return to the station for an hour or so, but I'll be back on guard duty later tonight."

I raised an eyebrow. "It's your day off—Jaz and Mac can handle the reports, surely?" I paused. "Or is this more a shower thing? As in, you hate ours."

His lips twitched. "That might or might not be a good guess."

"It's not that bad, seriously."

"I like a shower big enough to party in." He glanced at me, his blue eyes gleaming with mischief. "There's definitely no room in yours to do anything interesting."

I tsked. "A werewolf with no imagination is a very sad thing."

The gleam became heated. "Imagination is *not* a problem. I shall prove it to you once the current situation has been dealt with."

"I do wonder how, given the already mentioned party dimensions of your showers."

"There are small places aplenty in my house. We just haven't explored them."

"Then I look forward to doing so."

"Excellent."

I smiled and glanced out the window... and caught sight of a figure on the ridge of the hill several paddocks across. My stomach clenched and, for a second, I couldn't even breathe.

But it wasn't Clayton. Aside from the fact it wasn't tall enough to be Clayton, the figure on that hill had flowed from one form to another.

"Is there any reason for a werewolf to be running around up here?"

"No, why?"

"Because I just spotted one on the ridge several paddocks over. He's now running downhill through the tree line."

Aiden leaned forward and then frowned. "How the hell can you see that? I can barely see him, and I've wolf eyesight."

Once again unease stirred—as did the sudden desire to go talk to Katie. These changes—the sharpening of at least some of my senses—had only started happening since she'd inhabited my body. Maybe she—or even Gabe, whose soul now haunted the wellspring where he'd fused Katie to the wild magic and in the process lost his life—could tell me whether it was a temporary or permanent situation. Although given the time that had passed, it was looking more and more permanent. Which meant the real question was, how far would it go?

"The rising moon is fairly bright; I caught the glimmer of his coat more than anything." Which wasn't a lie, because that's what I was currently seeing.

He grunted—a sound that somehow managed to convey disbelief. "My first instinct is to go after the bastard, but the distance between us gives him the advantage."

"Against you. Not against magic. Keep driving." I quickly created a tracking spell and then wound down the window. The night air snapped in, cooling the cabin instantly.

The moon chose that moment to come fully out from behind the clouds, silvering the coat of the running form.

Aiden swore. "It's a goddamn O'Connor."

"Probably not from your pack, though."

"If he *is*, there'll be hell to pay."

As the moon's glow started to fade, I flung the tracking spell out of the window. It flew toward the running wolf, a small, tumbling mass of threads that shimmered in the moonlight. Our target obviously wasn't wearing much in the way of protection against magic, because the spell hit him dead center and instantly began tugging at my directional instincts.

"Got him," I said.

"Good."

He swung the truck off the track and accelerated across the paddock. As the wolf's speed increased, the spell's threads spooled out across the night, leaving a faint but shimmering trail for me to follow. I did wonder how in the hell he hoped to escape, given no wolf could outrun a vehicle—not over a long distance, anyway.

Then I spotted the truck near an open gateway. "I don't suppose you've spotted that man or the vehicle following us?"

"No, which means he's probably placed a tracker on my truck. He would have had plenty of opportunities today." He glanced at me. "If that *is* the case, then it's worth checking your SUV, too."

I rubbed my arms, but it did little to chase the chill that gathered once again. Aiden might be talking about physical trackers, but magical ones were easy to do and easy to conceal. Getting me—or Belle—cornered on our own would certainly be something Clayton would prefer. It's no doubt the reason I'd been drugged on my wedding day—it meant he didn't have to put in the time and effort required to seduce the unwilling.

The question that had burned in me since that dark day was whether my parents had been party to that drugging. While I could totally believe my father would have turned a blind eye, I really, *really* didn't want to believe my mother would have condoned it. I might have been a great disappointment to her, and she might have been a somewhat distant parent thanks to my lack of magical ability, but she'd never been deliberately cruel or uncaring.

As the wolf ahead neared his vehicle, he flowed back into human form and jumped into the SUV. I couldn't see the plate number from this distance, which was annoying because it meant we had no means of finding him if my tracker stopped working for some reason. Seconds later, he was speeding away from us. Aiden followed, gradually gaining ground as his truck bounced unsteadily over the rocky pasture. My grip on the grab handle was so fierce my knuckles glowed.

The wolf's SUV smashed through a gate, sending it flying as the truck spun to the right and barreled toward the road.

"You know," I said, as we hit another pothole and the truck threatened to topple. "It might be worth letting him think he's gotten away."

Aiden shot me a glance—something I felt rather than saw. "Are you sure the tracker threads won't snap or something if he gains too much distance?"

"I can't give you an ironclad guarantee, of course, but I'm pretty sure it won't."

He instantly slowed, and I eased my death grip on the handle. The SUV crashed out onto the road, its rear end fishtailing dangerously for several seconds before the driver got it under control and sped off.

"Either he's dragging a ton of fence line behind him, or he cut it earlier to get into the paddock."

"It's the latter," Aiden said, and immediately called the Barnetts.

I concentrated on the thinning spool of magic and on providing directions. We were soon cruising back to Castle Rock.

"Left into Forest Street," I said. "It feels like he's stopped."

"You want me to go slower?"

I hesitated. "Not yet. Turn down the third street on the right—it's just beyond that park."

We turned, the truck's headlights briefly spotlighting a couple walking on the gravel path that followed the left edge of the road. "We're almost on him now."

Aiden immediately slowed. We swept around the next

corner, and a number of buildings came into view. Directly ahead were several long tin sheds, and to our right was a single-story cream-and-red-brick pub that looked to have been around since the gold rush days. There were a number of cars parked out the front of it and at least six more in the vacant lot on the other side of the road. The SUV was nowhere in sight, but the tracking threads suggested our watcher had hightailed it into the pub.

"He's probably parked around the back." Aiden turned into a side street further up the road and then stopped.

"The minute either of us go in there," I said. "He's likely to run."

Aiden nodded. "I'm actually counting on it."

"How many exits are there?"

"Two aside from the kitchen, and he won't chance being stopped by the chefs or owner. There's an exit into the beer garden and another down the service hall, which contains the toilets." His smile was brief and sharp. "He'll no doubt take the latter the minute he spots you walking through the front door. Once I bring him down, you can make him talk."

"Oh, you can bet I will."

"Give me five minutes to get around the back without being seen, then head in."

I nodded. He climbed out, then leapt over the nearby fence and disappeared. I watched the clock count down, then leaned across the seat to grab his keys and climbed out. The moon was once again free from clouds, which was never a good thing when you had crimson-colored hair that burned brightly under *any* sort of light.

I tugged the hood of my jacket over my hair and walked casually toward the pub. There were six old weatherboard houses between it and me, but thankfully, the pub was wedge-shaped and the closest end had no windows. Even if our target was keeping watch, he wouldn't see me until I walked past the veranda.

The nearer I got, the more my heart raced. I flexed my fingers, trying to remain calm. At this point, we had no idea if this man was doing anything more than a bit of nefarious snooping. We had no idea yet if he was—in any way— connected to Clayton. Just because instinct was coming down on the affirmative didn't mean it was right.

I went past the section of veranda protected by plastic roll-down blinds and then stepped up onto it. A small sign to the left of the double wooden doors said Railway Bistro. I grabbed the handle, took a deep, settling breath, and then stepped inside. It felt like I'd stepped back in time. The ceiling was dark wood, the walls warm amber dotted with old photographs and land-scape paintings, and the antique furniture well-worn. There was a dining area on the left, a servery in the middle, and a bar area to the right. There were five couples and a family of six in the dining area, and half a dozen more people in the bar. The tracking thread led me to the right and, after a moment, I saw him. He was tall, rangy, with pock-marked skin—unusual in a were-wolf—and dark gray hair. He definitely wasn't from Aiden's pack, as they ran the full gamut of blond; gray only set in once age had started taking its toll. *This* wolf looked to be in his mid-thirties.

I pushed the hood off and walked toward him. The movement obviously caught his attention, because his gaze rose and met mine. Surprise flickered across his expression, followed swiftly by consternation. He pushed away from the bar and strode to the left, quickly disappearing from my sight.

As I rounded the corner of the bar, I saw a slowly

closing door that said Bathrooms and couldn't help smiling. Aiden had picked it right.

By the time I got there, the hallway beyond was empty and the door at the far end open. I couldn't see our suspect, but I could certainly hear him. He was cursing up a storm.

I stopped in the back doorway and watched Aiden drag the bound and handcuffed man closer.

"Told you it would work," he said cheerfully. "Let's go around to the beer garden—we can interrogate him there."

"I haven't been read my fucking rights," the man bellowed. "This is an illegal arrest."

There was a lilt to his voice that suggested he'd come from Ireland, but it was impossible to say how recently. Some people never lost their accent, no matter how long they stayed in another country.

"I'm head ranger and this is *my* reservation," Aiden said. "You were not only following us, but rather stupidly threw a punch at me. You have no rights."

"This is *bullshit*—"

"And it's bullshit that'll land you in a cell for several years if you're not damn careful and start cooperating."

"I demand you give me my phone call."

"Yeah, that's not going to happen." Aiden kicked a metal chair sideways, slung the stranger onto it, and then pulled one of the ever-present cable ties from his pocket, quickly connecting the stranger's bound hands to the back of the chair.

"Help," the stranger screamed. "Someone help me!"

Aiden rolled his eyes but strolled over to the double doors that led back into the bar and went inside.

I crossed my arms and glared at our captive. "I suggest you start cooperating, or you'll be forced to."

He snorted. "You don't scare me, witch."

I raised an eyebrow. "Really? I take it, then, that you've been given some form of protection against certain types of magic?"

This time, he controlled his emotions far better. There was barely a flicker to indicate my guess had hit the mark.

"I have no idea what you're talking about."

"That so? How, then, do you think we found you?"

He shrugged. "Your ranger friend is a wolf—they're good trackers."

"But not so good that they can follow someone in a speeding truck at a distance of several kilometers."

"I can't see your point—"

"The point," Aiden said, as he came back out, "is that you've got a tracking spell on you."

"That's impossible—"

"Says who? Oh, and don't bother with any more screams for help. The owner and patrons have been informed of the situation."

"And they'll be my witnesses when I sue your ass for false arrest and imprisonment."

Aiden smiled. "Oh, I don't think it'll get to that. Liz, do you want to check him?"

"Check me for what?" the stranger said, his voice indignant. "What the hell do you think I'm carrying?"

"Protection." I stepped to one side of the chair—out of feet range—and held my hand an inch or so above his body as I checked him from head to foot. It was only when I got to his boots that I felt the sting of magic. It wasn't Clayton's—aside from the fact it felt generic, it held none of his bite. I guess that was unsurprising—Clayton had been caught flat-footed once. I doubt he'd underestimate us a second time, and that meant he would not put his magical 'mark' on anything that could be traced back to him—not until he was ready to confront me, anyway.

It also explained why the tracker had stuck—the spell hadn't been designed to ward off something so simple.

I stepped back. "It's in his boot."

"Left or right?" Aiden said.

The stranger unwisely chose that moment to lash out with both tied feet. Aiden jumped back, then calmly grabbed the offending feet and upended him. As the stranger crashed back onto the grass and began uttering yet another string of curses, Aiden ripped off his boots and handed them to me.

I tipped them upside down; two small disks dropped onto the ground. The threads were pale and pulsed with a low-grade energy that definitely didn't belong to any blue-blood I knew.

Which didn't actually make me feel any easier. As I crushed them under my boot, Aiden said, "Right, are you going to cooperate?"

"Give me my phone call and a damn lawyer, and I might consider it," the stranger growled.

Aiden stepped back and waved elegantly toward our prisoner. "He's all yours."

I took a deep breath to center my energy and then began to spell as I slowly circled the prone stranger. I'd left the backpack—and my spell stones—back in the truck, and the metal chair wasn't really an appropriate anchor. It left me with no choice but to keep the spell open-ended, even as I activated it. That was never an ideal situation, but in this case, with him moving around so much, it at least gave me the option of pushing more energy and 'force' into the truth spell.

"Right," I said, as the spell's force pulsed through me. "He's ready to be questioned."

"No, he's fucking not," the stranger growled. "This has gone far enough—"

"Give me your name and pack," Aiden cut in.

The stranger's mouth opened and then closed several times, but in the end he couldn't escape the force of the spell.

"James O'Conner, Black Valley."

I frowned. "Where the hell is the Black Valley?"

"Ireland," Aiden said. "Why were you following us?"

Again he fought the press of the truth spell. Again he failed. "I was employed to follow the witch and photograph everyone she interacts with."

My gut clenched. I'd been right to fear Clayton might well target everyone else to get to me. "How long have you been doing that?"

"Five days."

Meaning a few days longer than I'd been sensing him. *Fuck.* "And have you been doing daily reports?"

"Yes, and being paid daily. You bastards will have no doubt cost me tonight's fee."

"Money will be the least of your problems when you're in jail," Aiden said, voice dry. "What's the name of the man who employed you?"

He bared his teeth, fighting the compulsion to reply, but in the end had no choice. "I don't know his full name. I was only given the first—Lawrence."

My heart stuttered to a brief halt and then broke into a gallop.

It wasn't only my husband here in the reservation. It was my goddamn father as well.

CHAPTER SIX

My knees buckled, and I would have hit the ground if Aiden hadn't lunged forward fast enough to catch me.

"Liz?" he said. "What's wrong?"

I didn't immediately answer. Couldn't immediately answer. I just sucked in air and tried to get the panic and fear under control. But not all of it was mine. Some of it was Belle's—her *fuck, fuck, fuck*, was a refrain that ran through the outer reaches of my mind, thick with the same fear that pulsed through me.

And with good reason—Clayton and my father were two of the strongest witches in Canberra. The combined might of Ashworth, Eli, and Monty might have been able to contain Clayton, but it was doubtful there'd be any such hope now that my father was also here.

You need to get out, Belle. You need to hide somewhere.

There is nowhere safe to run, Liz. Not now. Not when he's had the time to track all our movements and now knows who we interact with.

So grab a taxi and disappear. The sooner the better.

Me leaving this reservation weakens you. I can't and won't do that.

"Lizzie?" Aiden repeated. "Speak to me."

"My father's name is Lawrence," I croaked. "And that means he's here with Clayton."

"Are you sure?" Aiden said. "Lawrence isn't exactly a rare name."

"I'm sure." Even so, I pushed away from his arms and said to James, "Describe this man to me."

He shrugged. "Tall, broad shouldered, crimson hair and eyes like yours."

"Has he a port wine stain here?" I asked, running my fingers down the left side of my neck.

"I saw some dark mottling near his ear, but I couldn't say if it was a birth mark or something else. It's not like I was interested in getting to know him better or anything."

"How did he contact you?" Aiden said.

"He messaged me."

"Text or Facebook?" Aiden said.

"Neither."

I glanced at Aiden. "Meaning the messages were sent via magic."

It was a simple enough spell and one taught in high school, though it wasn't something I'd ever done. To be honest, I'd totally forgotten about it.

"And did you physically meet to hand over the information or did you electronically transfer?"

"Met. He didn't want any sort of electronic trail left behind. He even took the damn memory card out of my camera."

Aiden's smile held little amusement. "And you didn't have backups? I find that hard to believe."

"I don't really care what you fucking believe. I had no

choice but to hand everything over. He must have spelled me or something."

"And you still worked for him, despite this?" I rubbed my arms and somehow resisted the growing urge to run into the pub, order the largest bottle of whiskey they had, and get absolutely and totally drunk. "He must have been paying you a pretty penny."

"I'm not cheap." He studied me critically for a moment. "How did you two spot me? You shouldn't have been able to, given how far away I was."

"Your employer obviously forgot to mention the convenient fact that I'm a psychic. I've been feeling your presence for days; I just wasn't able to locate you until tonight."

James snorted. "Typical of a blueblood to leave *that* sort of information out."

It *was* actually typical, simply because to bluebloods psychic powers were of little consequence—which was why Belle had been able to overrun Clayton's thoughts so thoroughly. He hadn't believed her telepathy was strong enough to affect him.

He knew better now.

As Aiden continued to question James, I said, *Belle— I'm not leaving. Don't ask me to.*

I thrust down frustration and fear. *Then at the very least we need to find you somewhere safe to hide.*

Nowhere here is safe. Not from someone like him.

For no good reason, Maelle's comment rose. A tiny spark of hope stirred.

No way, no how, Belle said.

You'll be safe at Maelle's. It's the last place they'll think to look, and it's doubtful if either of them would dare attack a vampire's abode.

Because only an insane person would willingly stay on the premises.

Maelle owes us a favor—this will fulfill that. It keeps you close while keeping you safe.

From Clayton and your father, maybe, but not from her bloodsucker tendencies.

She swore an oath, Belle. She won't break that or her promise to help.

Are you sure of that?

Every instinctive bit of me is.

She swore softly. *Let me think about it.*

"I'll go get the truck," Aiden said, his gaze returning to me. "Will you be all right with the suspect?"

I nodded and dragged the keys out of my pocket. As he disappeared, I said, "When did Lawrence contact you?"

James shrugged. "A couple of weeks ago. He didn't appear in any sort of hurry to chase you up though."

He mightn't have been, but I doubt the same could be said of Clayton. "Did you ever speak to another man?"

"No."

So why, if my father had recently begun distancing himself from Clayton, was he now here helping to track down his escapee daughter? That really didn't make a whole lot of sense.

"How did he initially contact you?"

James shrugged. "I guess he got my details off my website and shot me a message. It was in-person from there."

"In your office? Or elsewhere?"

"Generally out in the open and away from any possibility of being seen."

"Where have you been meeting him here?"

James shrugged. "It varies—the last one was up at Jackson's Lookout."

Which wasn't that far out of Argyle, if I remembered properly. "Were you supposed to meet him there tonight?"

"No. He said he had other plans but he'd be in contact with a new meet location."

"How was he going to do that? Via messages magically transported to you again?"

He nodded. "They appear in my hotel room. And before you ask, they self-destruct two minutes after I've read them."

I smiled. Of course they did. My father was nothing if not cautious. "What time do they usually appear?"

"Around ten."

I glanced at my watch. It was just after nine now, but that still gave us plenty of time to get there if we left immediately. "Where were you staying?"

"At the Albion Motel."

Which wasn't a place I knew, but wouldn't be hard to Google. "Key?"

He blew out a frustrated breath. "Top pocket."

I stepped forward, carefully plucked the key free, and shoved it into my pocket.

Belle, you want to go for a drive?

It's a toss-up between that or drink myself into a stupor, and we do have to work tomorrow. She paused. *You don't think this could be a trap?*

There's no magic on James except mine now, and the protection disks weren't Clayton's or my father's, so neither of them would have felt their destruction. Presuming, of course, they'd been close enough to do so, and I doubted it.

And if, as I suspect, you find nothing there, why don't we then go on up to the clearing and talk to Katie? The sooner you get some answers to those questions you raised, the better.

Meaning she'd been listening in again.

I'm always listening in. It's what a good familiar does. She paused. *Well, except for personal times. Not interested in hearing any of that.*

I half turned as Aiden's truck appeared. *We should be there in twenty.*

I'll be waiting with coffee, extra holy water, and the location of his hotel.

Aiden tipped James upright, cut off the cable tie, and then dragged him across to the truck, shoving him into the rear and fastening him securely before starting the truck and heading off. It took just over twenty minutes to get back to the café; I leaned across the seat and quickly kissed him. "You still planning to stay overnight?"

He nodded. "I'll be a couple hours though—we'll need to question our suspect further and then process him."

I hesitated. "If we're not there, don't panic. I need to go talk to Katie."

His eyebrows rose. "Why?"

"Because she's in charge of the wild magic, and it might be possible for it to do some of the leg work for us. Clayton and my father might be able to hide from us, but no spell they could ever create will hide from the wild magic."

He frowned. "The wild magic in and of itself can't communicate with you though."

"No, but Katie will be aware the minute anything is found, and she can come find me. She's done it before."

He didn't look happy, but he cupped my cheek and brushed his thumb lightly across my lips. "Please promise me you'll be careful. Please don't do anything stupid."

"I won't."

I think he'll consider the two of us investigating the suspect's accommodation alone to be stupid.

Probably. We still have to do it, though. I kissed Aiden's thumb and then grabbed the pack and climbed out. Once he was out of sight, I flung the pack over my shoulder and then walked around to the parking area.

Belle came out of the rear door, two travel mugs and several bottles of holy water tucked into a cardboard travel tray. She locked the door with her free hand, then reached into her pocket and tossed a small round object my way. I caught it and realized it was Ashworth's diversion charm. It was a palm-sized wooden disk deeply etched with witch runes. Though its magic was currently inactive, its thick lines swirled around the disk, providing intriguing glimpses of the power and complexity of the spell. According to Ashworth, it would haze my aura and stop a tracer being used to find me. Whether it would stop a tracker on the truck, I couldn't say.

I pressed the center of the charm to activate it, shoved it into the backpack, and tossed *that* onto the rear seat. Then, slowly and carefully, I went over the entire vehicle, looking for a tracking spell. I found it attached to the exhaust pipe, of all places.

I squatted to study it. Once again, the magic within was neither my father's nor Clayton's, but it was a whole lot more powerful than the charms given to James.

Belle squatted down beside me. "Can you defuse it?"

"Maybe." I reached out and carefully plucked the outer thread free. The rest of the spell vibrated in response, but I couldn't feel anything to suggest additional layers had been added to prevent exactly what I was about to do. I narrowed my gaze and carefully deactivated the spell. Once inert, I plucked it free, then rose and tossed it into the nearby bin.

"Given how exposed our car is out here," Belle commented. "I think we should keep checking for trackers."

"And not just magical. Aiden said it's possible they're using electronic ones as well."

Alarm flitted across her features. "And how are we supposed to find them?"

"We don't—he will."

"Which isn't going to help us out at this particular moment."

"I know, but we'll just have to take that risk."

She climbed into the passenger side. "Let's hope we don't regret it."

I started up the SUV, reversed out, and then accepted my travel mug, sipping gratefully as Belle read out the directions. The SUV did have navigation, but we'd been without it for so long in our old wagon that it was taking some time to get used to using it, rather than Google Maps on our phones.

It didn't take us long to get to James's hotel, as it was only a couple of kilometers out of Castle Rock, well before Louton. Only trouble was, there was already a ranger vehicle stationed out the front of it. Jaz leaned against the passenger side of the vehicle, her arms crossed and stance relaxed as she watched us approach.

I stopped and climbed out. "Aiden sent you here, didn't he?"

"He did indeed," she said, clearly amused. "He figured you were up to something more than what you'd said. And, given you were alone with the suspect for a few minutes, it really wasn't hard to guess what."

"Damn, that man really *has* got your measure," Belle said with a laugh.

"That's because the pair of you have a history of saying

one thing and doing the exact opposite." Jaz pushed away from her SUV. "James's room is around the back. I got the key from the owner."

I cleared my throat. "And I got it from James."

She rolled her eyes. "That's evidence, you know."

"Yes, but I didn't want to break in and leave magical evidence behind."

"Because that makes total sense to someone like me. This way."

She led the way around the building. It was two-story and rectangular in shape, with a parking area out the back. Metal steps led up to the next floor, and rattled somewhat alarmingly as we went up. Jaz handed us gloves and then unlocked the top door. The hallway had six doors leading off it, three on each side. James's was the second on the left.

We stepped inside. The room was basic but clean. The queen-sized bed looked comfortable, the bedside tables clear of junk, and the bathroom—off to our right—looked small, but at first glance appeared clean and tidy.

"Nothing setting off your magical radars?" Jaz asked.

I shook my head. "But that's not really unexpected. He's a wolf not a witch."

"Then why did you come here if you didn't think you'd find anything?" She opened the small wardrobe and peered inside.

"Because James got his messages magically around 10:00 p.m., and I wanted to be here in case one arrived." I glanced at my watch. "We've only ten minutes to wait."

"Then we'll use the time to search the room. Belle, do you want to check the bed and bedside tables? Liz, can you go through the bathroom?"

I nodded and headed in. The first things I saw were the undies and two T-shirts hanging over the shower screen.

His shaving kit sat on the small shelf under the mirror and didn't hold anything unexpected. The two small drawers under the vanity were empty, as was the small cabinet behind the mirror.

"Nothing," I said, heading out.

"Ditto," Belle echoed. "The man travels light."

"Extremely light," Jaz agreed. "He's only got two changes of clothes in his bag."

"He's hand washed his—" I stopped abruptly.

The air between Belle and me had begun to sparkle, and the energy that followed was fierce and familiar—my father's. My gut churned, and I rubbed my arms, fighting back fear as the sparkle condensed and then faded. A single sheet of paper fluttered softly to the floor.

Jaz stepped forward.

"Don't touch it," I warned, "Magic lingers, and I'm not sure what it's designed to do."

"There doesn't appear to be anything written—" She stopped as a thin thread of gold appeared on the parchment-like paper and words appeared.

I stepped forward, even though part of me—a very large part of me—wanted to do nothing more than run.

We need to meet, daughter dearest, the message said. *Write when and where on this paper. You have two minutes before it is returned to me.*

"He knows you're here," Jaz said, her expression disturbed. "But how?"

"We think there's a tracker on our SUV," Belle said.

"And I take it from both your expressions that this parent isn't someone you want to meet?"

"No, not quite yet." Not until Ashworth and Eli got back into the reservation, at any rate. They may not make any difference in the end, but my father, at the very least, wouldn't do or say anything too drastic in front of such an audience.

"What are we going to do?" Belle said, her face pale.

"Answer the message, for a start." I glanced back at Jaz. "You got a pen on you?"

She tugged one out of her top pocket and handed it to me. I flicked the nib down, then, with only the slightest hesitation, carefully plucked the parchment. Magic stirred briefly across its surface, but I was wearing gloves, so anything he hoped to glean from my touching it would be voided. I walked across to the bedside table and began to write...

Meet tomorrow night, 8 pm, at our café. Don't attempt to see us tonight. We won't be there.

Then where the hell are we going? Belle said. *He likely knows all our contacts by now, and we can't put any of them at risk by landing on them tonight.*

We'll stay at a hotel somewhere. I picked up the parchment and returned it to its spot on the carpet.

That's not going to help if there's a tracker on the SUV.

We won't use our SUV.

I stepped back from the paper and glanced at Jaz. "What's the general range of trackers?"

She shrugged. "Anything up to half a kilometer or so, depending on the device."

"So it's possible he's not currently in viewing range."

"Very." A smile tugged at her lips. "I take it you want to swap vehicles?"

I nodded. "We need to keep out of his way until tomorrow."

"What's to stop him from coming into your café during the day?"

"Witnesses. He won't want them."

She frowned. "Which begs the question, why?"

I grimaced. "Long unpleasant story."

"Is it one Aiden knows?"

"Yes."

"So he'll be there at this meeting tomorrow night?"

"I doubt even the threat of magic will keep him away."

A smile tugged her lips. "He does get protective about those he cares about." She stripped off her jacket and made a give-me motion toward mine. "Keys are in the pocket. Keep the jacket's hood up when you're leaving, because that hair of yours will give the game away if he happens to be looking your way when you pass."

"We won't be going back the same—" I stopped as energy surged into the room again. A heartbeat later, the parchment was gone.

"I'm thinking now is a good time to leave," Belle said. "Before he decides to do a drive-by or something."

"Good idea," Jaz said. "Just be careful. The boss will be mighty miffed if you endanger yourselves—and we had more than enough of his foul moods when he and Mia split."

Mia being my nemesis—the wolf he'd loved and lost.

I handed her my coat and put on hers. "We'll be careful. Thanks, Jaz."

She grinned. "Repay me with a brownie, and we'll be good."

"Done."

We headed out. I told Belle to wait at the top of the stairs, then tugged on the hood and went to retrieve the ranger vehicle. I started it up and switched on the headlights but didn't immediately throw it into gear. Instead, I leaned on the wheel and scanned the night, looking for my parent or anyone else who might be a little too interested in what I was doing.

The moon was bright and my eyesight once again wolf sharp, but there was nothing that tweaked my instincts. If someone was out there, they were far enough back that they weren't within range of my senses—both my vastly improved regular ones and the magical.

I drove around the back of the hotel and pulled up next to the stairs. Belle jumped in and slid down the seat, out of immediate sight. I drove back onto the road, splitting my attention equally between where I was going and the rearview mirror. I couldn't see anything or anyone following us.

After a couple of kilometers, I said, "I think it's safe now."

Belle immediately sat up and pulled on the seat belt. "Are we still going to see Katie?"

I shook my head. "Neither of us can afford to be down on energy tomorrow night."

She snorted. "Like us being at full power is going to be of any use anyway."

"We won't be alone, and neither of them will do anything too radical in front of witnesses."

"Are you sure of that?"

"Yes." I just wasn't sure of anything else.

"Clayton won't leave it at just a discussion. We both know that."

"Which is maybe why my father is here. He's had close to thirteen years to reflect on his behavior—perhaps he's going to make amends."

Belle's laugh was short, sharp, and filled with disbelief. "We're talking about your father here—you know, the man who spent the first sixteen years of your life making you feel like a worthless piece of shit. If he's here, then it's for some other reason than making things right."

I half smiled. It was either that or cry, and tears weren't going to do anyone any good right now. "Stranger things have happened."

"Yes, but even this reservation can't produce *that* sort of miracle."

"That is possibly true." I paused. "I wonder if he came alone, or if Mom's here as well?"

"A question that will undoubtedly be answered tomorrow night. Where are we staying?"

"I don't know. You want to check out Google and find somewhere?"

"There's not going to be much in the way of choices at this hour." She pulled out her phone and started searching. "Do you want to avoid Castle Rock?"

I hesitated, then shook my head. "As long as we can park off street; the last thing we need is the gossips wondering why a ranger vehicle is parked outside a hotel all night."

She rang a couple of places and eventually found a room in an old lodge in the heart of Castle Rock. Thankfully, the manager didn't know us, and he certainly didn't ask any questions—he just showed us the room and wished us a good night.

While Belle rang Monty, I sent a text to Aiden, telling him about the change to our sleeping arrangements, and then a second one to Ashworth, updating them on events and asking him and Eli to be there tomorrow night. There was immediate and utter support from the two of them, and that only made the trepidation worse. So many things could go wrong; so many people could get hurt—people I cared about. People I loved.

As much as I believed neither my father nor Clayton would do anything drastic with such an audience, I'd been wrong before.

I just had to hope this wasn't going to be one of those times.

———

We got up early, had a massive breakfast of bacon, eggs, hash browns, and toast to fortify ourselves for the day ahead, and then returned home. The spells around the café were intact, and there was no sign of anyone keeping watch.

Even so, we entered cautiously, senses on full alert. Once again, there was nothing but the echoes of happiness.

I hoped those echoes made it through the oncoming night.

Business was brisk, which at least took our minds off the upcoming confrontation. Monty called just after midday, stating he'd drive by at five-thirty to pick us up, with no explanation as to why.

"I'm guessing they don't want us hanging around here too long alone," Belle said as she slid an order across the counter. Penny whisked in and picked it up. "We can't rely on Clayton or your father keeping to the set time, and we're basically sitting ducks here."

"True, but that does leave the café open to assault."

"Better they assault it than us."

"Also true."

I sent a message to Aiden to update him on what was going on, and told him I'd contact him when we were all heading back here.

His reply was a quick and abrupt *You'd better or we will have words.*

"The man definitely does care," Belle commented.

"*That* has never been in doubt."

"To you, me, and the world in general, yes. But I'm afraid he is in utter denial as to the depths."

"Maybe, but there's nothing I can do but accept it and move on when the time comes."

Belle smiled. "I like this new attitude."

"The new attitude is a product of realizing that, compared to what we are about to face, a broken heart is but a minor blip in the radar."

My tone was light, but it wasn't fooling Belle. She hugged me fiercely and told me it would all work out. I could only hope her instincts were right and mine were wrong.

The deeper into the afternoon we got, the more time appeared to slow. By the time we closed the café and shooed the staff home early, it was fair to say I was only a couple of strands away from falling to pieces.

We grabbed the backpack and our athames, threw additional layers of protection across the top of the stairs—more to know whether anyone went up there than to actually stop them—and then, at five-thirty, went out.

Monty pulled up right on time in an old Ford sedan. Belle grabbed the rear door and jumped inside, leaving me to take the front.

He'll take it as a step forward if I sit in the front, she said. *We may be in grave danger, but his marrying plans are never far from his mind.*

Even Monty isn't that shallow.

I wouldn't bet on it.

I smiled and did up the seat belt as he took off. "Where are we going? And where did you get this car?"

"Borrowed it from a neighbor, with the promise to

replace it if I wrote it off. Which I won't, unless Clayton and Lawrence do something totally off-piste. As to where we're going—" He paused to take the corner and headed out of Castle Rock. "I thought I'd shout you ladies a meal at a pub."

"I'm not entirely sure my stomach is up to eating," I said. "I gather the others are going to meet us there?"

He nodded. "I've booked a small function room so that we can talk and prepare without alarming anyone."

"Have you had any luck in tracking either of the men down?" Belle asked.

"No, nor did I really expect to." He glanced at me; there was something in his expression that had my breath stuttering in my throat. "I did contact a friend in Canberra, though. Your mother hasn't left."

My breath whooshed out. "I guess that's something."

"Yes, and it gets even more interesting. Apparently, she and your father have separated."

"*What?* Impossible. My mother would never contemplate such a move."

He raised an eyebrow. "Couples do fall out of love."

"Yes, but they were never *in* love. It was a union of political and power consolidation, nothing more."

"Which means," Belle said, "she must have a very good reason for putting him aside."

"Which I think Ashworth might be able to tell us about. Oh, and before I forget, Ashworth and Eli met the truth seeker and auditor at Tullamarine this afternoon."

I frowned. "They're not going to have time to record what happened to me. Not before the meeting tonight."

"No, but they can bear witness to said meeting as part of the information gathering process."

"Neither my father nor Clayton will admit anything in their presence."

"Which is why they will be recording the conversation from a safe distance."

"We'll all be recording the damn conversation," Belle commented.

Monty glanced briefly over his shoulder. "I think it likely they'll demand all phones turned off and placed on a table—especially given how cautious they've been to date."

"Which means they may also pat us down for listening devices."

"They may well, but they won't find it."

I raised an eyebrow. "Why not?"

"That, my dear cousin, will soon be revealed."

I rolled my eyes. "You fail when it comes to being all edgy and mysterious."

"Well, there goes one means of attracting my true love."

Belle snorted, and Monty's grin grew. I shook my head and said, "Is it actually legal to record a conversation without informing all parties involved?"

"I did check, and here in Victoria the answer is yes, just as long as the person who is secretly recording the conversation is one party of that conversation."

I frowned. "But they'll be elsewhere—"

"In this case, you're the person recording it, as you've requested their help to sort out this situation."

"Are they sure that will hold up in court?"

"Certain of it." He pulled into the driveway of a cream-colored, Victorian-style double-story building and parked around the back. "This way, ladies."

He jumped out and led us into the beautiful old building. After speaking briefly to the waitress who came to meet us, we were taken into what looked like an old Regency parlor. Maelle would have been very at ease in this place.

Belle and Monty ordered a meal and coffee. I stuck with tea and a bag of plain potato chips; anything else would have been dangerous given the uneasiness in my stomach. The drinks and the food arrived promptly, and we talked about everything other than the meeting that was now less than two hours away.

Just after seven, the door opened. Ashworth and Eli stepped into the room, followed by two women—one who looked barely out of her teens, the other in her mid-fifties.

Ashworth strode over to me and wrapped me in a big bear hug. "How're you holding up, lass?"

I smiled into his chest. "Better now that you and Eli are here."

"Wouldn't miss this confrontation for the world." He pulled back, then turned around and motioned to the two women. "I'd like you to meet Jenna Jones and Ruby Harrison, our truth seeker and auditor respectively."

I walked over to shake their hands. Jenna was the younger of the two, and obviously had some Sarr blood in her. Her skin was brown, her eyes gray, and her hair every bit as thick and lush as Belle's. Power surged as our hands met, but it was a mix of both magic and psychic energy. Ruby had strawberry-blonde hair—suggesting there was only a distant connection to one of the royal lines—bright blue eyes, and a gorgeously Rubenesque figure. Her grip held the same mix of psychic and magical energy.

"Thank you both for coming here today."

Ruby's voice, like her quick smile, was brisk and businesslike. "If Clayton Marlowe and your father are indeed complicit in arranging the marriage of an unwilling and drugged minor, then they must be brought to justice. The testimony of both yourself and your familiar, as well as the conversation we record tonight, will play a major part in the decision whether to take them to court or not."

I frowned. "If it's against the law, surely they must be charged."

"It depends entirely on the evidence, which we've not heard as yet." She flashed another quick smile. "Fear not, I've seen cases in court that have started with far less than what we already have here. Now, let's get you prepared."

She placed her briefcase on the table and pulled out a folder. The preparation involved me signing a formal request for their help, reading a pamphlet on truth seeking —what it involved and what the risks were—and then signing a permission form.

When that was done, she took a small silver jewelry box out of her briefcase and opened it up. Inside was an oval-shaped opal pendant about the size of my thumb. She lifted it by the chain and motioned me to turn around. I did, ducking down slightly so that she could place it easily around my neck. The back of the stone was metal and felt cold against my skin.

"The electronics are under the pendant's stone," she said. "You activate it by pressing the small button on the rear. We'll monitor, and can remotely deactivate if necessary."

"Why would you need to deactivate it?" Belle said. "Doesn't that defeat the whole purpose of the thing?"

"There've been some situations in the past where the suspects have swept the general area with a bug finder. While there's been no indication that either man has made inquiries for such a device, it's better for our case and for you if we proceed cautiously."

"Them finding the device wouldn't jeopardize the overall case, though," Ashworth commented.

Ruby glanced at him. "No, but it would make them aware that the Society is watching them, and that could make them react in unforeseen—and unwanted—ways."

"Given who we're dealing with, it's likely he already knows," Eli said. "I very much suspect him reacting in unforeseen ways is already on the cards."

His words hung ominously in the air. I briefly closed my eyes and fought to keep calm. Me becoming a messy bundle of nerves and fear was exactly what Clayton wanted; if we were to have any hope of surviving what was to come, then we had to keep strong and do the unexpected.

Ruby shuffled the paperwork back into her briefcase, then picked it up. "We shall get going. I prefer to scout the area a little before choosing a suitable—"

"Take Belle with you," I cut in. "She's my familiar, and I'd rather keep her out of Clayton's way."

"And why is that?" Jenna studied me through narrowed eyes. Though I couldn't feel the caress of magic or any step into my thoughts, I nevertheless had the feeling she was pulling forth secrets.

She won't get far, Belle said. *Not while I'm here.*

You won't be able to help me shield when she does her truth-seeking thing.

I know, but right now, she doesn't need to know all the gritty details. To Jenna, she added, "I placed a spell on him when I rescued Lizzie. Clayton is a man who doesn't like being bested, especially by a low-class witch like myself."

A small smile touched Jenna's lips. "That is indeed true."

"And makes this investigation a whole lot more interesting," Ruby said. "Come along, my dear."

With that, they turned and left. Belle raised an eyebrow at their abrupt departure, but nevertheless followed.

I glanced at Ashworth. "I'm guessing they hired a car at the airport?"

His smile crinkled the corners of his muddy silver eyes. "Broomsticks went out with the Dark Ages, lass."

"There was talk of a mechanical version a century or so ago—I saw the plans for it when I was working in the archives. It never got off the ground though." As our joint groans filled the air, Monty glanced at his watch. "We've got ten minutes before we need to leave. What's the plan?"

"I think it's better to go in with no plan," Eli said. He leaned against the wall, his thick salt-and-pepper hair gleaming in the room's light but his blue eyes deeply shadowed. "And definitely no magic at the ready. We're there as backup and witnesses. If we go in defensive, they'll react in kind. That's a situation that could get ugly all too quickly—and play in their favor when this gets to the courts."

"*If* it gets to the courts," I muttered.

Ashworth squeezed my arm. "The Society is confident they can follow this through to the end. Shall we go?"

He didn't wait for an answer, just led the way out. His truck was parked next to Monty's borrowed car.

"I think it best if we all park out on the street and use the front door—there's not much maneuvering room in the café's back hallway if things immediately go to hell," he added. "Is Aiden going to meet us there?"

"Yes. I've just got to send him a text."

Which I did once I'd climbed into Monty's borrowed wagon. It didn't take us long to get back to the café, where we were once again greeted by the shattered remnants of our protection spells floating on the breeze.

"Well, fuck," Monty said. "So much for thinking my alarm spell would give us advance warning."

"You're dealing with two of the strongest witches in Canberra," I said. "Don't feel bad."

"I don't. I'm just pissed off—I was assured that spell would work no matter how strong the witch it was warding against."

"It doesn't really matter now." My gaze was on the open front door. It was an invitation to enter—one we couldn't really refuse. "Park up the road. We'll walk down."

As Monty obeyed and Ashworth stopped behind us, Aiden appeared. He opened my door and offered me his hand. I gripped it tightly and let him help me out. But as much as I wanted to hang on to him, I couldn't. I had no doubt Clayton and my father were watching us, and I wasn't about to give them any more ammunition than they'd already collected when it came to my private life.

"What's the plan?" His gaze swept the four of us. "Where's Belle?"

"Safe with the auditor."

"Ah. Good."

"Let's go, lass," Ashworth said softly. "Better to get this all over with sooner rather than later."

"I'm not entirely sure I agree with that statement."

But I nevertheless activated the listening device, then slung the pack over my shoulder and strode down toward the café.

The four men followed me, their steps echoing with purpose and strength. It should have comforted me. It didn't.

I neared the door but didn't alter my pace; if I faltered now—in any way—I'd end up running. The time for *that* was over.

The café's lights were all on, and in their warm glow the shattered remnants of our protection spells were very visible. The threads that contained the wild magic *did* at least remain intact, and I wondered why, given they'd probably had plenty of time to utterly strip all protections from the café. It did at least mean that with those strands still active, we still had some protection against any move my father and Clayton might make.

The two of them were sitting at a table in the middle of the room. They were both tall and somewhat slender, with silver eyes that gleamed coldly even under the warmth of the lights. Both could be termed handsome men, though Clayton's face was deeply etched with lines that hadn't been there twelve years ago. The sheer force of their joint power oozed through the room and snatched my breath.

But only Clayton's aura ran with black and purple.

He was deeply, disturbingly furious.

My steps faltered.

Not because of what I saw in him, but rather what I felt in *me*. I'd expected fear. I'd expected panic. I'd expected that the mere sight of him would have me reverting to the frightened sixteen-year-old who had no means of fighting the man tearing at her clothes and bruising her flesh.

What I *hadn't* expected was the deep and utter rage.

Only it wasn't aimed at Clayton.

It was aimed at my father.

CHAPTER SEVEN

That rage rolled over me, a red wave so strong I couldn't have combatted it even if I'd wanted to. It fueled me, strengthened me, swept away thought and fear and common sense.

As the two men rose to their feet, I took several quick steps forward, drew back my fist, and punched my father so damn hard, his head snapped back. He crashed backward, blood spurting from his mashed nose.

I stood over his prone form, my right fist aching but both clenched against the pulsing need to punch him again and again while he was down. But as strong as the rage was, awareness lingered deeper down. One punch might be forgiven in court; two or more would play into his favor.

Magic surged, its intent so obvious that the remaining unbroken threads in our protection spells began to pulse.

"I wouldn't finish that spell, Clayton," came Monty's soft warning. "You've had long enough to study the magic in this place to know any such response would be unwise. Attempt any *physical* action and you'll find *my* fist in *your* face."

Monty stood to my right, so close that I could smell the sharpness of his aftershave. Aiden had stopped to my left, his body practically humming with rage. I didn't have to look at him to know his fists were clenched and knuckles white. He remained in control of his werewolf instincts to protect, but only just. Ashworth and Eli were several steps further back, positioned either side of Monty and Aiden.

Clayton's magic stilled, but his fury washed dark waves of anger over me as I continued to glare down at my father.

Lawrence calmly tugged a white handkerchief from the top pocket of his suit jacket and gently pressed it against his broken and bloody nose.

"That, daughter, was uncalled for."

The red wave rose again, and I dug my nails into the palms of my hands in an effort to combat it.

"Uncalled for?" I growled. "You forced me into a marriage I didn't want and a wedding night in which I was nearly raped. You're my fucking *father*. You should have protected me instead of pawning me off to the highest bidder in an effort to get rid of me."

"It would seem our memories of that situation are somewhat different." Clayton's soft voice was cool and calm, totally at odds with his aura. "There was no exchange of money—dowries went out with the Dark Ages—and there was certainly no rape."

"Only because you were goddamn stopped—"

"If you didn't want my attentions, you should have spoken up."

"And how was I supposed to do that when—"

"Enough," Lawrence commanded again. He picked himself up off the floor and then stepped out of immediate reach—it was a small retreat, but it nevertheless gave me immense satisfaction. "Before we go any further, I'll ask you all to turn off your phones and place them on the table. This conversation is one I'd prefer to keep between us."

I snorted. "Gee, I wonder why?"

"Your sarcasm will not improve this situation."

"Newsflash, Father dearest—I don't fucking care. You were dead to me the minute you forced me into marriage with the rapist here."

"Again, that was *not* the case. Phones, gentlemen?"

His continued denial made me wonder if he suspected the conversation was being recorded from a source other than our phones. He didn't appear to have any sort of radio frequency detector to hand, and I couldn't hear anything to suggest a sound jammer of some kind was being employed. Which didn't mean it wasn't. They'd been in the café for who knows how long and had had time to do anything.

"We'll lay ours down only if you two do the same," Ashworth said.

My father's gaze moved past me. "And who might you be?"

"These fine gentlemen," Monty replied before Ashworth or anyone else could, "are our witnesses. They might also be magical backup if you two start getting antsy."

Clayton's lip curled, but once again, he held back from commenting. Which was so far beyond the norm for him it made me wonder how my father had managed to leash him.

I took out my phone, turned it off, and placed it on the table. One by one the others repeated the process; my father and Clayton were the last to do so.

"Right," I said. "What are the two of you doing here?"

"You're my fucking wi—"

"Clayton, enough," Lawrence snapped.

His voice had lost little of its usual power despite the handkerchief now shoved up his nostrils in an effort to stem the bleeding. It had to be hurting his mashed nose, but I couldn't for the life of me feel a spark of sympathy.

Clayton took a deep breath, and the viciousness once more melted from his features, but not his aura. While it was beginning to seem like my father *had* come here to sort out the mess he'd made, Clayton definitely had not.

He wanted revenge.

Not just on me, but on Belle.

The only reason he was even here in the café with my father was the spell she'd placed on him, I realized. After all, he couldn't finish what he'd started all those years ago if he couldn't actually get it up.

Which is a damn good reason for me not *to lift the spell,* Belle said. *He won't keep any deal made—that much is pretty obvious.*

I agree, but let's concentrate on one thing at a time.

"The situation cannot be allowed to stand as it is," my father said. "It's affecting the future of you both—"

"There's only one way this situation is going to fucking end." Anger made my voice vibrate. The red rage remained close to the surface, and I couldn't be sorry about it. It kept me from giving in to the fear and the memories that still burned deep down. "And that's for the marriage to be annulled."

"That would not be our first—"

I snorted. "Of course not, because marriages can only be annulled if one of the parties did not give their consent or consent was obtained by duress or fraud." My gaze shot to Clayton's. "Imagine what *that* would do to your reputation if it got out."

Heat shot into his cheeks, but once again he held his tongue.

It might be wise not to antagonize him any further came Belle's uneasy comment. *He looks ready to kill.*

It was only then that I realized she'd deepened our connection so that she could see through my eyes.

Yeah, sorry, she said, *but I needed to understand exactly what's going down. I think the rage stopped you sensing it.*

Probably.

"A divorce would be more convenient," my father said.

"Oddly enough, I'm not in the mood to make things convenient for *either* of you."

Anger flared deep in his eyes, and just for an instant, his power surged over me, momentarily scalding my senses and sending the café's remaining spells into a frenzy of activity. Lightning flickered out from the layers of wild magic, jagged little warnings of what waited if they didn't watch what they were doing.

Unfortunately, it also served as a pointer that all was not as it seemed—not with me, not with the magic that still protected this place.

"Interesting" was all my father said. But his gaze, when it returned to mine, was speculative.

"Not so much," Monty replied. "Not if you know the recent history of this place."

"The magic of a wellspring can affect spells, but what just happened here is extremely unusual, and we all know it."

"Except," Ashworth drawled, "for the fact that the wild magic within this reservation does many things it should not —and I suspect you've both read my reports and Monty's and are well aware of that."

"Meaning you're Ira Ashworth," Lawrence said. "That would certainly explain recent events in Canberra. But back to the matter at hand—if we agree to an annulment, there must be suitable terms on both sides."

"And what would you consider suitable terms?" Monty asked. "Given you forced a sixteen-year-old into a marriage she didn't want, I'm thinking it might be better for you both to simply get the annulment ASAP and walk away. We all know you have enough tame judges in your pockets to get it done quickly and quietly."

"That might well be possible," my father said. "But we want the spell on Clayton removed, and I want you, Elizabeth, to return to Canberra and undergo a full magical audit."

I forced a smile, even as my gut clenched. A full audit would reveal the ongoing changes within me. "So that you can drug me into another marriage? I think not."

"Fine. We'll do it here—I don't particularly care."

Of course he didn't. Not when it might reveal that the daughter he'd tossed away like so much rubbish might actually hold some worth. The anger of the child who'd never been good enough rose, but underneath the hurt remained. Despite everything, there was some small spark of that child still aching for the love of her father.

"And why would I put myself through that again, Father dearest? I had sixteen years of being told I was a worthless disappointment. I don't need to add an exclamation point to what is already common knowledge."

"Oh, I think we do." He studied me for a long minute, and I rather suspected he was seeing the things I was trying to keep hidden. "These are my terms. Do you agree to them or not?"

"If I say not?"

He smiled. It was cold and hard, and sent trepidation crawling across my skin.

"Then I shall release the leash."

"That," Monty said, "sounded a whole lot like a threat. And in front of witnesses."

"No, it was just a statement of fact. I'm here to broker a deal between two legally bound parties, one of whom is not in the best state of mind currently. If terms cannot be agreed on, we will return to Canberra. I cannot be held accountable for what may happen after that."

"If he comes into this reservation," Aiden said, voice deceptively mild, "and makes any sort of threat or move against Liz, I'll rip his goddamn throat out."

Clayton's laugh was a short, sharp sound of contempt. "You won't get within ten meters of me, wolf, and that little trinket around your neck won't in any way protect you."

"Perhaps not, but you might be wise to remember that wolves *always* hunt in packs."

Clayton bared his teeth, but at my father's curt "Enough, both of you," refrained from replying.

Monty thinks we've really got no choice but to agree to the terms, Belle said. *If the audit is done here, then you're at least fully protected against anything they might attempt afterward—especially if you're right in believing the wild magic won't release you.*

I resisted the urge to scrub a hand across my eyes. *I hate the thought of doing another audit.*

With a whole lot of justification. But if it gets Clayton out of your life without any collateral damage, it might be a small price to pay.

The key word there is 'might.' And even if we do agree and my father does drag Clayton back to Canberra, would he stay there now that he knows where we are?

I seriously doubted it.

As do I, but to echo your earlier statement, let's deal with one thing at a time.

"Daughter? Do we have an agreement?"

"I want the marriage annulled—and I want the paperwork in my hands—before we either remove the spell or I'm audited again." I paused. "And I want assurances that once the spell *is* removed, Clayton won't seek any sort of retribution for our past actions."

"I so swear," Lawrence said. "Clayton?"

"You have my word I will not seek retribution. I will, however, need to return so that the spell may be removed."

"Indeed—but not alone. I don't trust you, Clayton. I don't trust you'll hold to your word."

"He will."

I glanced at my father and wondered if he was being willfully obtuse or whether the years of friendship between them were blinding him to Clayton's ultimate intent.

"He'd better, because I'm not that frightened sixteen-year-old anymore, and I *will* do whatever it takes to protect both Belle and myself."

My father studied me for a moment, then nodded once. He understood and accepted what had been left unspoken. I doubted Clayton did.

"Then we have an agreement." He removed a small metal object from his pocket and placed it on the table. I wasn't entirely sure what it was and was disinclined to admit it. "It has been recorded for posterity."

"I want an unredacted copy of that audio," Monty immediately said.

"And I will ask the same of whatever record you might have of this meeting." His gaze came to mine. "While I certainly *did* consider you a disappointment when it came to power, I never thought you were stupid, Elizabeth."

I snorted. "And that's supposed to make me feel better?"

His smile was cold—distant. "I suppose it *is* too late for that."

"You suppose right."

He nodded and glanced at Clayton. "We may leave, now."

Clayton picked up his phone and immediately strode from the room. But not without one final glance back at me. His silver gaze promised retribution. Promised hurt in more ways than I could even imagine.

I crossed my arms and glared back at him. I refused to show him fear, if only because that's exactly what he wanted.

The strength imbued by the red rage held until my father had left. Then the utter enormity of everything that had happened hit; I began to shake so fiercely that my knees gave way and I would have fallen had Aiden not lunged forward and somehow caught me.

He didn't lower me onto a chair. He simply wrapped his arms around me and held on tight as I shook and shivered and generally unraveled.

"It's okay." His voice was soft—soothing. "It'll be okay. The worst of it is over now."

No, it wasn't, I wanted to say, but the words remained stuck in my throat.

I remained in the security of his arms for a very long time, drinking in his scent and trying to find the courage to step back, to stand once again on my own two feet. To once again gather strength in order to fight on.

Because I would have to, before all this was over

"What we all need is coffee," Belle said, as she strode in through the door. "And cake. Big slabs of cake."

"Sounds like a plan to me," Monty said. "Where are Ruby and Jenna?"

"They can't fraternize with witnesses—it could lead to accusations of tainted evidence." She took a small black device out of her pocket. "They've said we should keep this on hand; if we have any further meetings or confrontations with Clayton, we need to record them."

"Did they manage to record this confrontation?"

"Yes and no. Whatever device the bastards were employing to jam the frequency worked well enough that their recording was patchy."

"That's what the silver disk was," I said.

"Most likely," Monty said. "Though I'd have thought holding it on their persons would also disrupt their own recordings."

"Not necessarily," Aiden said. "There're jammers that can block specific frequencies, and they're likely to have set their recording frequency to one of the unblocked ones."

"Monty," Belle said, "come and cut up the cake while I make the coffees."

As he obediently followed, I finally pulled away from Aiden. His grip slipped from my waist but he hovered close, ready to catch me should I go down again. Which was possible, given the utter weakness still washing through me. The red wave had taken a very physical toll on my body, which was decidedly odd.

"Where are Ashworth and Eli?" I said, suddenly noticing they weren't in the room.

"Following Lawrence and Clayton to make sure they're leaving the reservation as promised."

"I've no doubt they'll return to Canberra," I said. "It's the whole 'not coming back' bit I reckon will cause us problems."

"Even Clayton wouldn't go against your father," Monty said. "He wouldn't dare."

"Except that he and Father have had a falling out, remember?"

"Just like him and your mom," Monty mused. "I wonder if it has anything to do with his odd comment to Ashworth?"

I moved across to another table and sat down. Not just because it was bigger, but because the air didn't hold any lingering scents, be it their anger or the woody scent of Clayton's aftershave.

Neither of which you should be able to smell, Belle commented.

I frowned. *Since when have I not been able to smell aftershave?*

I was fully connected, remember? Trust me, what you smelled and sensed wasn't normal for anyone other than a wolf. We really do need to speak to Katie and uncover what the hell is going on.

Yes, but not tonight. I haven't the strength.

Tomorrow night, then.

I was going to suggest tomorrow morning, before we open.

Aiden's knee pressed against mine as he sat next to me; the contact had the still-churning inner nerves easing just that little bit more. The man definitely made me feel safe, even if it was more illusion than truth when it came to the likes of Clayton.

That would mean getting up before dawn. It'll be cold.

Freezing. But it's our best chance to get answers without having anyone tagging along with us.

Meaning Aiden.

Yes.

He's aware of the changes in you, Liz. He wants answers, even if he's not currently pressing.

He's not pressing because he's waiting for his perfect wolf to arrive.

Not true.

I frowned. *Meaning what?*

Oh, he is *waiting for Miss Perfect, but that has nothing to do with his concern for you.* Out loud, she added, "What odd comment are we talking about?"

She picked up the tray of coffees and brought them over. Even from where I was sitting, I could smell the alcohol she'd added to hers and mine. The sooner we got the whole marriage mess sorted the better, or we were going to end up alcoholics.

Monty followed with three plates of black forest cake and a fourth containing a stack of brownies.

"I'm not sure even *I* can get through that many slices," Aiden said, accepting the plate with an amused smile.

"I have every faith in your eating prowess," Belle said, sliding a steaming coffee mug across to him.

Monty handed out the remaining plates, then leaned the tray against the table leg and sat down. "On discovering who Ashworth was, Lawrence said 'that would certainly explain recent events in Canberra.' I took it to mean Liz's parents' recent separation."

I frowned. "But how would learning who Ashworth was —" I stopped. "He knows Ashworth's sister is head of the Black Lantern Society."

"Which is?" Aiden asked.

"According to Ashworth," I said, "It's a secret society of witches, werewolves, and vampires who work behind the scenes to right wrongs and bring justice to those who escape it."

"Sounds more like a vigilante group," Aiden commented. "And it can't be too secret if your father knows about it."

"The Society is whatever it needs to be." Monty glanced at me. "And if Lawrence is now aware of it, they must have recently contacted your parents. It would certainly explain your mother's sudden decision to separate from your father."

"And *that* would explain why he's now attempting to make amends for his actions thirteen years ago," Belle said. "It's still all about power and his need to retain it rather than any desire to put things right for his daughter."

I picked up my fork and scooped up a thick bit of chocolaty goodness. "To be honest, I don't care what his motivations are, as long as it ends in an annulment. But I don't for one minute believe Clayton will leave it at that."

"He has to," Monty said around a mouthful of cake. "He swore an oath, and that's something no witch would go against lightly."

"Maybe sane witches, but I'm not entirely sure Clayton could be classified as that anymore." I remembered the look in his eyes and shivered. "His aura was nigh on black, and it wasn't grief. It was a fury so fierce it consumes him."

"Somewhat understandable if he's been incapable of getting an erection for nearly thirteen years. That might send any man mad." Monty scooped up more cake. "What I'd like to know, though, is how the damn spell lasted so long. Don't take this the wrong way, Belle, but it really shouldn't have. At the very least, he should have been able to unpick it without much hassle."

"I know, and I can't explain it." She shrugged. "It's not like I was actively thinking that night—I was running more on instinct."

"Were the two of you connected?" Aiden asked. "Is it possible that some of Liz's magic leaked over to Belle and fortified her spell?"

Monty pointed his fork at Aiden, his expression excited. "By God, I think he nailed it. It explains *so* much."

"My magic wouldn't have worried Clayton any more than Belle's," I commented.

"Except," Monty said, "if the wild magic somehow got involved. It explains their desperation to find you—it wasn't *just* the erectile dysfunction spell, but what that spell revealed."

"Good theory, but there *is* one—"

Monty held up a hand. "Yes, I know, the seeker should have been able to use the still-active spell to track you and Belle down. But here's the thing—that spell, if I'm right, was a combination of both of your magics *and* the wild magic, and therefore unviable as a means of tracking."

"At least until we came here, and the wild magic within your DNA was activated again," Belle said. "Which certainly explains the seeker's sudden appearance."

"All possible except for one thing," I said. "The wild magic didn't actually make an appearance in *any* of my magic until we came here."

"When it comes to conscious magic, that's certainly true, but what if it was done subconsciously? What if the situation and your fear combined to tear through whatever barrier had previously prevented you accessing your inner wild magic for those few vital minutes? It's not like either of you have been in such a dire situation since then—"

"Thank heaven for *that*," I muttered.

"It could also provide a reason as to why the wild magic here responded to you," Monty continued. "The barrier had already been breached and it sensed a kindred spirit, so to speak."

Or rather, Katie did, Belle said. *It makes a weird sort of sense, given that until you came into the reservation she had no conduit for the power she was now a part of and no means of communicating with anyone.*

I guess Monty's theory would also explain why it took so long for the inner wild magic to make its presence felt—the barrier had been torn rather than destroyed. It took a while— and multiple connections—for it to fail.

Yes. And I'm guessing that's the real reason Clayton came here today—he wanted to see if there was wild magic within you.

Did my shield hold?

Yes, but the reaction of the wild magic woven into the café's spells would have given him enough reason to believe its source was you rather than an accidental inclusion.

"I'm thinking," Monty said, voice dry, "that there's a whole different conversation happening between you two. How about you illuminate the poor males in the room?"

I flashed him a smile and picked up my coffee. "Sorry, we were just discussing the merits of your theory."

"And?"

"It really only amplifies the danger we're still in." I glanced at Aiden. "And before you say it, you can't keep sleeping on the sofa. It's impractical."

"You're making him sleep on the sofa?" Monty's eyebrows shot upward. "Why?"

"It's part of our no-sex-under-this-roof rule," Belle said. "Which we undertook after several bad relationships stained the atmosphere in previous homes."

Amusement crinkled the corners of his eyes. "Which means you'll just have to move out when we get married."

Belle snorted and flicked a bit of cream at him. He laughed and dodged. "Seriously though, if Clayton comes here against his vow, he risks his position on the High Council and generally being ostracized—especially with your father as a witness."

"Because my father will always protect *his* position and power base first and foremost." I couldn't help the edge in my voice. "And *that* brings a secondary problem—he'll want to use me as a bargaining chip once he's got confirmation of my ability to use wild magic."

"It won't do him any good if you can't leave the reservation," Aiden commented. "And let's all be honest, few high-blood witches would deign to leave their lofty positions in Canberra to live here. Hell, look at the lack of choice we had when it came to the reservation witch position."

"That lack of choice did lead you to the best choice," Monty said immodestly.

Amusement lurked around the corners of Aiden's eyes. "The best of a bad bunch isn't really something to boast about."

"You've obviously been hanging around Ashworth far too much."

Aiden's smile broke loose. "He does have a way of cutting through the bullshit that I quite like."

Monty rolled his eyes and returned his gaze to mine. "While I think it unlikely Clayton will break his vow, I'm also aware that we can't ignore your premonitions—even if they're fear based. Which means we need a—"

He stopped at the sharp ringing of a phone. Aiden grimaced and said, "Sorry, I've got to take this."

He rose from the table and walked a few yards away.

"That," I said, watching the tension ripple across his shoulders, "isn't good news."

"Another death?"

"I think so. Whether it's related to our recent ghoul attacks or something else, I can't say."

"Just as well I'm back to take up the investigating reins, then," Monty said. "I doubt you're up to visiting a crime scene right now."

"Actually, it'd probably take my mind off deeper, darker matters." I sipped my coffee and half wished Belle had been a little more generous with the whiskey. "Did you get any information from the friend you went down to Melbourne to meet?"

"I did, but I'll have to update you tomorrow." He gulped down the rest of his coffee and rose as Aiden approached. "We've got another one, I take it?"

"Uncertain." Aiden's gaze met mine. "Are you sure you don't want me to return tonight?"

I nodded. "Even with tame judges in their pockets, it's going to take a few days to get the annulment. We have breathing space."

His gaze remained on mine; judging my words, looking for lies. Eventually, he bent and kissed me. "I'll see you tomorrow, then."

"For breakfast?"

"That would be appreciated."

"It really would," Monty said.

I grinned. "You're usually here for breakfast these days anyway, so I just took it as a given."

"Excellent." He slapped Aiden's shoulder lightly. "Shall we go hunt us up a ghoul?"

"When it comes to hunting, I prefer rabbits and foxes." Aiden sent a wink my way, then turned and walked out.

Once Belle had locked the door behind the two of them, she said, "Are we really staying here tonight?"

"I think we'll have two safe days up our sleeves; after that, it's all bets off."

Belle plonked down and nursed her coffee mug between her hands. "Surely it's in your father's best interests to keep an eye on him? Especially if you're right and he's already formulating plans to pair you off to a more suitable blueblood beau?"

I shuddered at the thought. "You're forgetting how long they've been friends. It'll never occur to my father that a witch of Clayton's standing *wouldn't* honor a vow."

"So, what are we going to do?"

I shrugged. "Given we can't afford to close the café—"

"If there's one thing I'm certain of," Belle cut in, "it's the fact he won't attack us where there're witnesses."

I grimaced and drained my mug. The alcohol within the coffee didn't really do a whole lot to ease the inner tension. But I doubted even a full bottle of whiskey would do that.

"I actually don't think he'll attack me at all. I think he'll go after you first. And if he can't snatch you, then he'll go after Aiden or Monty. They've been following us for a week, remember? They know our movements and ties."

"We could camp up at Katie's wellspring," Belle said. "If we're not safe there, we won't be safe anywhere."

I hesitated, then shook my head. While we now had permission to enter the clearing whenever necessary from the Marin pack—on whose land the wellspring was situated —I doubted they'd be too happy about us camping there for any length of time. Werewolves were notoriously protective of their privacy and their compounds. Humans found wandering around without permission soon found themselves spending quite a bit of time in jail. Unlike most in the reservation, I'd been privileged enough to see both the Marins' and O'Connors' inner sanctums, but only because they'd needed the use of my psi skills. Even though I was Aiden's girlfriend, I was not—and never would be—fully welcomed into their midst.

"I don't want him or anyone else from Canberra finding that wellspring. Besides, the final confrontation will get nasty, and we can't afford to shed blood in that place."

Belle blinked. "I'm not liking the fact your premonitions have jumped from revenge to bloodletting."

"It was always going to come down to that. It's just a matter of whether we'll all survive said letting." I pushed up from the table. "And on that cheery note, I'm going to bed."

Belle's concern ran through my mind. "Are you okay?"

"Yeah. I'm just dead tired." I paused and added with a somewhat wry smile, "Which is better than being dead any day."

She snorted and flicked a leftover bit of cake at me. I dodged it with a laugh and headed upstairs. The spell across the top was still intact, which at least meant neither my father nor my husband had snooped. I set the alarm on my phone, then stripped off, climbed into bed, and was quickly asleep.

And dreamed of destruction, bloodshed, and death.

Whose was the one point the dreams refused to answer.

I shivered in my coat and then slammed the SUV's door shut. The stars were bright overhead, but the moon was on the wane and her power little more than a distant hum. The mountain was an indistinct shadow that loomed above us, and the surrounding scrub was filled with the scrabbling of small animals, though whether they were bush rats, possums, or some other kind of nocturnal hunter, I couldn't say.

Belle flicked on her flashlight and shone the beam on the barrier that signaled the end of the dirt road and the beginning of the goat track that led up to the wellspring's clearing.

"I'm not looking forward to doing this in the dark," Belle said. "It was bad enough climbing the damn mountain in full daylight."

"At least this time, we're better prepared." Not only were we wearing proper hiking boots, but I also had water and energy bars in the backpack. I slung it over my shoulder, switched on my flashlight, and resolutely strode toward the track.

It seemed rougher—and the incline steeper—than I remembered. It didn't take long for the burn in my legs to begin, but I ignored it and strode on resolutely. While my breath quickly became short, sharp pants for air, I noted with at least a little satisfaction that—unlike the last time we'd been here—I didn't have to stop multiple times. My somewhat haphazard fitness routine was at least having *some* benefit.

We paused about halfway up to grab some water and munch on a protein bar. I tugged off the coat and tied it around my waist, but left the sweater on. The night was bitter, and I didn't want the sweat chilling on my skin. The last thing I needed was a cold right now.

The scrub and trees became much denser the farther up the mountain we got. Unlike the forests around Castle Rock, this area didn't have much in the way of old mines or tailings. It was so quiet that the sharp sound of our puffing echoed through the trees.

Eventually, the path leveled off. The trees around us

were thick and tall, and shut out both the stars and the moon's waning light, leaving the vast areas not lit by the flashlights in deep shadow.

But shadows weren't the only things here.

There was magic.

Wild magic.

Katie's magic.

She was waiting for us.

CHAPTER EIGHT

The sting of energy got stronger the closer we drew to the clearing. While this wellspring was far younger than the other, it was giving every indication it would end up being as powerful, if not more so, than the older one.

From up ahead came the soft glimmer of lights—wisps of wild magic, drifting on the breeze. Waiting for me, as Katie waited for me. My fingers twitched in response, and something within began to hum, as if in answer to unheard music.

We reached the edge of the forest and stopped. The clearing wasn't very large, but it was strewn with rocks and other debris from the landslip that had taken out a good portion of the cliff directly opposite. At the base of this was an ankle-deep rock well. Water bubbled up from a seam near the cliff's base, lapped over the edge of the basin, and then wound its way down the gentle slope, where it would no doubt join forces with the stream further down the mountain.

The tiny well was the source of the wild magic, and the air above it shimmered with its force. It had certainly ramped up since the last time we'd been here, and I couldn't help but wonder if that had anything to do with Katie's presence.

I raised a hand; the tiny threads of magic danced toward me and then curled around my fingers and wrists. They were as fragile as moonbeams and yet pulsed with power. Within that power was a sense of acknowledgment. Of kinship—and it was one that had nothing to do with Katie.

It should have frightened me—and I suppose in the saner portions of my mind it did—but this wild power was part of my being and coming here felt like a homecoming.

Your whole body hums came Belle's awed comment. *You're totally in tune with the music and power of this place.*

I glanced at her. Her eyes glowed with echoes of the energy that pulsed through me. *It's not Katie who won't let me go. It's the wild magic itself.*

Because you're a part of it.

I nodded. *The origin of my wild magic might not be this wellspring, but it all comes from the one source deep within the earth.*

The delicate threads of power began tugging me forward. Katie's doing rather than the wild magic's.

I'll wait here, Belle said.

You're safe from the wild magic. It won't ever hurt you.

A smile touched her lips. *I know, but I think it better at least one of us remains fully aware of what is going on around us.*

Good point. Just because I believed we were safe from Clayton for the next couple of days didn't mean we should throw caution to the wind—especially when there was a murderous ghoul roaming around the reservation. It might have kept its kills to newlyweds, but that didn't mean it wouldn't broaden its tastes if the opportunity presented itself.

I switched off the flashlight and shoved it into my pocket as I stepped into the clearing. The gentle moon-beams spun around me, their music echoing through my mind, the notes alien and yet not. It was a sound I'd heard intermittently and distantly over the years, and long ignored.

It was through that sound—through the power of it—that I could now see Katie. Her form was ghostly, but she very much looked like a younger version of Ciara.

Standing behind her was a pale, wispy figure. I knew who it was without his features being clear—her husband, Gabe, who'd died here during the process of melding Katie's soul to the wellspring.

"You have questions?" Katie's voice was soft—melodious.

"Yes, about the wild magic and what it's doing."

Her gaze swept me; I suspect she missed little. She motioned toward the wellspring. "Let's sit. I like being close to our energy source."

'Our' meaning not just hers and Gabe's, but also mine. Interestingly, the closer we got to the wellspring, the more Gabe's body solidified. He reached out and pressed his hand against Katie's spine, and the two shared a glance. The sheer joy and utter love so evident in their faces had me blinking back tears.

No wonder she liked being close to the wellspring—it enabled the two of them to physically interact.

I crossed my legs and sat in front of the basin. Its energy was fierce and skittered across my skin like thousands of tiny fireflies, a warm rush that both burned and welcomed. Katie elegantly sat opposite me. Gabe remained standing.

"Why do I suddenly appear to have wolf-like senses?" I asked, once she was comfortable.

"I think it's a combination of me briefly taking over your body and my presence within the wild magic. Some sort of bleed over has occurred."

Which was exactly what I'd thought might be happening. "How far do you think the changes will go?"

A smile touched her ghostly lips. "Not far enough for you, I suspect."

"I don't want to be a werewolf."

She raised an eyebrow. "Not even to catch one?"

"That's never going to happen—even you know that."

"I know the heart usually wins, even when the head wishes otherwise." She glanced up at Gabe. Love shone like a beacon from her eyes and her body.

It made me feel like I was intruding. Made me envious of what they still had.

I cleared my throat. "In the case of your brother, his heart has already been taken, so it's really not a contest."

"Perhaps," Katie said, amusement gleaming in her eyes, "and perhaps not."

I raised my eyebrows even as my heart began to beat a little faster. "Meaning that you've now revised the warning you gave to both your mother and Aiden?"

"No. What they both wish will come to pass—that, I'm afraid, is inevitable now. It's what happens *after* she returns that remains unclear."

Meaning there was no escaping heartache for me. Great.

Katie's hand lightly touched mine. Her energy fizzed across my skin, as electric as lightning. "Hold on to hope. What isn't yet written can always be changed."

My smile no doubt echoed the sadness within. "Except

for the fact my own dreams are telling me a very different story."

"Your dreams aren't always right. You've admitted that multiple times."

Not to her I hadn't, which meant that even when I couldn't feel her presence or that of the wild magic, she was aware of everything that was going on.

"Not everything," she said. "But I do tend to keep an eye on the people I care about as well as the people *they* care about."

I stared at her for a heartbeat. "That thought wasn't spoken out loud."

"Because we don't need to now, thanks to your strengthening connection to the wild magic. Voicing our thoughts is more a pleasant habit than a necessity."

"Does that mean I can summon the wild magic from anywhere within the reservation? Even if it isn't in the area?"

"I don't know, so maybe you should try it next time you're out in the middle of nowhere." A smile tugged at her lips. "But, for modesty's sake, perhaps not when you're with Aiden."

"On that I agree." My voice was dry. "There're definitely some things a sister shouldn't see."

She chuckled. "I was talking about your modesty rather than mine. Wolves tend not to worry about such things."

"Even werewolves aren't into public displays."

"Depends entirely on the werewolf," she said, cheeks dimpling.

I snorted softly. "How much sharper do you think my senses are going to get?"

She shrugged. "Who knows? By rights, Gabe's spell shouldn't have worked. By rights, you should have died in utero. If I had to guess, I'd say that—while there's no denying the wild magic protects and strengthens you—it will also be the reason why the changes you're currently experiencing will go no further than sight, sound, and perhaps strength and endurance."

I frowned. "Why?"

"Because the wild magic is so deeply embedded that even if it *were* possible for your DNA to be enhanced to the point of enabling change, I don't believe the magic within would allow it."

A vague spark of hope stirred. "What about any children I might have?"

Amusement crossed her features. "Are we specifically talking part werewolves here?"

"In theory. Just in case, because hey, sometimes miracles do happen."

"And I'm proof enough of that." She paused. "In truth, that's another question neither of us can answer, as no one, as far as we're aware—and the songs and memories of the wild magic stretches back to the beginning of time itself—has ever survived complete immersion in the way you have."

Which only made that vague flicker of hope shine brighter.

"So it *is* remotely possible that if I did happen to marry a werewolf and we did happen to have children, they'd survive the problem your mother described in great detail?"

"Mom means well, but she's an alpha and can sometimes be very overbearing."

"To say the least," I muttered.

Katie's smile shone. "To answer the question, what protects you should also protect your offspring, but there's no guarantee, and Mom is right—the consequences of such a marriage can be heartbreaking."

I hesitated. "And yet it's a risk you and Gabe were willing to take."

"It was never a risk, because death was my fate. Had it been otherwise?" She looked up at Gabe. Both their faces glowed. "I'm not sure what we would have done. Not had children, most likely."

"That won't be my fate. There's at least one child in my future—a little blonde-haired girl." Whether it was Aiden's or someone's I'd yet to meet was unclear.

"Then I'll keep all things crossed that she *is* an O'Connor. I fancy being an aunt." She paused. "Is there anything else you need?"

"At this point, no." I hesitated. "Do you keep watch over the reservation's borders at all?"

"No." She studied me shrewdly for a moment. "I take it this is about the men who were in your café last night?"

"Yes. I don't suppose you know where they were staying?"

"No, and I can't say I felt their presence, either. Why?"

After I'd quickly explained the situation, she added, "And you fear Clayton will take his anger out on Aiden as much as Belle?"

"Yes. Are you—via the wild magic—able to protect him?"

"My connection to the wild magic continues to grow, and it may one day be possible that I can use its energy to defend my own. For now, however, I'm limited."

"Define limited."

Gabe's ghostly form shifted, and Katie glanced up at him. I couldn't hear what he was saying, but after a moment, her gaze returned to me. "I can prevent a magical assault—as I did when you and Aiden were attacked in the graveyard—but at this point I cannot prevent a physical assault or retaliate against a living person without your presence to direct the force of the wild magic."

"Why? Wasn't the point of all this"—I waved a hand at the wellspring—"for you to become the reservation's guardian?"

"Yes, but there's no certainty that I'll ever fully command the wild magic in the manner you can. The spell binding a soul to a wellspring was an untested—and unfinished—theory. We have no real idea how deep the immersion will go."

Meaning I'd been right in guessing the spell's origin had been Gabe more than some long ago forgotten spell, and that made it even more vital we kept this wellspring's existence secret. If word got out about what he'd managed to do, it would bring half of Canberra here to interrogate him and to study Katie's immersion. And while he and Katie had had nothing but good intent, that might not be the case with others. If a dark soul ever managed to merge with a wellspring, there was no telling how far the stain of evil might spread, especially given all wellsprings came from the one source deep within the earth and were ultimately all connected. Such an event could have dire consequences for any community situated near a wellspring.

"Protecting him from a direct magical assault, even if only for a few minutes, might be all that's necessary."

Especially if I wove a warning spell into the charm he was wearing. Unless Clayton got hold of something personal of Aiden's, any spell he'd created to snare Aiden would have to be done in his immediate vicinity. A warning of incoming magic would give Aiden time to either run—or, knowing the man as well as I did—track Clayton down and stop him.

"That I can do—shall I start immediately?"

"No—I'll send word via the wild magic." I pushed to my feet. The tiny moonbeam threads immediately gathered around me, their song tinged with sadness at my leaving.

"One day, perhaps, you might remain here permanently with us," Katie said. "But that's a way off yet."

"I long way off, I'm hoping."

She laughed, a soft sound that had the moonbeams dancing. "So am I, because three would definitely be a crowd."

I smiled and left. The moonbeams trailed us for quite a while but eventually turned and scooted back to Katie.

"Well, that was interesting," Belle said as the path became less treacherous again. "Although we didn't really get that many answers."

"No, but it did give me some hope." I flashed her a grin over my shoulder. "The future isn't as set in stone as I'd feared."

"Perhaps, but I wouldn't be pinning too many dreams on that comment just yet. Not when she also said Mia coming back is inevitable."

"I know—just as I know we'll break up when she does and I'll be a sobbing mess. But at least there's now a possibility he and Mia won't last."

"They might not, but what happens when the next wolf comes along? Or the one after that? Unless he decides to marry you, you're setting yourself up for continuous heartbreak. You'll be better off ending it cleanly with Mia's return, because if he *does* marry you, he'll have to turn his back on his pack, his parents, and his position as alpha-in-waiting. That's a big ask, given he is, above all else, an honorable man with a deep sense of duty."

I scowled, even though I knew the truth of her words.

"I'm not listening to you. I'm going to enjoy dreaming about future possibilities for the next few days at the very least."

She chuckled softly. "Good, because I'd rather you concentrate on *your* future rather than mine for a goddamn change."

I laughed, a sound that echoed across the stillness of the surrounding trees. In the distance, something altogether much darker responded.

I paused, forcing Belle do a quick jump sideways to avoid crashing into me.

"What?" she said, her voice hushed.

"I don't know." I scanned the trees but couldn't see anything out of place or unusual. And yet... my 'other' senses were stirring.

It's very quiet out there, Belle said. *Unusually so, given dawn isn't that far away now. Could it be our ghoul?*

Possibly. Whatever it was felt dark.

Do you want to investigate?

No.

But you nevertheless will.

Her mental tone was dry, and a smile tugged my lips. *Also true.*

She made a sweeping motion with her hand. *You lead, I'll follow.*

One of these days that's going to get you into deep trouble.

I wouldn't have it any other way.

I chuckled softly and cautiously stepped off the path. Dawn was only just beginning to stain the sky, and deep shadows still haunted the trees. The flashlight's bright beam pierced the darkness directly in front, but somehow deepened the ink on either side.

Leaf matter crunched under every step and, like my

laugh, it spun loudly through the silence. This time, there was no response. I wasn't entirely sure whether that was a good thing or bad—especially given that wisp of darkness remained.

The ground dipped sharply into a ravine that could only be described as wild. Blackberries were so thickly clustered along the ravine's bottom that, although I could hear water, I couldn't actually see it. It was the sort of place snakes and rabbits loved because so few predators dared risk the thick thorns. I was suddenly glad that it was winter—at least snakes weren't going to be a problem.

The path was another steep goat track littered with loose stones and treacherous drops. We followed it cautiously, but were little more than halfway when my foot slipped and I went down hard, bruising one knee and skinning the palm of the hand I threw out to save myself. I cursed loudly; the sound echoed once again, but drew no response from the shadows still haunting the brambles below.

Fuck, are you okay? Belle grabbed my arm and helped me upright.

Yeah, I think so. I brushed the dirt from my knee, then inspected my hand. The scrapes were minor, even if they stung like blazes.

You were damn lucky you didn't break your wrist or leg given the way you fell, Belle said. *Do you want some water to wash those cuts out with?*

When we get down to the bottom. It's pointless doing it before then, because I might just fall over again.

Even you're not that clumsy.

Maybe not, but the damn path does get steeper.

I picked a small stone out of one of the wounds and then walked on, this time concentrating on every single step rather than getting distracted by the darkness still tugging at my senses.

We made it to the bottom of the ravine without any further problems. I swiped at the sweat dribbling down my cheeks and scanned the nearby scrub and blackberry canes. Despite the fact they'd looked like an unbroken wall, there were quite a few usable paths meandering through the various clumps. Whether roos or werewolves had created them, I couldn't say, but it did at least mean we weren't in immediate danger of being scratched raw by blackberry thorns.

We followed a path that meandered through the canes and crossed over the small, stone-lined creek several times. Though the sky was now a riot of color, shadows still lurked down here. With the growing dawn came life, and the noise of unseen creatures skittering away from our approach filled the air.

The path crossed the creek one more time and then split in two—one track heading back up the ravine, the other moving into thicker canes.

Left or right? Belle directed her light toward the path leading upward. *I'm guessing since that track looks less forbidding, we'll be going left.*

I grinned. *I think you're getting the hang of this.*

I'd rather not.

What happened to that 'you lead, I'll follow' sensibility you were spouting not so long ago?

It got snagged on blackberry thorns and torn away.

Amusement bubbled through me, but it didn't last long. As the path led us into the thicker grove of blackberries, the canes closed in and their thorns were impossible to avoid.

After multiple snags and scratches, I was just about ready to call off the hunt when the breeze sharpened, rattling the canes and bringing with it an odd, metallic scent.

I knew what it was almost instantly, having smelled it on more than a few occasions since we'd set up shop in this reservation.

Blood.

I drew in a deeper breath, but there was little hint as to what else might lie up ahead. There was no sense of magic and nothing to suggest that anything living—or dead, for that matter—lay in wait. I nevertheless wove a repelling spell around my fingers and cautiously moved on.

After a few more meters, the blackberries gave way to a small cleared area. The creek bubbled along one edge, and there were several small dirt pits to my right that suggested foxes or maybe even stray dogs had been making themselves at home here.

In the middle of the clearing was a large bloodstained area.

Belle stopped beside me. "The first thing that strikes me as odd is the fact that there's no skin or bones. Even scavengers wouldn't erase all evidence of a kill."

"I don't think the blood came from a kill."

She glanced at me. "Why?"

"Because it has the taint of darkness in it."

Her gaze shot back to the bloodied patch of ground. "Do you think it's from the ghoul?"

"Possibly." I hesitated, remembering the weird images I'd gotten from the victim's mind.

"Even ghouls can't break the laws of life," Belle said. "If this thing *actually* tore itself apart, it would be dead."

"If it was a ghoul, yes, but we're obviously dealing with something very different."

She rubbed her arms. "Do you think it'll be possible to track this thing through its blood?"

"Monty would probably know that better than I would."

"You want me to ring him?"

I glanced at her, amusement lurking around my lips. "You're volunteering to do that quite often these days."

She gave me a deadpan look. One that said 'step no further'.

My grin broke free as I raised my hands. "It might also be a good idea to ring Penny and see if she and Celia can open up for us. I'll check out the blood."

As she got out her phone, I walked across and squatted next to the stain. This close, it looked surprisingly fresh, which no doubt explained why darkness still radiated from it. Droplets gleamed on the tips of the grass, and pools little bigger than a twenty-cent piece had yet to soak fully into the ground.

I hesitated and then reached out to—but didn't quite touch—the nearest pool of blood. My fingers tingled and warmed, and my psi senses stirred. This tiny patch of blood still held its secrets, but they were fading as fast as the blood was drying.

I withdrew my hand and turned as Belle hung up and shoved her phone back into her pocket. "Monty and Aiden are on their way."

"What happened with the other murder?"

"It was a family argument that got nasty and loud, but thankfully no one was killed."

That was at least good. "And the café?"

"No problem. Apparently, Celia's staying with Penny until she gets enough money for a place of her own, so she'd welcome the extra shift."

Celia was Penny's niece and had only recently arrived in the reservation from Geelong after an apparently acrid split with her boyfriend.

"You find anything?" Belle added.

"As yet, no, but I think I can read the blood."

She blinked and stared at me for a second. "Seriously?"

"You already know the answer to that."

"Well, yes, but... how is something like that possible? You've never been able to do it before now."

"It's not like we've had a lot of opportunities—"

"Since coming here, there've been ample," Belle cut in. "Hell, the watch you found in the forest had dried skin attached, and you didn't get any images or memories off that."

"Maybe because I was trying to pull something from the watch rather than the skin."

And even when I *had* touched the skin, I'd been unable to sense anything more than death simply because the watch had been in the ground too long. I glanced back at the blood. That was not the case here.

Belle swung her backpack off. "If you're going to do this, I'll set up a protection circle. If that blood does belong to a ghoul then it might still be nearby. I don't want it catching us unawares."

I waited as she set out her stones and then activated them. Once she was sitting comfortably on the other side of the stain, she dug her phone out of her pocket. "I'll record what you're seeing, but please remember to speak, otherwise Aiden will be annoyed." She paused. "Or rather, more annoyed. You should have told him we were coming up here."

"He's not my keeper, Belle."

"But he *is* a wolf, and they tend to get all territorial and protective over people they care about."

I wrinkled my nose. "We're in Marin territory—nothing untoward is going to happen to us here. Besides, I couldn't have asked the questions I did if he'd been there."

"Which doesn't negate the fact that when it involves his sister—or anyone else in his pack, for that matter—you should have mentioned it. Ready?"

When I nodded, she hit the record button. I took a deep breath to center my energy and then carefully placed two fingers into the small, somewhat sticky pool. I didn't have to reach for my psychometry abilities—they surged to life the minute I touched the blood, and filled my mind with sensations: hunger, frustration, pain, and anger. The latter was a fierce, deep burning. I pushed deeper into the wave of emotion, not only trying to catch some reason for the anger but also some sense of who and what we were actually dealing with.

"Lizzie," Belle said softly. "Tell the recording what you're seeing."

"Old hurt," I said with a frown. "Old anger."

"Any reason why?"

"No." I hesitated as the shadows within the blood shifted, revealing vague images. "It's something to do with a wedding—and being betrayed."

"Was she the bride?"

I pushed more energy into the connection, trying to deepen it. I might as well have tried to catch a wisp. "I think so."

"What was she doing here? Why is there blood on the ground?"

More indeterminate images stirred. "She was splitting."

"Splitting?"

I nodded. "It's what I saw in the victim's mind—she can sprout bat wings, and in taking flight, her torso tears away from the rest of her trunk and legs."

"And this blood is the result of that?"

"Yes."

I tried to catch more, but the images were now so vague —the pulse of darkness so faint—that there was little to see other than smoky wisps that held no form and made no sense. I withdrew my fingers and quickly wiped them clean on the dirt.

"So if she separated, where's the body?" Belle said. "Even if foxes or other vermin had discovered it, surely there'd be remnants left."

"Unless she's also able to reattach. It's possible if we're dealing with something other than a ghoul."

"Anything else to report?"

"No. But if we want to use the blood to trace this thing, I'd better preserve some pretty quickly. Its power is fading fast."

I swung my pack around and pulled out a plastic Ziploc bag and a pocketknife. While I was also carrying my silver knife, using it would erase any lingering remnants of darkness within the blood.

I carefully cut out a good clump of soil that still held a sticky globule of blood and then carefully constructed a spell that would both contain and also 'freeze' the blood in its current state; hopefully that would make whatever impressions remained in the blood last until Monty got here. Once the threads of magic were tightly wound around the chunk of earth, I activated the spell and then carefully prodded it. The darkness that stirred lightly across my fingertips was no fainter than before. Hopefully, it would remain that way.

Belle deconstructed her protection circle, then we moved across to the small creek and perched on a couple of handy rocks. As the red-and-gold fingers of dawn faded and the day became brighter, the faint sound of approaching sirens ran across the silence, growing sharper before abruptly cutting off.

We heard Monty long before either man appeared—he was swearing like there was no tomorrow.

"He's obviously having a lot of fun with the blackberry canes," Belle said, amusement evident.

"Well, he's broader than either of us, so he's probably getting caught more often."

"I'm not hearing Aiden complain."

"No doubt because he's in wolf form and can move through them easier."

It was a guess that was proven correct a few minutes later as Aiden stepped into the clearing, his silver coat gleaming in the soft morning light now filtering through the trees. He glanced at the two of us—and even in wolf form, the gleam of annoyance in his blue eyes was very evident— then padded across to the bloodstain and sniffed it. His nose wrinkled in distaste, then light shimmered across his body, briefly concealing the change from wolf to human.

Before he could say anything, Monty all but erupted out of the blackberry cluster. His jacket was shredded and there were bloody scratches across his face and hands.

"Well, fuck, that's an experience I'm not looking forward to repeating." He plucked a short cane from his hair and flicked it away. "So, was the effort worth it? Did you get anything from reading the blood?"

I couldn't help smiling. "The blood belongs to the ghoul, and the ghoul can sprout wings and tear itself in half."

"Ha! Then I guessed right," Monty said, delight evident.

"Care to share said guess with the rest of us?" Aiden said, voice dry.

"What we're dealing with is a Manananggal, and it's not really a ghoul. It's more a vampire-like monster or witch who—depending on which myth you read—preys on either sleeping pregnant women or on newlyweds. The latter is apparently due to it being left at the altar."

"So what happens to the lower part of its torso when it separates?" Aiden asked.

"It's left standing wherever the Manananggal separated. The easiest way to kill it is to find the abandoned torso and then sprinkle a mix of salt, crushed garlic, and ash over and around it. This prevents the two parts rejoining, and means the Manananggal will perish on sunrise."

I frowned. "Why, when it can obviously survive without half its body?"

"All magic has its limits and all supernatural beings at least one vulnerability. Obviously, needing to rejoin its body before night is over is this creature's."

"Does that mean it's the inability to become one again that kills it, rather than sunlight?" I asked.

"Good question—and one I can't answer."

"Is preventing it rejoining the only way it can be killed?" Aiden asked.

"I daresay the usual methods to kill a vampire would work with this creature." He walked across to where Belle and I were sitting. "Can I have a look at the blood sample?"

I handed him the Ziploc bag. He undid it and rolled the thread-wrapped piece of dirt into his hand. "There's not much of a pulse, despite the spell around it. Which, by the way, was well done."

I smiled. "Will you be able to use it to do a location spell?"

"Maybe." He silently studied the bloodstained dirt for a few seconds. "If we're to have any hope of it succeeding, it'll need to be done straight away. And I'll need your help, Liz."

I frowned. "Why? You're the stronger witch and—"

"In spellcraft yes, but it's rather debatable when it comes to actual power." His voice was dry. "But that's beside the point. I can do a locator but if the dark thread contained within the blood fades too much more, then our only hope might be your psi skills."

"I've already used psychometry on the blood, Monty. The images were vague—"

"Maybe the connection was simply too faint because the creature is too far away."

"Blood is a connector?" Aiden asked, surprise in his tone.

Monty glanced at him. "With many supernatural creatures, yes."

"Then why haven't we used it to locate these things before? If there's one thing we haven't been short on in the recent spate of murders, it's blood."

"Yes, but I rather suspect it's a skill that's only recently developed." Monty's gaze returned to mine. "Am I right?"

"Yes." I shrugged. "It would seem the wild magic is altering—either by enhancing or changing—some of my psychic abilities and my sensory capabilities."

"Is that why you came up here to talk to Katie?" Aiden asked.

I met his gaze evenly. "Yes. And no, I won't inform you every time I go see her, Aiden. That would be impractical and intrusive."

"On her life? Or yours?"

I smiled, though it held little humor. "Can we save this discussion until after we've caught this ghoul or vampire or whatever the hell it actually is?"

He studied me for a minute, then nodded once. The annoyance in his eyes remained—and sparked an echo inside of me. He had no right to anger; not when the Marin pack had given us clearance to enter that clearing as and when necessary.

He wasn't my keeper. Not now. Not in any future scenario I could imagine. And I'd have thought he'd know me well enough by now to be aware of that fact.

Except he's not only a werewolf, Belle said, amusement in her mental tone, *but also a man. And we all know that their brain and instincts don't always listen to each other.*

I snorted mentally and tried to ignore the niggling annoyance as Monty wove a spell in and around my preserving spell. It was so delicately done that although the two spells were intimately entwined, neither interfered with the other.

"Right," he said after closing off the last thread and then activating the spell. "The trail leads up the hill."

Belle pushed to her feet. "At least we don't have to tackle the blackberries again."

"Depends on where the trail leads us," Aiden said. "They return with a vengeance in the next valley."

"Something else to look forward to," I muttered, casting a look Aiden's way.

He simply raised one eyebrow and motioned me forward. I swung my pack over my shoulder and followed Monty up the hill. I was puffing badly by the time we reached the top, so when Monty stopped, I took the opportunity to grab a drink.

"Has the trail gone cold?" Aiden asked.

"Maybe." Monty held the spell-wrapped piece of dirt away from his body and moved slowly around. After doing one complete circle, he turned back to the right. "There's a slight pulse coming from down that trail, but I'm not entirely sure it's a true reading."

I frowned. "How can it not be a true reading?"

His expression was troubled. "I don't know. It just feels... off."

"I'm not smelling anything out of place," Aiden commented.

Neither was I. But if Monty said something was wrong, then there definitely was. "If you peel back your spell, I'll see if the blood can give us any further clues."

He nodded and immediately did so. I carefully pushed a finger through the threads of my preserving spell and lightly touched the dried blood. Though there was very little in the way of response, Monty was right. Something felt different.

I withdrew my finger and studied the faint path that disappeared into a thick strand of trees lining the ridge. "Whatever's caused the change in the response we're getting, I don't think it's too far away."

"I'll go investigate—"

"Both of us will. It'll be safer." I glanced at Belle and Aiden. "Wait here. We won't be long."

Aiden's gaze narrowed, but he didn't argue.

Be careful was Belle's only comment.

I turned and followed Monty along the top of the ridge. The windswept trees gathered close to the path, and though the sunlight filtered through them easily enough, a vague caress of evil began to stain the air.

"Monty—"

"I know." His voice vibrated with tension, and magic

sparked across his fingertips—a containment spell. "It's coming from around the curve ahead."

"It doesn't feel like the creature." I silently followed his lead and cast my version of his spell across my fingertips. "It's not solid enough, if that makes sense."

"It does." His pace slowed as we neared the curve. "It vaguely feels like magic."

"Oh, that can't be good."

"I'm thinking that's an understatement." The spell twined around his fingers glowed brighter. "I'm not seeing any threads though."

I stepped sideways to get a better view. The path ahead continued to curve around to the right; despite the shadows and the faint caress of evil and magic, there was no indication a spell had been activated. "Maybe she's hidden them."

"Maybe." There was doubt in his tone.

"Has the pulse from the blood changed at all?"

"It's almost nonexistent now. But that could simply be because it's dried and the connection's been severed."

I eyed the path ahead with trepidation. "What do you want to do?"

"We have to go on—I don't think we've got any other choice. The last thing we need is for a werewolf or a hiker to spring a trap set for us."

"Agreed, although can I just state that I'm not altogether happy about *us* springing the trap, either."

He glanced at me. "You can remain behind."

"And risk losing the only relative I actually like? No."

"The problem with *that* statement is the fact that if you get hurt, my future wife won't be happy."

Too right, Belle said. *And seriously, tell him to cut it out with the 'future wife' stuff. It's getting annoying.*

"The future wife," I said obediently, "wishes you to stop calling her that."

He chuckled softly and, in that moment, we heard it.

A soft snap.

We both stopped and glanced down.

The sound hadn't come from Monty stepping on a bit of wood or anything else so mundane.

Its source had been a spell—a thread of magic we hadn't seen and still couldn't see. The broken remnants of whatever spell had been stretched across the path remained invisible—only the slight echo of its power floating away on the breeze gave its presence away.

For several heartbeats, neither of us moved. The broken threads continued to drift away, but there was no immediate indication that anything untoward was about to happen.

"Maybe it was just an alarm of some kind."

His whisper scratched across both the silence and my nerves. I scanned the area, looking for anything that suggested there were caves or some other kind of hiding spot nearby. There wasn't any sort of rock outcrop, big or small. Nothing but trees clinging to the edge of the path, partially hiding the steep drop down to the ravine.

"Why would she set an alarm here?" I whispered back. "It makes no—"

I cut off the rest of the sentence as the ground vibrated. It was little more than a faint tremble that came and went, but it nevertheless had tension ramping up several notches.

A heartbeat later, a second shudder ran through the ground, sharper and stronger than before. This time, it came from behind us rather than underneath us.

Understanding hit, though it came from my connection to this mountain—to the magic that welled from deep within it—rather than any understanding of what the spell had been.

I thrust a hand onto Monty's back and shoved him forward. "*Run!*"

He flailed for a heartbeat, then caught his balance and did so, all but flying across the top of the ridge. The rumbling grew stronger, louder, and the trees around us quivered and shook.

This goddamn section of the ridge was about to slip into the ravine.

"Faster, Monty!"

He swung up an arm to bat away the branches of a tree that swayed so badly it looked storm-tossed. "I'm running as fast I fucking can!"

I leapt over a branch that crashed between us, slipped on sliding soil, and stumbled forward several steps before I caught my balance and ran on.

Huge chunks of ground were now breaking away, taking with it scrub and smaller trees. It forced us to dodge and weave, which slowed us and only increased the danger.

Then, with a *whoomph* that hurt my ears, the entire section we were on collapsed into the ravine.

CHAPTER NINE

I dropped like a stone for several feet, a scream on my lips and terror in my heart. I hit the broken earth hard enough to have pain shimmering up my spine and tumbled forward, surrounded by a deadly rain of earth, rocks, and broken bits of trees. Felt the surge of magic when I hit the ground a second time, felt it rise around me. Saw a flash of blue to my right and instinctively flung out a hand, somehow grabbing Monty's. His fingers twitched, tightened on mine, even as the magic continued to surge. It wasn't witch magic, but wild. It flowed over me, over Monty, forming a connection that somehow pulled us into each other's arms even as it created a shimmering barrier between the worst of the landslide and us.

But it didn't stop us falling; didn't stop the bruises and cuts as we rolled and bounced sideways down the hill.

Then, abruptly, my back hit stone and we stopped. I cursed, blinking back tears of pain and sucking in air as hurt rolled through every inch of me. The broken hillside continued to slide past us, but the shimmering barrier of wild magic forced the worst of it away from us.

Neither of us moved. I don't think either of us dared. Eventually, the tumble of debris eased. As the shimmer of wild magic faded, I became aware of the wave of pain washing through my thoughts and sent a panicked, *Belle? Are you okay?*

Yes. Aiden sensed the onset of the landslide and got us both off the ridge.

Then why are you in pain?

I twisted my ankle on the way down. Aiden went into hero mode and carried me. She paused. *What about you and Monty? We couldn't see what happened from where we were.*

We sprung the Manananggal's trap, which is what set off the landslide. The wild magic saved us, Belle. I didn't call it —it just came.

Meaning the connection is deepening into an instinctive response level—and I guess that's no real surprise given it's embedded in your DNA.

Yes, but it's problematic. I definitely don't need an instinctive-level response to anything Clayton might do or try.

"Lizzie?" came Aiden's shout from somewhere above us.

"Here!" I replied.

"And Monty?"

"Also here."

"Stay where you are. The hill remains unstable, so I'll be down as soon as I can." He paused. "Are either of you hurt?"

"Nothing's broken, as far as I'm aware." I glanced down as Monty stirred. His face was bloody thanks to a large cut above his left eye, and his right cheek was scraped and bruised. "You?"

"Same." He coughed and then winced. "The bruises are going to be horrendous, however."

"If bruises and a few cuts are all we come out with, then I'm not about to complain. We should be dead."

"That was certainly the bitch's intention. Thank God you called the wild magic into action."

I didn't disabuse him of the notion. Right now, it wasn't important. "Can you sit up?"

"Yeah, I think so." He carefully pushed away from me and then levered himself upright, his expression a mix of determination and pain.

I carefully followed suit, but a dozen different hurts flared the length of my body, and the world briefly spun. I sucked in a breath and then raised a hand to the tender spot on the top of my head; my fingers came away smeared with blood. At least it wasn't profusely bleeding—unlike the cut above Monty's eye. I swung my battered backpack around and pulled out some tissues. "Shove these on the cut."

He did so. "Well, one good thing did come out of all this —we now know our Manananggal is magic capable."

"Which is no doubt how she sensed us—she must have felt me spelling her blood."

"And *that* is going to cause problems, because if we can't use magic to track her, finding the bitch is going to be a whole lot harder."

"Maybe." I shifted position, trying to ease the ache in my back. "And maybe not."

He raised an eyebrow. "Meaning what?"

"Meaning, how is she finding her victims? Either she's hanging around wedding venues or she's casting a spell of some kind to find newly married couples."

"I guess a love spell could be perverted in such a manner." He swiped at his cheek, smearing blood across the few bits of skin that weren't either bloody or dirt caked. "But the reservation is a big place, and we'd have to be close enough to detect the spell's formation."

"What if we stake out local weddings? There can't be that many booked—not when it's almost winter."

"Not everyone dreams of a summer wedding."

"Of course not, but numbers have to be down—why else would most of them offer deep discounts during the winter months?"

"I guess." His expression remained doubtful. "The other problem is the fact that the rangers haven't the manpower to watch all possible venues. We certainly haven't the witch power."

I glanced past him and saw Aiden sliding toward us. Relief stirred, along with an odd feeling of security. Of being completely safe, even though that was as far from true as it could get given both Clayton and the Manananggal were still casting long shadows over us.

"Then how are we going to find this thing?"

"I don't know yet." He glanced around. "Nice of you to join the party, Ranger."

"Nice to see you're obviously well enough to joke about the situation." He squatted between us, his gaze briefly sweeping me and coming up relieved. "How the hell did you survive the collapse?"

"Luck and magic." I touched his arm lightly. "Help me up."

"It might be better to wait for the medics—"

"How long will they be? And what about Belle?"

"Aside from a sprained ankle, she's fine."

"I know *that* much—I meant, are the medics going to her?"

"No, because Mac and Jaz are currently carrying her out to them."

"If this ravine is anything like the other," Monty commented, "the medics aren't going to reach us very easily, especially when they're carrying all their equipment. It'll be better all round, Ranger, if we just walk out."

He hesitated, studying Monty and no doubt seeing the determination there. "I think it's foolish, but I can't actually stop either of you. But please, can you both agree to being fully checked out at the hospital?"

"Agreed." Aside from the fact I *wasn't* stupid, the doctors could provide the industrial-strength painkillers I was no doubt going to need once all the aches and bruising fully developed.

He hesitated and then helped me upright, his grip moving from my hand to my elbow as my legs wobbled alarmingly. Once I was steady, he released me, then helped Monty to his feet.

He studied the two of us for a second, and then shook his head. "This way."

Our pace was slow, and it seemed to take hours to get out of the damn ravine. I was sweating and aching by the time we reached the road and the waiting ambulance officers. Belle had already been taken to the hospital, but the medics assured me it was nothing more than a precautionary measure and that her sprain wasn't that bad.

Monty and I were bundled into the waiting ambulances and taken to the hospital. It was a good five hours before they'd run all their tests and confirmed what I already knew —aside from cuts and bruising, I was perfectly fine. They loaded me up with painkillers, told me to rest up over the next couple of days, and then shuffled me out the door— where I discovered Aiden waiting for me.

"Hey," I said, rising up on tiptoe to kiss him. "I thought you were working?"

"I am, but I'm also the boss." He opened the truck door and ushered me in. "And we need to talk."

I waited until he'd jumped into the driver side. "If this is about Katie—"

"It's not so much about Katie, but rather your continuing refusal to fully trust me."

I frowned. "That's not true—"

"Isn't it?" He pulled out of the parking area and then glanced at me. "Then why not simply tell me you were going to see Katie and that you didn't want me along?"

I wrinkled my nose. "Because I thought you'd insist."

"I would certainly have asked why, but I wouldn't have insisted. I'm a werewolf, not an ogre."

A smile tugged at my lips. "I know, and I guess I do owe you an apology. It's just that I have a hard time—"

"Trusting anyone other than Belle. I know. But you've formed a family of choice here, Liz, and you very much need to believe in and trust *all* of us."

Family. It was something I'd long searched for, something that was finally within my reach.

And something Clayton could so very easily destroy.

I blinked back tears and stared out the side window for a couple of seconds. When I was certain my emotions were back under control, I told him everything Katie had said about the wild magic; everything except the whole baby thing. There was no real point in mentioning that, simply because—however much I might hope otherwise—the little girl I saw in my future might not be his.

"She also confirmed that I can't permanently leave the reservation."

"Which is a good thing, isn't it? It means that Clayton can't swoop in and spell you away."

"In theory, yes." Although given both Clayton and my father had hidden their presence from Katie, there was no absolute certainty.

He slowed as the lights ahead went red. "And the stuff about the wild magic protecting you? Is that what happened today?"

"Yes."

"Which means Clayton can't actually hurt you."

"He can hurt me by hurting Belle. Or you. Or any of the others."

Aiden frowned. "Do you really think he'll go to those extremes?"

"I don't know. I don't know him. I've never really known him—he was my father's friend and a second cousin. I had very little to do with him."

At least until my father decided the best way to deal with a problem child was to basically sell her off to a friend desperate to have a wife young enough to have lots of children.

"Then you need to talk to someone who did," Aiden said.

I snorted. "Like who? My goddamn father?"

"Well, no. I was thinking more along the lines of your mother."

"*What?* Why?"

The lights went green. He slipped the truck into gear and took off again. "Well, if she's now left your father because she was told what he and Clayton did, she may well not only welcome the contact, but the chance to make amends."

"You don't know my mother." I couldn't help the bitterness in my voice. "She and I were never close."

"Which doesn't mean she won't be feeling some regret over the situation." He glanced at me again. "What have you got to lose? Given you've been found by them and you can't run anymore, you've got no real choice but to face up to your past—*all* of it—and move on."

"Fine advice coming from a man still haunted by his." It was out before I could stop it, and I silently cursed. I didn't need to be stirring *that* up right now.

"She doesn't haunt me," he bit back. "Not anymore."

I glanced at him. "So if she came back tomorrow—"

"That's very unlikely to happen."

It was said with a bitterness that spoke volumes and basically confirmed future heartache. "But if she *did*?"

"Then I'd deal with it." He stopped in front of our café. "But it's not my past causing us problems right now, and I can't see the harm in reaching out."

"I'll think about it." I undid the seat belt and leaned across to kiss him. "Are you coming around for dinner later?"

He shook his head. "It's Dillon's fourteenth birthday, and I said I'd be there for the celebration."

Which was just another reminder that no matter what happened between us, that part of his life was something I would never share.

"I'll see you tomorrow, then."

I grabbed my backpack and carefully climbed out. The various aches protested the movement, and I walked somewhat stiffly into the café. I didn't look back. Didn't wave goodbye. The man was too astute and might have seen the brief sheen of self-pitying tears.

"And why might they be happening?" Belle said, as I

locked the café door and hobbled toward her. "Or is that a stupid question?"

"The latter. Why are you on your feet—weren't you told to rest that foot?"

"Yes, and I am, but I needed coffee and there was no one here to make it for me." She limped over to the table and sat down. "I chatted to Penny, by the way. Everything went smoothly with the café today, and I asked Celia to work for the rest of the week. I figured neither of us will be up to running around too much."

I nodded. "I'm heading upstairs for a long hot bath. I think we'll do takeout tonight."

"Excellent idea. But before you go—are you up to a session with the truth seeker and auditor?"

"Tonight?"

She nodded. "They want the files ready in the event of your father or Clayton changing their minds about the annulment."

"My father won't change his mind. Not now that he's aware I can interact with the wild magic."

"Yes, but it's not your father who has to sign off on the annulment, and Clayton's just as aware of your abilities."

"True." I hesitated. "Aiden suggested I ring Mom and get the gossip on him."

She blinked. "You know, that might not be a bad idea."

"I don't know, Belle—"

"She won't reject you, Liz. She never did, even if she wasn't the most caring parent."

I took a deep, somewhat shuddering breath. Rejection certainly was a fear, and its origin wasn't the years of being told I wasn't good enough, but rather the reaction of *both* my parents when we'd lost my sister, Cat. They'd blamed me for her death; hell, *I* blamed me, simply because, in the end, I hadn't been strong—

"And if they'd actually *listened* to you—or actually believed your psi abilities just that *once*," Belle cut in tartly, "your sister might well have survived. Her death is on *their* shoulders, not yours. I've long thought their over-the-top reaction was in part due to that knowledge."

"You've never said that to me."

"I did. You never wanted to hear it."

Probably because thinking about *that* time—about *them* —sparked all the fear, disbelief, and horror to life. And I really *wasn't* looking forward to reliving them under the truth seeker's ministrations.

"I'm not entirely sure what ringing my mother will actually achieve aside from awkwardness. It's been too long—"

"For both of us," she said gently. "But for your peace of mind, more than your mother's, you need to speak to her. If nothing else, you can ask her why she never objected to the so-called marriage."

"I guess." I wrinkled my nose, not really wanting to think about it *at all* right now. "Have you contacted your mom yet?"

"I tried calling her cell phone but she must have changed numbers. I left a message on the home phone instead." Belle laughed softly. "She always was a social butterfly."

She was also kind, generous, and loving. She—and her contacts—was also the reason the two of us had been able to disappear so thoroughly. "I'd love to be a fly on the wall when she finally listens to that message."

"Yeah." Belle's smile was bright with anticipation and absolute happiness. "I'll probably have to hold the phone away from my ear for several minutes while she gets her screaming and sobbing over with."

This moment had been a very long time coming for Belle, and I couldn't have been more pleased. She'd given up so much more than I had when we'd both gone on the run. "She probably won't be the only one sobbing."

"Absolutely not." Belle made a motion toward the stairs. "Go soak in the tub for an hour or so. I'll ring Jenna and let her know we'll be ready by eight."

I nodded and wearily climbed the stairs. Once I'd filled the bathtub, I threw in some Epsom salts as well as a mix of lavender and rosemary oils, then spent the next hour doing nothing more than topping up the water's heat and listening to music.

Dinner was a chicken, avocado, and cheese pizza with barbeque sauce for me, and a traditional Aussie pizza for Belle, followed up by coffee and the last two slices of banana bread cheesecake. To say I felt better after that mountain of food was an understatement. Maybe the changes I was undergoing thanks to the wild magic were also altering my appetite; if that was true, I just had to hope it also adjusted my metabolic rate. I was happy with my current weight and really didn't want it to go up—or down, for that matter.

The two women appeared right on the dot of eight. Ruby strode in and scanned the café with interest. "Lovely atmosphere in this room, but it's really not suitable for what we have to do. Have you got somewhere more comfortable?"

"We've a sofa upstairs," I said, "but the four of us won't fit on it."

"That's fine—we'll be quite happy with one of the café chairs. It's more your comfort during the reading that we're worried about."

I directed them toward the stairs and then said, "Would either of you like tea or coffee?"

"A green tea would be lovely," Ruby said.

"I'll have a revitalizing potion, if you don't mind making it," Jenna said. "This process knocks me about a fair bit."

As they continued on, I made the drinks and then carried them up on a tray. The coffee table had been shifted to one side, and the two chairs we kept on the balcony had been dragged inside. One had been positioned in front of the sofa and the other was off to the side.

I placed the tray on the table, handed out the drinks, and then sat beside Belle on the sofa.

"So, what's the process?"

"It's quite simple, really." Jenna perched on the chair in front of me, then placed the potion on the floor. "Or will be, once you drop those mental shields of yours. You simply have to think back to the moment you were first told of the marriage, and I'll take it from there."

I frowned. "So you'll just be verbalizing my memories for the sake of the recording?"

"No, I'll actually be bringing your memories to life so that the camera can record them. They'll basically be a movie that plays out in the space between us for as long as my mind is connected with yours. I'll be verbally overlaying that with both your thoughts and replies, as the two aren't always the same."

"That's one hell of a variation on telepathy," Belle commented.

"Yes, and there're few who can do it—and fewer still who actually *want* to do it."

"I'm guessing that's why you asked for a potion," Belle said.

"Truth seeking is a young person's game, to be sure,"

Jenna agreed. Her gaze returned to mine. "Drop your shields and relax. Once I make the connection, I'll ask you to think back to the day you were first informed about the marriage and then I'll control the direction from there."

I nodded and drank some coffee. It didn't help with the nerves; didn't help ease the churning in my stomach.

Belle removed her fortifications, and then I let my shields fall. I felt naked without them; vulnerable.

"I should warn you," I said, "One of my psi skills is psychometry so—"

"That's fine," Jenna cut in. "Skin on skin contact isn't necessary."

She scooted the chair forward until our knees touched, then placed one hand palm up on my thigh and the other palm down.

"Right," she said. "Think back to the first time you were informed about the marriage."

I took a deep breath and then closed my eyes and reached for the memories I'd long kept shuttered. For an instant nothing happened; I'd built the walls around them very well indeed. But, gradually, the memories stirred. *Walking into my father's study, stopping when I see Clayton. Hating the way he looks at me, like I'm a prime piece of meat, ready for the market. My father, telling me he has some news, asking me if I want a drink, giving me a Coke that's already been opened. It tastes odd, and that oddness sweeps through me. I sit frozen, unable to move, to react, as thin threads of his magic curl around me—through me—pushing away my growing fear, holding me still.*

Clayton has petitioned for your hand in marriage, my father says, and I believe it would be a good match.

No, I want to scream, No!

But I'm held immobile as my father continues, I have given my consent. All we need now is yours.

I open my mouth. Try to say no. What comes out is yes.

Horror sweeps through me. Horror and hurt and a deep sense of denial. Clayton steps forward to kiss me, his lips consuming mine, cold and horrible. I shudder, shake, but cannot deny him. Cannot move. I stare at my father beseechingly, but all I see is anger. Anger and a deep need to get rid of the child he believes should have been the one taken.

Clayton releases me, steps away, and the two men shake hands. The agreement is finalized, the marriage to be formalized within the next week.

I sob but the sound never makes it past my lips... not then, not later. The spell lies within. No one sees it. Only Belle knows that something is wrong...

The images stop, only to jump forward to my wedding day. Or night, as it's late. No white dress, no fanfare, and no bridal flowers. The ceremony is a simple one, performed at home with only my parents present. The spell still controls me. I speak as required and obediently sign all the documents. There's no celebration. No congratulations. Nothing is said. I'm simply handed over to my new husband and led from the room.

Again there's a time jump. *I'm in Clayton's house, in his bedroom, and he's pawing at me, ripping my clothes from me, touching and kissing me, his hands cold and clammy, his breathing hot and heavy. I want to fight, want to run, but I can't. I scream and I scream but there is no sound, no means to call for help.*

But my rage—my fear—finds voice in another. Belle. She breaks into the room, her hands alive with power unlike anything I've ever seen before; it's hers and mine and something else, something that looks like lightning and moonlight combined. He reacts, his magic spitting out almost instinctively. She knocks his attack away and casts a spell that freezes him, casts another that causes his erection to deflate, then pushes him off me. As he crashes from the bed to the floor, she grabs me, pulling me to my feet and helping me dress.

We run. Into a waiting car, into the arms of Belle's mother...

The memories fade, and it's only then I realize that I'm shaking and sobbing. Belle's holding me fiercely, her tears wet against my cheek, her body trembling as badly as mine.

Jenna removed her hands from my thighs, but for several minutes, no one says anything. Eventually, I take a deep breath and gently pull away from Belle. "Well, that was every bit as bad as I thought it'd be."

"I can see why you shored those memories up so tightly." Ruby's voice held no emotion, but her fury rolled across my skin. "I think there's more than enough here to start an investigation. I don't believe we need further testimony from Belle."

"Are you sure?" she said, doubt evident. "I'd rather get it over with now and have a watertight case against these bastards."

"We've already filmed your mother's memories—"

"She did that?" I cut in. "Willingly?"

"Yes," Ruby said. "Her memories corroborate some of what we've just seen."

"And the ones that don't?"

"Involve situations where you were not present."

I hesitated, but couldn't help asking, "How did she react when you told her the marriage was forced?"

"I'm afraid I can't say—audits are confidential."

"What about my father, then? Have you talked to him as yet?"

Jenna bent to pick up the revitalizing potion. "No."

"Why not?"

"Because we must speak to all witness and view all statements before approaching suspects. But I have no doubt it'll happen once the board sees your memories."

"And the chances of any prosecution being successful?" Belle asked.

Ruby hesitated. "If your father continues his attempts to make amends, it'll count in his favor. I'm afraid many will view his behavior—in arranging a marriage, not in coercing via magic and drugs—as nothing out of the ordinary. Such arrangements have been happening for eons, after all."

Meaning he'll likely be handed some fines, then patted on the back and told not to do it again. Belle's mental tone was angry.

You know what? I think I could live with that, as long as Clayton goes down hard.

Personally, I'd like to see both of them face the full weight of the law, but I guess one of them facing it is better than nothing.

It was certainly more than we'd ever hoped for.

Jenna finished her potion, then pushed the chair back and rose. "We'll head back to Canberra in the morning. It'll take a day or so for the full board to arrive, so don't expect any immediate action."

"Will you contact us once the board has made its decision?" I asked.

Ruby placed her teacup on the coffee table and began dismantling her tripod. "You'll receive official notification of our acceptance—or indeed rejection, if that does happen to occur—of your case and then be kept updated on proceedings."

I nodded. "Thank you both for doing this."

The smile that touched Ruby's lips had a slightly anticipatory edge. "Oh, trust me, it's no hardship. Especially when it comes to Clayton Marlowe."

I raised an eyebrow. "You've a personal gripe against him?"

"I wouldn't be here if I did, as that could lead to claims of bias from his lawyers." Ruby swung her backpack over her shoulder. "But there are many on the board who have run afoul of the man in recent years. He's not what he once was."

I frowned. "He didn't seem any less powerful when he was here the other night."

"The weight of magical power alone does not give you standing or respect in Canberra," Jenna commented. "Actions also count."

Which backed up Ashworth's comments that Clayton had done himself no favors over the last few years.

"I don't suppose you'd care to share what he's done?" I said.

Ruby shook her head. "That would be gossiping, and not in our brief. But if you want to know, you could check out *The Canberra Times*. You might find some illuminating news reports."

"I'll do that. Thanks."

She nodded, and the two of them left. I locked the door behind them and then said, *Belle, I'm going to repair the protections and then stay down here and do some prep for tomorrow. Do you want another coffee?*

No. And you should be resting.

I feel the need to cut things. Besides, I'm not going to be able to sleep just yet. The memories I'd long denied were too damn close to the surface right now.

You want me down there to help with the spells?

No, I'll be fine.

Are you sure?

Yes.

I walked into the reading room, pushed the table and carpet aside, and then sat cross-legged on the floor. It took a while to repair what my father and Clayton had destroyed but it didn't leave me as physically drained as it had previously. Perhaps my spelling muscles were getting stronger.

With that done, I headed into the kitchen. Once I'd scrolled through my music to find a suitably rocky playlist, I spent the next couple of hours preparing tomorrow's food and singing loudly. It was close to midnight by the time I went to bed, and to say I crashed would be an understatement.

But that didn't stop the dreams.

This time, they weren't filled with bloodshed.

Instead, they were warning of smoke and fire.

The café had been open for a good hour the next morning by the time Aiden and Monty arrived to claim their usual corner table. Monty moved like an old man, and his facial bruising had developed into a rich kaleidoscope of color, which made the white tape across the cut on his forehead stand out rather starkly.

Aiden's gaze swept me as I approached. "How are you feeling this morning?"

"Battered and bruised, but at least I look far better than Monty."

"Roadkill looks better than Monty right now," Aiden commented, amused.

"Oh, ha ha." Monty gingerly leaned back in his chair. "I got a call from Ruby this morning—she said they were leaving. I take it they did their session with you last night?"

"Yes. Do you both want your usual breakfast?"

"Given the swift change of subject," Monty said, "I'm gathering the process was unpleasant?"

"I had to drag up memories I've spent close to thirteen years suppressing—what do you think?"

"I think I would have spent the rest of the evening getting drunk." He touched my hand lightly. "I'm sorry you had to go through all that, but if it helps stop Clayton—"

"We'll know in a few days what they decide. In the meantime, food—yes or no?"

"When have I ever said no to food? The usual, please."

I snorted and glanced at Aiden. "You too?"

"Just a coffee for me. I ate up in the compound."

I nodded and went into the kitchen to place their orders, then leaned against the counter while Belle made their drinks.

"Are you coming over to the table for a chat?" I asked. "It's about time you took a break and got off your foot, isn't it?"

"The foot's fine, and I don't want to give Monty any ideas." She paused. "Any more ideas, that is."

I grinned but held back my comment as she raised a warning finger. Once their coffees and my tea were made, I picked up the tray and returned to the table. I also raised the privacy spell around the table to ensure those nearby couldn't hear what we were saying.

"How did your brother's party go last night?" I asked as I sat down beside Aiden.

He smiled and slid one hand over my thigh, a gentle caress that had desire curling through me. "As well as any party with a bunch of rowdy fourteen-year-olds could. I'd rather have been here sleeping on the sofa, to be honest."

"That's the sort of comment grumpy old men make," Monty said, amused.

I smiled and poured my tea out. "That's because he is. He'll be thirty this year, remember."

"Positively ancient," Monty agreed.

"Says the two people who are, what—a whole year?—behind me." His voice was dry.

"Almost a year and a half in my case," Monty said. "I was always the baby of our group at school. I think that's why Belle has never taken me seriously—she's got something against younger men."

I smiled. "Aside from the fact you're my *cousin*—"

"Which doesn't mean squat, because Belle isn't related to either of us."

"We grew up with you. It's almost the same thing."

"Hardly. And growing up together should count for rather than against me. She knows exactly what she's getting—"

He stopped as a balled-up piece of paper hit the back of his head and bounced away. He glanced down and then around and blew Belle a kiss. She rolled her eyes and shook her head, her expression one of tolerant amusement.

I smiled but refrained from saying anything. Not that it really mattered, given Belle was well aware of my thoughts —and gave me a narrow-eyed warning glare to prove it.

I took a sip of my tea. "So, the Manananggal—Monty and I came up with a couple of ideas on how we might catch this thing."

"I'm guessing the first suggestion is to stake out wedding venues for the next couple of days," Aiden said.

"Good guess," Monty said.

Aiden gave him a deadpan look. "I do *do* this whole investigating thing for a living."

Monty chuckled and thanked Penny as she appeared with his breakfast. "How many weddings are we talking about?"

"Only three—one tonight, two tomorrow."

"I think she's more likely to attack tonight," I said. "That quake would have taken a lot of energy—she'd have to replenish her reserves sooner rather than later."

"Unless she did so last night," Monty said. "She may prefer her victims newly married, but that doesn't mean she can't feed on anyone else. And the reservation does have a lot of remote properties."

"There's been no reports of missing or murdered persons as yet," Aiden said.

"If she went remote, would there be?" Monty asked.

"There's nowhere truly remote in a werewolf reservation," Aiden said. "The scent of blood and death can carry quite a way."

"Well, if she didn't feed last night, she'll have to tonight." I reached across the table and stole a bit of bacon from Monty's plate. He chased my fingers with his fork, his expression one of mock outrage. "How are we going to trap her if we can't use magic?"

Aiden frowned. "Why can't you use magic?"

"We suspect that's how she knew we were tracking her —she felt Liz's spell entwining around her blood."

"Which leaves attending the weddings to keep an eye on things as our only real option—especially given the

Manananggal has to be tracking her victims via some sort of spell—"

"Why?" Aiden cut in. "The first victim was attacked when he was alone at the reception."

"Which could have been just an unfortunate matter of timing on his part," Monty said. "He'd been going to check something in the car, remember. Maybe our ghoul was in the process of casting her tracker spell when he made his appearance."

Aiden frowned. "Why would she be placing spells on vehicles when she can separate and fly?"

"I'm guessing because she has to keep her lower body safe when she's separated—as evidenced by that damn clearing where Liz found the blood."

"If that's the case," Aiden said. "Then we simply have to watch the cars and grab her before she places the spell."

"It might be better to let her place the spell," I said. "Monty and I can then exchange places with the intended victims and bring this bitch down where there's less possibility of innocent bystanders getting hurt."

"Good idea except for one thing—she's magic capable," Monty said. "It's possible she'll sense our presence."

"How close would she have to get to do that?" Aiden asked.

Monty shrugged. "She's obviously a strong witch given what she did on that ridge; it's totally possible she could sense our presence from quite some distance."

"Not if we both shield our magic, surely?" I said.

"There are some witches who can sense a shield almost as easily as they can magic—and *this* witch isn't exactly regular flesh and blood."

"Then perhaps it would be better if Liz and I act as bait,

and you and my team wait for the Manananggal to appear from a safe distance," Aiden said. "That should split up the power output and lessen the prospect of her sensing you too early."

"It could work." A devilish glint entered Monty's eyes. "But you two will need to keep alert. No role playing while on duty, please."

"We rarely even *kiss* when he's on duty," I said, voice dry. "So that's not going to be a problem."

"And for good reason." Aiden's expression hadn't changed, but there was a subtle edge in his voice as he added, "People don't get hurt that way."

My eyebrows rose. "That very much sounds like the voice of experience speaking."

"Not mine, but a friend's." He gently squeezed my thigh. "I vowed to never get caught in the same situation. I'm doing my best to keep that vow—though it's been a whole lot more difficult of late."

'Difficult' is such a romantic word to use, Belle commented, mental tone wry. *And why hasn't he mentioned this before now?*

Because the friend is probably a werewolf, which means it slips into the 'can't share with the human' basket. But hey, at least he did admit it had been more difficult lately. That's something, right?

As far as morsels go, it's pretty poor.

Given how reticent the damn man is about verbalizing his feelings, I'll take any morsel I can get. Out loud, I added, "What time does the wedding start?"

"Ceremony is at four, reception at seven."

"She's unlikely to trouble the ceremony," Monty said. "Sunlight kills her, remember?"

"We don't know that for sure," I said. "But it's likely

she'll use a proxy of some kind. She knows we're onto her now, so she'll be extra careful."

Monty frowned. "Everything I've discovered about Manananggals suggest they're loners by nature—"

"Given the level of supernatural nasties we've been attracting of late," Aiden cut in, "I don't think we can rely on this thing following the general script. To be on the safe side, I'll get Jaz and Mac to tail the bride and groom from their accommodation to the church. I also think you should be there, Monty—you *are* the reservation witch, after all."

"I like the way you remember that fact only when it suits you." Monty's voice was dry. "Do we know where they're staying the night?"

"In one of the cottages in the venue's grounds—it's a winery."

"Are there guests in the other cottages?"

"The bride's parents, who are up from Melbourne, and some interstate guests."

I frowned. "So how is our ghoul going to find her victims? Putting a tracker on the car is one thing, but that's not going to help her once she's at the venue. It's not like being newly married has a specific scent."

"Actually," Aiden said, "it does. It's generally a heady mix of sexual pheromones, thick desire, love, and excitement."

"Is that why werewolf weddings tend to be held within compounds?" Monty said. "The scent gets everyone high and shenanigans ensue?"

"Let's just say that there's often more than one relation-ship cemented at a wedding." Aiden raised his coffee, but it failed to hide the amusement flirting with his lips. "But back to the topic—I'll arrange for the guests in the other cabins to be evacuated—"

"Have emergency accommodation at the ready, by all means," Monty cut in, "but don't make the final decision until we know what kind of spell she—or her proxy—puts on the vehicle."

I frowned. "How is that going to help?"

"Because there're spells that can be passed from an object to a person on touch," Monty said. "Although if that's what she's using, we'll have to make sure one of you snares it rather than the couple."

"Which means Liz and I will also have to be at the ceremony." Aiden glanced at me. "I'll pick you up around three forty-five."

Obviously, the church was a local one. I nodded and quickly finished the rest of my tea. "I'd better get back to work."

Aiden squeezed my leg and then released me. I rose, picked up my mug and the teapot, then dumped both into the kitchen before moving around the counter to help Belle with the cake and coffee orders.

The rest of the day passed reasonably quickly. I sent Belle upstairs to rest her ankle once the lunch influx had eased and spent the rest of the afternoon doing some food prep. Penny and Celia handled the cleanup while I dashed upstairs to change clothes. We might do nothing more than sit in the truck, but on the off chance that we did have to get out, I didn't want to look out of place. By the same token, I didn't want to be running after the Manananggal in a dress and high heels.

"Go with the black pants." Belle crossed her arms and leaned against the doorframe. "Team it with that green shirt, and you're good to go."

"Thanks." I glanced at her. "What are your plans for the evening?"

"I might go through the books we have here and see if Gran had any spells that'll protect the café from Clayton. I wouldn't put it past the bastard to destroy this place before he tries the same on us."

The memory of fiery dreams rose, and alarm prickled across my skin. "It might be also worth looking into stronger flame-retardant spells."

"I'm gathering that's *not* a random comment."

I grimaced. "No, but I couldn't actually *see* what was burning."

"Your dreams are damned annoying sometimes."

"And yet they're still nowhere near as bad as your spirit guides." I paused. "I don't suppose they've had anything to say about the Manananggal, have they? Or even Clayton?"

"Other than saying it's best to avoid them both? No."

I snorted softly and shoved my feet into my shoes. "I'd better go wait for Aiden."

Belle pushed away from the door. "Be careful out there tonight. There's an ill wind blowing, and that usually means trouble is about to hit."

"I don't think there's any doubt about *that*." But I also didn't think it would come from the Manananggal. Not tonight, anyway.

Of course, I'd been wrong before, which was why I detoured into the reading room to pick up the backpack before heading out to meet Aiden.

He pulled up in front of the café and then leaned across to open the passenger door. "You look rather nice this afternoon."

"Meaning I normally don't?" I climbed in and buckled up.

"Maybe I should have said extra nice."

"I figured it wouldn't hurt if, for some reason, we had to

go mingle with guests." I glanced at him as he pulled out into the traffic. He'd changed out of his ranger gear and was wearing black pants and a dark blue shirt that emphasized the color of his eyes. "Looks like I wasn't alone in thinking that. The shoulder holster does spoil the look, however."

"The jacket will cover it. How close do you need to be to feel the spell being placed?"

"Monty will probably feel the magic easier than me, but if she's using a proxy of some sort we may not sense anything. It'll depend entirely on what sort of spell she's using."

"And the proxy? Do we need to do anything about him or her?"

"If we stop them—or attempt to de-spell them—it might well warn the Manananggal. We're better off grabbing a photo of them for identification purposes, so we can find them again once we've caught our ghoul."

He swung right into Hargraves Street. "Do you think the proxy will be in any danger?"

"I have no idea. I guess if things go wrong tonight and the Manananggal escapes, it's totally possible the proxy will become dinner."

"I'll get Tala to ID the photo ASAP; if things do go wrong, we can hightail it over to the proxy's location and protect him or her."

He made another turn and then slowed down. A large, white-painted church building dominated the grounds of the school to our right. He pulled up in front of the drive leading into the church grounds.

"Is this the only entrance?" I asked.

"No—there's another the bridal car will use. They'll drop the bride and bridesmaids at the church steps, then park in the area on the other side of that fence."

"That fence is damn inconvenient. It's too tall to see over."

"Monty will be our eyes—he's standing over near the water tanks and has a good view of the entire parking area."

I raised an eyebrow. "And you know this how?"

"I was speaking to him just before I picked you up."

"Huh." I studied the beautiful old church for a moment. "Were you and Mia planning to get married in a church?"

I could feel his gaze on me, but I resisted the unspoken demand to turn and look at him.

"We split before we got around to details like that. Why?"

I shrugged. "Just curious."

"For what it's worth, I'm more a civil ceremony on home grounds type guy, but let's be honest, a wedding day is never about what the groom wants."

I laughed and glanced at him. "I'm sure Mia will appreciate that sentiment when she finally gets back here."

The words were out before I could think about them, and I silently cursed as he went utterly still.

"What makes you think she's coming back?" His voice was flat; his expression shut down. "Or that I'd even want her to?"

"You heard what Katie said when she was talking to your mother. We both know—even if you don't want to face it—that she was referring to Mia."

"Yes, but that doesn't answer the second—"

"Oh, I think your reaction says everything that needs to be said. Don't get me wrong, Aiden. I'm hoping like hell she doesn't arrive anytime soon. But I also know you're in an emotional holding pattern and have been since she left. That won't change until she *does* come back."

"If that were true, I wouldn't be—"

He cut the rest of that sentence off, leaving me wondering just what he was about to admit. I had imagination enough to believe he'd come close to admitting his feelings for me. And yet the fact that he'd cut the declaration off meant that no matter what his heart might be saying, his mind had other plans.

And they currently *didn't* include a crimson-haired witch. Not in the forever together, white picket fence and babies kind of way, anyway.

The truck's com system buzzed, breaking the brief but tense silence. Aiden pressed a button on the console and then said, "Jaz? Is there a problem?"

"No—just giving you the heads-up; the bridal car is about to pull into the church's driveway. Do you want us to remain here or shall we move across to the reception venue?"

"Head on over to the venue and keep alert."

"Will do, boss."

Once she'd signed off, he contacted Monty and updated him. Thankfully, we didn't have to wait that long for trouble to stir.

The wedding cars had barely driven past our driveway to park in the allocated area when my instincts prickled. I frowned and glanced around, but there was no one in immediate sight, either in the church's grounds or on the street ahead. I flipped down the sun visor and looked behind me.

An oddly dressed man walked toward us. While he was wearing black dress pants, he'd teamed it with an orange cardigan and a green cravat. He was also wearing mismatched shoes—one was black, one was brown. He moved in an almost robotic way, reminding me somewhat of a marionette. And while I couldn't immediately see the strings of magic, they were obviously there. The distress in his face, the panic in his eyes, all spoke of a man who wasn't in control.

"Our proxy is approaching," I said softly.

Aiden twisted around. "The oddly dressed man?"

"Yes. I can't see a spell, but he's definitely under one."

Aiden picked up his phone from the center console. "Warn Monty. I'll send some pics to Tala and get her to ID him."

I sent Monty a text and continued to watch the stranger. Though he didn't turn his head or look at us when he neared our car, his expression twisted and his mouth moved, as if he was desperately trying to say something. But the creature that held his leash kept him moving forward.

My gaze slipped down to his hands, and after a second, I spotted a telltale shimmer. The spell had been concealed —that's why I hadn't seen it earlier. I narrowed my gaze and tried to push past the blockage, to no avail. But that wasn't really a surprise; the magic of someone capable of bringing down half a mountain was never going to be easy to unpick —especially by someone as untutored as me.

The colorful stranger disappeared behind the fence line. Aiden's phone beeped, and he glanced down. "Our suspect has stopped a few meters away from the cars and is studying the area."

"The Mananangal is suspicious."

"Which isn't surprising now that she knows she's facing at least one witch. I'm actually surprised she's remained in the reservation."

"As you've already noted, when has a supernatural nasty ever done the sensible thing here?"

"I keep hoping that one of them eventually will." His phone beeped again. "Okay, suspect is now making his way toward the bridal car. Monty's unable to see what sort of spell is involved from where he's standing."

At least it wasn't just me. I studied the fence, wishing for X-ray vision or at least a lower fence.

Aiden's phone beeped again. "The spell has been placed. The suspect is heading our way again."

He'd barely finished saying that when our oddly dressed gentleman appeared in the driveway, did an abrupt turn, and walked back up the hill. I twisted around in the seat to watch him, instincts twitching. "I might follow him."

"I don't think it'd be wise to go alone—not after what happened at the ridge."

"Monty has to check out the spell, and you have to touch the thing so it transfers to your hand rather than the groom's. I'm all that's left."

"And you're sure he needs to be followed?"

"My instincts are."

He blew out a frustrated breath, then twisted around and grabbed a green windbreaker and a beanie from the back seat. "Take these. I'll track you down once we've dealt with the spell."

I grabbed the coat, beanie, and my backpack, then scrambled out of the truck. Our oddly dressed gentleman had already disappeared into what looked to be a pedestrian laneway between two houses. I chased after him, damn grateful for flat shoes rather than heels.

I swung into the lane, saw him at the far end, and immediately slowed. I had no idea how the Manananggal was controlling him or whether she had access to his senses, but the last thing I wanted was for him to look around and spot me. He'd seen me sitting in the truck outside the church, and while he might not think much about that, the

Manananggal's suspicions would rise if she noticed I was now tailing him.

He turned right and disappeared again. I broke into a run to close the distance, keeping to the grass that lined the edge of the old stone path so that my footsteps didn't echo. I paused at the end and peered out from behind the safety of a scrubby-looking bush. My quarry was striding down the middle of the road, seeming oblivious of the footpath that ran along the left of the street.

I sent Aiden a quick text and then pulled on his coat, tucked my hair up into the beanie, and stepped out into the street. The wind swirled around me, filled with the scent of rain and promising yet another cold evening. But it also held a thick thread of fear and uncertainty.

The stranger didn't want to go wherever the Manananggal was forcing him to go.

The footpath gave way to rough stone and a steep hill. The shadows closed in, as did the silence. The houses on either side of the road were dark, seemingly empty of life.

I pulled out my phone again. Aiden might be able to follow my scent, but given the wind, I wasn't about to take a chance. I really didn't like the feel of this situation.

We continued on for another ten minutes, and I suddenly realized we were heading for Kalimna Park—the forest where I'd found the teenage victim of a vampire. The man ahead might be under the spell of a lesser-known type of vampire, but I seriously hoped the outcome of this hunt would be very different to that other.

The road ended in a T-intersection. The stranger hesitated, staring at the forest on the other side of the road for several minutes, and then turned right, heading up the hill on a no through road.

I paused at the corner, waiting until he'd reached the

top before crossing over to the park side of the road, then continuing on. Dusk was closing in, but at least the odd silence had given way to the sounds of a normal evening—people talking, TVs blaring, kids screaming, and, in the forest itself, small rodents skittering away from my approach.

I reached the top of the hill. My quarry was nowhere in sight.

I swore and quickly looked around; how could anyone so brightly dressed disappear so quickly? Had he gone into the house? Or into the forest?

I eyed the latter uneasily. The last thing I wanted to do was traipse through the scrub in growing darkness. Not only was it possible that the Manananggal was now mobile, but it might very well be a damn trap.

I glanced back to the house. It was a rectangular-shaped, flat-roofed brick building that had been painted white. A large carport was attached to one side, with a small Honda parked underneath. There were no lights on in the house and no indication—

A scream cut across the rest of that thought.

A scream that was high-pitched and filled with agony.

The scream of someone staring into the eyes of death.

CHAPTER TEN

I t hadn't come from the house.

It had come from the goddamn forest.

I held still against the instinctive urge to rush headlong into the forest after the colorful stranger.

Maybe once, I might have done exactly that, but I'd come too close to death far too many times now to do anything without taking at least *some* additional precautions.

I sent Aiden and Monty a quick text and then pulled a packet of salt from my backpack. Once I'd raised a containment spell around my fingers—and crossed all things that it was strong enough to at least temporarily contain the Manananggal—I went in.

The screams cut off as abruptly as they'd started, but there was no sense of death, only a thick wave of satisfaction.

Trepidation stirred across my skin, and my steps slowed. This *was* a trap, and while I had no idea what the Manananggal intended, I wasn't about to run headfirst into it.

The spell threads rolling across my fingertips provided just enough light for me to pick my way through the trees. Leaves crunched under each step, and the sound seemed extraordinarily loud in the expectant hush that once again held the forest.

I swallowed heavily, though it did nothing to ease the dryness in my throat, and kept following the vague wisps of terror that now stained the wind.

The sense of expectation grew stronger. I slowed even further, my gaze searching the growing darkness, looking for the creature that was out there somewhere.

Leaves crunched behind me. My heart leapt and I raised my hand as I swung around, the spell buzzing angrily around my fingertips.

It wasn't the Manananggal. It was Aiden and Monty.

I took a deep, very relieved breath and lowered my hand.

Aiden's gaze scanned me, and some of the tension in his body slipped away. "I smelled blood and thought it was yours. Very happy to see it's not."

"How far away is the scent?"

"About a hundred meters."

"The Manananggal's also close," Monty said. "Her magic itches at my skin."

"Any idea just what that magic might be doing?" I turned and kept following the twin scents of terror and anticipation, my pace quicker than before. Caution might still be needed, but at least I didn't have to deal with this thing alone.

"No," Monty said. "But at least the thickness of the canopy prevents her from dive bombing us."

"I think the chances of her dive bombing us are far less likely than her casting another—"

I cut off the rest as another scream rent the air. The hairs at the nape of my neck rose in response—not so much at the sheer force of agony and suffering evident within that scream, but because it was undoubtedly the Manananggal's way of directing our action.

She didn't want me walking through the trees. She wanted me rushing headlong through them.

Me. Not Monty, not Aiden. Me.

The insight had me stopping abruptly.

"Problem?" Aiden said, voice soft but edged.

"You could say that." I scanned the darkness, looking for the creature even though I was well aware I wouldn't see her until she wanted to be seen. "The Manananggal knows I'm here. It's waiting for me."

"How?" Aiden said, at the same time that Monty said, "Her blood."

I nodded. "Using her blood to track her has somehow allowed her to gather far too much information about me. We'll need to split up."

"While her awareness of you is unfortunate," Monty said, "I don't think that's a very good idea."

"We have no other choice. She's torturing that poor guy in an effort to make me rush headlong into whatever trap she has waiting ahead. She's got my measure—"

"She might have the measure of your regular magic," Monty cut in, "but not the wild."

"I can't use the wild magic willy-nilly, and I certainly can't use it to kill."

Another scream. The Manananggal was desperate to keep me moving. Fear stirred, but I thrust it down. The wild magic had already proven that it could protect me against her magic.

"Our best chance of getting this bitch is to attack from

two fronts," I continued. "I'll keep her attention on me while you two sneak around behind her."

Aiden hesitated and then touched my arm and moved past me. Monty murmured a quick "be careful," then followed Aiden into the scrub.

I took a deep breath that did nothing to ease the sick tension within, then did a sharp left and crashed through the scrub. The noise echoed, and the sense of anticipation sharpened.

No more screams rent the air, but the pulse of death was sharper—closer. Time was almost up for the colorful stranger; even if we could wrest him from the ghoul's grip, life was not now guaranteed...

I thrust the thought away. While there was life, there was always hope.

Remember that, an inner voice said, *when Clayton crashes through your world...*

My fingers clenched involuntarily, making the spell fizz brightly. I took another deep breath and pushed past the terror that particular premonition raised. One danger at a time; one monster at a time.

The smell of blood sharpened abruptly. I paused and scanned the scrub ahead of me. There was nothing to indicate a trap about to be sprung; no spell threads, no pulse of magic, and absolutely no sign that a monster was close.

But she was.

And so was the stranger. It wasn't just the smell of blood that was strong now. The stench of his agony filled my nostrils and burned across my senses. He lay in the clearing just beyond the thick line of bushes ahead of me.

The Manananggal, however, was in the sky. I might not be able to see her, but I could sense her. Could sense her thickening desire to rip my heart from my body and taste the power in my blood.

I took another of those useless deep breaths and hoped like hell that Monty and Aiden had managed to get around the back of her. We needed to end this—end her—tonight.

I pushed through the bushes and then stopped on the edge of the clearing, the spell fizzing brightly around my fingertips. The stranger was missing the brown shoe, and his bare foot was torn and bloody. His orange cardigan had been shredded, as had the shirt underneath. His exposed torso was bloody and torn, his innards oozing out across his stomach. The Manananggal might be capable of finesse, but she'd not used it here.

Because of me. Because she wanted to feed on me. On my heart. On my blood.

My gaze jumped skyward. I couldn't see her, but that was unsurprising given she was magic capable. There were plenty of invisibility spells out there; you just had to have the power to perform them. This bitch obviously did.

To draw her out, I'd have to step away from the trees and into the target zone.

I scanned the trees lining the other side of the clearing. Though I couldn't see Aiden or Monty, a familiar scent had my nose twitching. They were close. And waiting.

My gaze fell back to the gutted stranger. Saw the rapid rise and fall of his chest. *While there was life, there was hope...* but only if we hurried.

I briefly closed my eyes and then, before courage fled, strode out into the clearing.

I'd barely taken five steps when the spell rose around me, a powerful wave of deadly intent. I dove away from the tendrils of energy that reached for me, seeking to bind, to hold. To *cage*.

I hit the ground hard enough to force a grunt of pain, then became aware of the rush of wind. Looked up, and saw a nightmare.

One that trailed its intestines behind it like a tail and whose bat-like wings ended in claws thicker than my wrist.

I swore and flung the containment spell at her. She screamed and veered sharply away. I changed the direction of the spell, but she ducked and weaved, all the while continuing her dive. She was going to get me before my spell stopped her.

I got up and ran for the trees. Saw, out of the corner of my eye, a black wing and the gleam of claw. I swore and dodged left; heard the rip of material, felt the trickle of warmth down my arm.

I twisted around and ran back across the clearing. Felt the surge of Monty's magic; saw the shimmer in the air as his spell arrowed directly at me. Waited until the very last moment and then dropped low and twisted around as the spell flew over my head.

The Manananggal spotted it and veered upward sharply. The spell followed her trajectory, quickly latching on to a bloody bit of trailing intestines. As the spell unwrapped and the threads of the containment portion crawled toward her torso, she screamed in fury and then, with one sharp claw, sliced the spell—and the section of intestine it had latched on to—away. As the bloody bits tumbled toward the ground, she did an abrupt turn, tucked in her wings, and dove.

Straight at me.

There was no time to spell. No time to run. She was so damn close I could see the gleam of victory in her blood-colored eyes.

The bitch thought she had me.

The bitch was wrong.

I flung a hand upward, and bolts of sheer energy leapt from my fingertips and arrowed toward her. Surprise flicked across her expression; she rolled to one side, her wings pumping furiously as she tried to outrun my lightning. I spread my fingers wide, breaking the bolt into five arrows of light. Every single one hit her; the first one burned into her torso while the other four melted holes in the membrane of her wings. Her flight became erratic, but she somehow continued to gain height despite the tattered state of her wings.

Five gunshots rang out in quick succession. The Manananggal's body twitched and bled, but her frantic flight wasn't stopped. Wasn't even slowed.

Another surge of magic, and then Monty's spell was again chasing her. This time, it was nothing more than a simple tracker, which was perhaps why the Manananggal didn't appear to notice when it hit the severed edge of her torso. She just kept flying, blood dripping from her body like black rain.

I pushed up and ran over to the stranger. He was still breathing, but how long he would remain that way when he'd been gutted I couldn't say. Death might be hovering, but she hadn't yet stepped close to claim his soul.

There was still hope.

I swung my backpack around, then glanced up as Aiden and Monty entered the clearing. "We need an—"

"Already called. Tala's going to meet and lead them in." Aiden's gaze fell on the stranger's stomach, and his expression darkened. "They may not get here in time, though."

"We can't all stay here and wait for them," Monty said. "We need to go after that bitch and stop her."

"You two go." I pulled the small medical kit and a bottle

of holy water from my pack. "I'll wait here for Tala and the medics."

"Perfect plan," Monty said. "Aiden?"

Aiden's gaze held mine for a heartbeat; deep in the depth of his bright eyes, I could see the battle between heart and duty.

"Go," I said softly. "I'll be fine."

A smile twitched his lips, then he nodded and said, "This way."

As the two of them ran from the clearing, I carefully removed the shredded remains of the stranger's clothes from the edges of the wound and his exposed intestines, then undid the small bottle of holy water and poured it over the sterile dressings from the medical kit. I didn't bother trying to push everything back into his body; I'd read enough books to know that generally wasn't a good idea. Instead, I simply covered the wound and protrusions to keep them sterile. There was nothing else I could do for him; nothing except free him from whatever spell might still remain. If death *was* his destiny, the last thing he deserved was for his soul's journey to be hampered in some way by the Manananggal's magic.

The only trouble was, the binding spell she'd placed on him wasn't visible even though the dark caress of its energy made my skin crawl. Embedding spells in this manner wasn't something I was familiar with, and I had no idea if dismantling it would be dangerous. Which meant I'd better call Belle in.

I sat cross-legged on the ground near his head and reached for her. *You busy?*

If you consider eating a great big bit of chocolate cake busy, then yes. You need help?

I'm about to break whatever magic lies on the victim of

the Mananangal. I just need you to keep an eye on proceedings.

Her surprise ran through me. *Said victim is still alive?*

Long story, but yes, because she used him to lure me into a trap.

Confusion replaced the surprise. *How?*

I somehow created a connection between us when I used her blood as a tracker. She must have guessed we'd be staking out local weddings and used the stranger as bait.

Getting rid of the local witch is the sensible thing to do. You okay?

Yes, but the lure isn't. The ambos may not get here in time, and I don't want to leave the stain of her magic on him.

Good idea. Even if it doesn't hamper his journey, it might somehow alter the trajectory of his rebirth.

That's what I thought. You comfortable?

Yeah, go for it.

I took a deep breath to center my energy, then carefully reached out with my 'other' senses. What I couldn't physically see instantly became visible. The spell was a fist-sized mass that sat just above the long cut that had gutted him. Tendrils not only ran up to his brain but also around his heart; the latter explained his pasty skin and blue lips. For whatever reason, she'd been controlling his heart rate.

Perhaps she didn't want him going into cardiac arrest and damaging his heart before she'd had a chance to dine on it. Belle's mental tone was grim. *The spell's construction is somewhat unusual, isn't it?*

She knows she's dealing with another witch, so I suspect she's taken steps to prevent interference.

A final snare?

More than likely. I scooted around to the side of his body and studied the spell from a different angle. And

caught, through a slender gap between two of the concealment spell's threads and a still gaping bit of wound, something that looked a whole lot like metal. Darkish-colored
metal. I shifted again and leaned closer. It was definitely
metallic...

A horrible suspicion stirred. Hoping like hell that I was
wrong, I peeled back the nearest section of dressings and
used them to carefully open the wound up. It revealed
exactly what I'd feared. The final trap wasn't just magical; it
was also physical.

Something had been shoved into the internal cavity
created when she'd gutted him. Something I rather
suspected might be a grenade, given the little I could see of
its shape.

*Which means the spell has probably been designed to
remove the pin the minute anyone tries to dismantle it,* Belle
commented. *How the hell are we going to counter that?*

I don't think we *can.* I simply didn't know enough about
this sort of magic. *I think our best bet would be to remove
both the spell and the grenade from his body.*

What if it's primed to go off if it's moved?

That's more than possible. I put the dressing back over
the wound, even though there was probably little point to
worrying about infection now. Not when a grenade had
been unceremoniously shoved into his gut. *I think I'll
call—*

I stopped, my heart leaping at the sound of a twig snap-
ping. A second later, Tala stepped into the clearing. She
quickly scanned the area, then looked at me. "The area's
safe to enter?"

"For now. Where are the ambos?"

"Waiting for the all clear. Define 'for now.'"

"There's a spell-wrapped grenade shoved into his stomach; I can't dismantle it, and I'm not sure if it's safe to remove it."

She stared at me for a second. "Seriously?"

"Very."

"Why the hell are you still sitting next to him, then?"

"Because it's the only way I'll feel the spell—" I stopped as the stranger's breathing changed—became a desperate rattle. "Shit, he's going. Get the ambos in here."

"I can't if we've an active threat—"

"He's going to die—"

"Better one than four." Tala's voice was grim. "It's procedure, Liz. Until the device is deactivated, I have to cordon off the area—"

"Damn it, Tala—"

I stopped again. The rattle in the stranger's breathing went silent. Several seconds later, his soul rose.

There's no stain of her presence or magic attached, Belle said softly.

I closed my eyes against the sting of tears. While I knew his death wasn't my fault, guilt nevertheless swirled. If I'd only known more...

You wouldn't have been able to save him, Belle said. *If his soul moves on rather than linger, it was his time.*

Knowing that doesn't ease the guilt, Belle. Out loud, I said, "It doesn't matter. He's dead."

"That doesn't alter the existing problem—the explosive device in his stomach. Where are Aiden and Monty?"

"Going after the ghoul. I think we need to call Ashworth in—given how long he's worked for the RWA, he's more than likely dealt with something like this."

Tala immediately pulled her phone out of her pocket and made the call. "He'll be here in twenty—will you be okay while I go meet him?"

I smiled faintly. "A dead man holds no fears for me."

"Maybe, but this dead man is primed to explode."

She offered no further objections, however, just turned and disappeared back into the forest. I heard a brief conversation a few minutes later—she was obviously updating the ambulance crew—then silence fell. I had no idea if the crew remained; the stranger's body would have to be taken to the morgue once it was rendered safe, but it seemed impractical for them to be waiting around here when they could be tending to other emergencies.

I returned my gaze to the stranger and the magic that still resided within him... and noticed it had changed. The spell's tendrils no longer restricted his heart, and the ones that had bound his mind were also in retreat. The main mass had also altered; it was now longer—thinner—than it had been only minutes ago.

Then it hit me—she would have felt the stranger's death, given she'd still been connected to his mind when he'd died.

She also might have been aware that I was here given our tenuous connection. If the magic was altering rather than simply deactivating, there could only be one reason.

She was pulling the pin.

I thrust to my feet, grabbed the backpack, and ran like hell for the trees.

I had no idea how long it took for a grenade to explode after the pin was pulled, but it surely couldn't be more than four or five seconds. A silent countdown began in my head; I hit the tree line at three.

The grenade went off at four.

CHAPTER ELEVEN

The blast wave hit and briefly sent me flying. Bits of metal tore through the leaves and branches of the shrubs above, sending a rain of green all around me. I hit the ground with a grunt of pain and tumbled into some sort of depression—the hollow caused by an uprooted gum tree, I realized, spotting the huge root ball looming above me. I curled close to the edge of the hollow, trying to present as small a target as possible, waiting for the destruction to end. Waiting for bits of flesh and body parts to stop splashing wetly onto the ground only meters away.

Heightened senses, I thought grimly, weren't always a bonus.

"Lizzie?" came a shout. "You okay?"

Tala, not Aiden.

"Here." I uncurled and sat up. I hadn't entirely missed the destruction—blood stained my left calf, and there was wetness seeping into my shoe. I carefully rolled up my jeans and had a look—the wound was long, but only one small section of it was deep. Whatever had caused the cut had also sliced into my boot; while my foot didn't feel injured or cut in any way, I left the boot right where it was. Just because it didn't feel injured didn't mean it wasn't—the boot might be the only thing holding my foot together.

I glanced up as Tala appeared. "Those medics still nearby?"

"On the way back." She squatted at the edge of the depression, her nostrils flaring as her gaze scanned me. "Any other wounds?"

"Not that I'm aware of."

"Good." Her gaze moved to the right, and her expression became grim. "What happened?"

"At a guess, she felt him die. Either that, or the spell was primed to react once he was dead." I hesitated but felt obliged to add, "If we had taken him to the ambulance, the blast would have killed us all. It was the right call."

A faint smile touched her lips. "Of course it was—but thank you. Is it safe to go out there?"

"As safe as it ever can be with a ghoul hellbent on killing loose on the reservation."

"So there's no lingering magic I have to worry about?"

"Not that I can sense, but if you give me a hand—"

"You're not going anywhere except to hospital."

"But—"

"I trust your instincts," she said, and then added somewhat wryly, "And *that* is a statement I never thought I'd be uttering."

It certainly wasn't one I'd ever expected to hear, especially given her initial skepticism when it came to my abilities.

She pushed to her feet and then looked around. "Jen, she's over here."

Jen was one of the ambulance crew and in no time at all

had me treated, bundled onto a stretcher, and whisked away to the hospital for a full checkup.

Thankfully, the cut on my leg only required a couple of stitches and my foot was, as I'd surmised, uncut. But I was certainly gathering a good selection of bruises.

I caught a cab home, and Belle met me at the door, ushering me in before handing me the biggest revitalization tonic I'd ever seen. It was probably also one of the foulest smelling.

"That's just your heightened sense of smell kicking in," she said. "It's no worse than usual, I assure you."

I wasn't so certain of that given the gleam in her eyes, but nevertheless shut my eyes and gulped the thing down. It tasted as bad as it smelled.

I shuddered and thrust the empty glass at her. "You lie."

She chuckled softly. "One of these days you'll stop believing me when I say things like that, and I'll have to start making them palatable."

I snorted softly. In truth, adding sweeteners to most potions actually diluted their potency. It was possible to use Manuka honey—which was well known for its restorative properties—but Belle was old-school like her mom when it came to potions. The thicker and fouler, the better they worked.

I hobbled toward the stairs and slowly started up; despite my caution, my calf ached in protest. The painkillers they'd given me were beginning to wear off.

"Have you heard anything from Aiden or Monty?" Belle stayed behind me, obviously intent on catching me should I fall—although given her sprained ankle, I wasn't sure how she'd manage that without sending us both tumbling. "Do you know if they caught the Manananggal?"

"No, and I'm thinking that's not a good thing."

"Unless they've got her cornered and are waiting for daylight. Given her magical strength, that would be the prudent choice."

I couldn't help grinning. "Prudent isn't a word I associate with Monty."

Belle chuckled. "That is for sure. But Aiden's not one to take unnecessary risks."

Especially when it came to his heart... I pushed the thought away and dropped down onto my bed. "I think I'll have to park behind the coffee machine tomorrow. I'm not going to be much use for anything else."

Belle raised an eyebrow. "Didn't the doctors tell you to rest up?"

"They told you the exact same thing—are you?"

Her grin flashed. "When it comes to orneriness, we're both as bad as each other. I'll do the coffee, you handle the cakes. Penny and Celia can handle the rest."

"Sounds like a plan." My phone rang, the tone telling me it was Aiden. A ridiculous surge of happiness hit.

"It's hardly ridiculous when you're in love with the man." Belle tapped my shoulder. "I'll leave you be. Don't spend all night talking dirty to him—you need to sleep."

"Spoilsport." I hit the answer button as she left. "Did you kill the Manananggal?"

"No. How badly were you hurt this time?"

"I wasn't. How did she escape?"

"She didn't." Exasperation filled his tone. "Define wasn't."

I smiled and lay down. "I cut my leg, but it's not serious."

"So no stitches?"

"Just a couple."

"Fuck, Lizzie—"

"I'm fine. Really."

"You keep saying that, and it's never entirely true." The exasperation in his voice might have been high, but so was the caring that ran underneath. It wrapped around my heart and made me giddy. "I really wish I could take you home tonight."

"I really wish you could too." I kept my tone deliberately light. "Maybe once the whole Clayton situation is sorted—"

"You'll give in to the inevitable and move in with me."

I'd love to. I really would. I closed my eyes and kept the words locked inside. "You know why I can't."

"Liz," he said gently, "the return you fear might not happen for months or years, if at all. Why let the possibility of future heartache disrupt the happiness of the present? Especially when you've spent most of your life running from one rather than enjoying the other?"

It was tempting. So very tempting... I took a deep breath and released it slowly. "Because—"

"You're afraid," he cut in again. "And we both know your fears are well founded. I might not be looking for my werewolf mate, but I can't guarantee she won't ever step into my life. What I *will* promise is that I won't toss you aside as cavalierly as you fear. I care for you. Deeply. Hurting you is not something I ever want to do."

"I know that, but I'm just..." Scared that this time—this split—would be the one to utterly break me.

And yet, heartbreak would happen whether or not I was living with him. The dice had been cast on the day we'd met, and nothing was going to alter the course on which I was now set. Why not grab as much happiness as I could, while I could, before fate threw her spanner into the works?

I took a deep breath and slowly released it. "Okay then."

There was a long pause. "Is that a yes?"

"Yes."

His joy practically vibrated down the line. "I'll start making room in my wardrobe."

I laughed even as my heart did another of those ridiculous little dances. "I can use the one in the spare room."

"I've seen your wardrobe—trust me, there'll be plenty of room in mine. Besides, how can I have the pleasure of watching you dress if you're doing so in the other room?"

I laughed again, though this time it was a deep and husky sound. "I'm thinking said watching might just lead to other things."

"Oh, I'm counting on it."

Anticipation shot through me. Of course, it was a little preemptive given the whole Clayton situation. "Are you coming around for breakfast tomorrow? You can catch me up on why the Manananggal escaped you both then."

"She didn't escape. Monty's tracker is still on her."

"Then why—"

"She's holed up in a cave surrounded by some pretty strong spells. Monty thinks it better if we attack her in the morning, when she's more restricted."

"Daylight might kill her, but we've no idea if it'll weaken her magic."

"No, but the fact she hasn't managed to take another victim will."

"What if she leaves the cave?"

"Then we'll deal with her."

"You're still there?" I asked, surprised.

"Yeah, although I don't think Monty is too happy about spending the night out in the open."

"He does like his creature comforts." I hesitated. "It might be wise if he calls in Ashworth, just to be safe."

"Ashworth is already on the way here, though I suspect the only reason Monty asked him was so he could bring a supply of coffee and food."

"I suspect you might be right. Be careful out there."

"Always," he replied. "Sweet dreams, and I'll see you in the morning."

He hung up, leaving me feeling slightly left out. I wasn't the reservation witch and certainly didn't have the power or the knowledge to counter the bitch's spells, but I really wanted to be out there with them.

I sighed and put the phone back on the bedside table. Once I'd stripped off, I climbed into bed and went to sleep.

And for the first time in ages, dreamed of a future filled with happiness rather than death and destruction.

To say the three men arrived at the café the next morning looking less than happy would be the understatement of the year.

"Let me guess," I said, as I closed the door behind them. "She wasn't there; only the tracker spell was."

"She had an escape route all ready." Monty dropped heavily onto a chair. "We only discovered it after we'd peeled back her spells and went in after her."

I hobbled around the counter and began making coffee. "You didn't check for other exits?"

"Of course we did," Aiden said. "Problem was, she'd already left by the time we'd arrived—something we didn't know until we entered the cavern itself."

"Can't you use a piece of her magic to track her with?" Belle came out of the kitchen carrying plates stacked with bacon and eggs. "You said you peeled it back, not destroyed it."

"That's what we're intending," Ashworth said. "But the laddie here insisted we wait until the sun had fully risen."

"Makes sense," Belle said. "When the sun is at its strongest, she'll be at her weakest."

"That's exactly my reasoning," Monty exclaimed.

"Your reasoning," Ashworth said, amusement evident, "has more to do with that rumbling stomach of yours than the best time to attack the Manananggal, and we all know it."

Monty grinned and didn't deny it. As Belle returned to the kitchen to grab the rest of the food, Aiden took the tray of drinks from me and carried it over to the table.

"How are we going to tackle her capture?" Belle placed a stack of toast on the table, then plonked down beside Monty.

"We?" he said, eyebrows rising.

"It was a metaphorical we," Belle said. "Curiosity, not stupidity."

"Except if I know my cousin, she wants in."

I smiled faintly as I made myself a bacon sandwich. "She certainly does, but she's also aware that if things go wrong, she can't run."

"She can't?" Monty glanced down. "What happened to your leg?"

"A dead man exploded. Aiden didn't tell you?"

"That he was dead, yes, but not that he'd exploded. How the hell did that happen?"

I quickly updated him and then added, "She's probably got more than one grenade at hand, so you'll have to watch for physical traps as much as magical."

"Wouldn't be the first time a ghoul has tried to blow me up," Ashworth said. "I daresay it won't be the last."

"That's undoubtedly true," Monty agreed, his tone grave but his eyes twinkling, "Especially given how old and crotchety you are."

"You, laddie, need to respect your elders more, or they'll box you around the ears." He glanced at me. "I don't suppose you've heard anything from Canberra?"

I shook my head. "Ruby said it'd be a few days before the decision is made. You're more likely to hear something than us right now."

"Sophie tends not to say much—"

"I wish *that* ran in families," Monty murmured.

"—when it comes to active cases," Ashworth continued, obviously deciding to ignore him. "Which in this case suggests they're taking it on. It'll have to be ratified before the full board before you're advised though."

"Ruby said as much." I bit into my sandwich and munched on it for a bit. "I'm worried about Clayton, though. Anger consumes him, and all he wants is revenge. I don't think whatever control my father has on him will last beyond the annulment."

"The Society has people keeping an eye on him, lass," Ashworth said. "The minute he makes a move to leave Canberra, we'll know about it. It'll give us plenty of time to prepare."

But would those preparations be enough? Every instinct screamed no, but maybe that was just the fear of the sixteen-year-old seeping through yet again.

Aiden slipped his hand over my thigh and lightly squeezed. My gaze met his, and deep in those depths, I saw a promise—one to keep me safe no matter what.

But that's exactly what I feared—that his life might be

forfeit right alongside Belle's if Clayton did make it back here. Not only because they were the two most important people in my life, but also because Belle had taken Clayton's manhood and Aiden had claimed what Clayton had been denied—me.

Aiden's phone rang. He glanced at it and then rose. "Sorry, have to answer this."

As he moved to the other side of the room, Monty said, "I'm betting that's the report of another body."

"That's a bet no one in this room would take," Ashworth said. "The Manananggal had plenty time after escaping us last night to find someone to feed on."

"Was last night's bridal party relocated?" I asked.

"Yes," Monty said, "and Aiden triggered her spell rather than the groom, so she won't be able to find them."

I took a sip of coffee. "Do you think the spell is the reason she knew you were after her? It's not like you had time to nullify it last night."

"Doubtful," Ashworth said. "As it's not in an active state."

It was a comment that had me glancing at Aiden's right hand; spell strings still clung to his fingers. I frowned. "Why haven't you removed it?"

"Because if we can't track her this afternoon," Monty said, "we may have to use him as bait."

"You'd better keep him safe if you do, or I'll cut off something vital."

"My future wife might not be too pleased with that," he commented, shooting a clearly amused look Belle's way.

"I was talking about access to free breakfasts, but I'll happily shift focus to your manhood if you want." I glanced past him as Aiden returned. His expression suggested Monty's guess had been spot-on. "Another murder?"

He nodded. "And it's in the same area we believe the Manananggal is."

Monty drained his coffee and then stood. "Are we dealing with a single or double death?"

"Single." Aiden's gaze met mine. "Dinner later?"

I nodded. As he headed for the door, Monty a couple of steps behind them, Ashworth rose and said, "Thought you might like this."

He pulled a folded piece of paper from his pocket and handed it to me.

I accepted it with a frown. "What is it?"

"Your mother's phone number."

My stomach did an odd flip-flop. "How'd you get it?"

"She asked Sophie for your contact details. Sophie got hers instead. The choice should be yours as to whether you want to talk to her or not."

I didn't say anything. I really couldn't. I just stared at the white bit of paper, a dozen different emotions tumbling through me. Belle and I might have discussed the possibility, but this little bit of paper meant I now had to make a decision.

My inner child still wanted nothing more than to run and hide from the possibility of hurt that the contact would bring. The adult I'd become wanted answers, even if they did hurt. I wasn't entirely sure which half of me was stronger.

Ashworth lightly gripped my shoulder. "I'll not advise you one way or another, lass. Just know that Eli and I are here if you need us."

I blinked against the sting of tears and briefly gripped his hand. "I know. Thank you."

"I haven't got a daughter," he said, his voice a little gruff.

"But if I had, I sure as hell would have been proud if she'd grown up like you. Your parents are idiots."

And with that, he turned and marched out the door.

"We definitely struck it lucky when he and Eli came into our lives," Belle murmured.

"And part of me thinks I should be happy with that and not look backwards."

Belle glanced at me. "You've spent all these years second-guessing your mom's part in this. If nothing else, you deserve to have some answers. You don't have to have any sort of relationship with any of them beyond that. As Ashworth said, the choice is yours."

The choice might be mine, but would my father take any notice? Now that he was aware of my link to the wild magic, I very much doubted it.

I took a deep breath and released it slowly. One problem at a time was a motto I needed to follow for the next few days.

My father could wait until *after* I'd decided what to do about my mother.

In the end, the adult—and the need for answers—won.

But my hands shook as I slowly keyed in her phone number, and it took what seemed like forever before I could press the green call button.

The phone rang... and rang.

My stomach was twisting so badly it physically hurt. I wanted to hang up, to say I'd tried and leave it at that. And yet I didn't want to spend the rest of my life wondering what would have happened if I'd only held on and asked my questions.

Whether I could actually trust the answers I got over the phone was another matter entirely. My mother, like my father, had played in the political arena for decades, and was well versed in the art of subtle manipulation.

Finally, the ringing stopped and a cool voice said, "Eleanor Marlowe speaking. How may I help you?"

The sound of her voice after all these years sent a wild mix of joy, anger, hurt, fury, and sorrow tumbling through me, and it momentarily robbed me of the ability to speak. This woman was my mother, but she'd always been something of a stranger.

"Hello?" she repeated. And then, with the slightest catch that spoke of uncertainty, added, "Elizabeth?"

"Yes." The response was whispered; my throat was so damn dry I couldn't manage anything else.

"Oh." She paused. Gathering herself, I suspected. Controlling her emotions—or was that merely the wishful hopes of that lonely inner child? "Thank you for calling. I wasn't sure—"

"Neither was I." And I still wasn't, if I was being at all honest. I took a deep breath and plunged on before courage fled. "But I needed to know why you didn't stop the marriage. You must have known I'd have never willingly agreed to it."

There was a longer pause. "You really must believe that I had no idea your father had used a combination of drugs and spells—"

Anger—and old hurt—stirred, making my response sharper than I'd intended. "Did that response wash with the Black Lantern people? Because it certainly doesn't with me."

"It's the truth."

"You might not have known about his use of drugs," I

retorted, "but you're every bit as strong as him magically—why didn't you see the threads of his spell on me?"

"Because you and I rarely interacted after Catherine's death. There was little opportunity or time—"

"There was nothing stopping you from *making* the time." It was angrily said, but I didn't really care. After so many years of holding back, it felt good to finally unleash. Which might not have been wise, but I wasn't really in the mood to be wise right now. "I'm your goddamn daughter—did it never cross your mind to at least *ask* if I was okay?"

"No," she said softly. "It did not."

Four words. Four simple, brutally honest words that were nothing but the truth and yet still so unexpected. I'd grown up well aware of my own insignificance within our family, but hearing it confirmed like this, however regretfully...

My anger fled, leaving only a deep and empty sadness behind.

I'd spent nearly thirteen years hoping that she'd had no part in pawning me off to Clayton. Thirteen years of hoping that when she did find out, it would somehow bring us closer together.

The truth was, nothing would ever do that. She simply didn't care enough about me.

And while I'd always been envious of the relationship she'd had with Cat and my brother, Juli, I now had to wonder just how much of that was due to their worth, power-wise. In the cold light of this conversation, I rather suspected it had played—and, in the case of my brother and his offspring, still did play—a major role.

I scrubbed a hand across eyes that ached but had no tears to shed, and said wearily, "Why on earth did you ask to contact me?"

"Because it was the right thing to do."

Of course it was. Why would I think anything else when I'd grown up well aware that *appearing* to do and say the right thing was all that really mattered. "I suppose that's why you broke up with Dad?"

"His actions in this whole farce have put me in an intolerable position." She paused, as if suddenly realizing how all that sounded. "Which doesn't mean I'm not sorry for what happened or for my own lack of foresight and support. I am. It's just—"

"That you care more about your standing in Canberra than the daughter who offers you so little."

"That is unfair and untrue."

"It's nevertheless how I've always felt."

"Then I am doubly sorry—"

"It doesn't matter anymore," I cut in. "It really doesn't."

Even as I said that, a weight lifted. It was the truth. I had a life—a good life—and people who loved me as my parents never had. The inner child might have wanted reconciliation but the reality was, what I'd found in Castle Rock was far more real than anything I'd ever get from my parents.

She didn't immediately reply and—though it was probably nothing more than imagination—her hurt filled the silence. I let it stretch.

Her next question, when it eventually came, did surprise me.

"Is there anything I can do for you, Elizabeth? I know nothing can ever make up for the trauma you went through, but..."

Her words trailed off. Perhaps she realized it was a case of too little, too late.

"There is something," I replied evenly. "Make sure the annulment is pushed through quickly."

"Your father is attending to that, but I'll ensure there are no delays."

Meaning that despite their so-called split, the two remained in contact. No doubt once this had all blown over and my father was given whatever meager punishment the council deemed appropriate, they'd renew their alliance and continue on as if nothing had ever happened.

"The other thing you can do is keep an eye on Clayton. If he leaves Canberra, please let me know immediately."

"Clayton would not be foolish enough to leave Canberra when the specter of an investigation haunts him. It would be testament to guilt."

"Have you spoken to him since he and Dad returned?"

"Of course not, but—"

"Then you can't speak to his state of mind. Trust me, he wants revenge. On me, on Belle—" I paused as instinct stirred. "When did you last speak to Dad?"

"Yesterday—why?"

"It's possible Clayton might well hold him ultimately responsible for the marriage and its consequences."

I could almost see her frown. "What consequences?"

"Belle placed an anti-erection spell on him. According to what he said when we met, it still holds."

"*Belle* did that?" Her disbelief echoed.

"She's far more capable than any of you ever imagined, but that's not the point. Check Dad. My instincts are saying he might be in trouble."

"Clayton is hardly that foolish, but I'll nevertheless do as you ask. Your psychic skills were always your one strength."

"And here I was thinking you considered them a frightful anomaly and an affront to the Marlowe name."

There was another of those long pauses. "It was never my intention to make you feel so unwanted, Elizabeth. You're my daughter, and no matter what you think, I do love you."

An apology of any sort was something I'd never expected, but I couldn't help asking, "Then why did you never try to find me?"

"Because I was told you didn't want to be found."

"Who by?" But I knew, even as I asked the question. There was only one person who knew why we'd fled—Belle's mom.

"Ava Sarr," she confirmed. "And at least now I understand her comment to me when she was interviewed about your disappearance."

"Which was?"

"Any mother who stands by and allows such abuse deserves to lose her daughter." She hesitated. "I really *am* sorry, Elizabeth."

"Apology accepted." There was no point in harboring resentment. No point in holding on to bitterness and anger. I'd already wasted years of my life to it. It was well past time to move on. I glanced at my watch and saw it was close to six. Aiden would be here soon. *He* was my future, not the woman who gave birth to me. "I need to go. We'll talk again soon."

"I'd like that."

With that, she hung up. I stared down at the phone and wondered if I'd ever hear from her again... and realized in that moment that I didn't care either way.

Aiden had been right. Talking to her really had been the best thing I could have done.

"That," I said with a sigh as I pushed my plate away, "was divine. Thank you."

Aiden had suggested we go back to his place rather than a restaurant when he'd picked me up, and I'd readily agreed. After everything that had happened over the last few days, I really wanted some alone time with him. Especially given it might be the only chance we had for a little while. Clayton would be here soon—I felt that within every psychic inch of me—and we simply couldn't afford to be caught alone. I might have the wild magic on my side, and Clayton might not be aware how deeply ingrained it was within me, but he did at least know I could weave it through spells. He'd find a means of countering it before he came here, of that I was sure.

"You cook for me often enough. It's only fair that I return the favor." A smile tugged at Aiden's lips as he collected the plates and took them over to the sink. "Luckily for us both, I'm very good at making steak and chips."

"Does that mean there's no dessert?"

A wicked light flared in his eyes. "That depends on your definition of dessert."

I raised my eyebrows even as desire began to unfurl. "I was talking about a sweet that is usually eaten after a main course."

"Oh, so was I."

Anticipation stirred. "Are we talking before coffee? Or after?"

"Lady's choice."

I pursed my lips, pretended to think about it. "Perhaps I need to sample said dessert, just to see if it's worth my time."

"More than happy to provide said sample."

He moved around the long counter that separated us but didn't claim his seat next to me as I'd half expected. Instead, he brushed my hair from the nape of my neck and then kissed my bare shoulder, his lips so warm against my skin. Delight skidded through me, and I closed my eyes, savoring the sensations that tumbled through me as his kisses trailed from my shoulder to my neck and then on to my ear.

"Enough? Or shall I go on?"

"Oh, please," I murmured huskily, "do go on."

He chuckled softly. "As my lady wishes."

His lips left my skin, but only long enough to turn my barstool around. He dropped tender kisses on my forehead and my cheeks before finally claiming my mouth. But this kiss was no tease; it was searing hot, filled with desire and demand. It left me breathless. Left me wanting. Badly.

"Does the sample please my lady?" His heated breath brushed my kiss-swollen lips, and his blue eyes gleamed with heat and hunger.

"It does." It was little more than a breathless whisper.

"Shall I continue?"

"Please do."

"With pleasure." He slipped his fingers under the dress's straps and slid them down my shoulders. I wasn't wearing a bra, and his gaze devoured me, leaving me hot and breathless and wishing he'd eat me in truth.

When he did, I could only groan in complete and utter bliss.

I was right on the edge of coming when the phone rang sharply. Aiden stopped, and my groan became one of frustration.

"I have to take that."

"I know."

"I'm sorry."

"I know." I lifted his face to mine and kissed him softly. He tasted of heat and desire and me. "Go."

With a low growl, he pushed to his feet and strode across the room. "This had better be—"

He stopped. Though my hearing had sharpened over the last few months, I could still only hear one side of the conversation. But that was enough to know there'd been another murder. I slipped off my stool and quickly redressed.

"Be there in twenty." He hung up and thrust a hand through his thick hair. "We've got another death."

"The Manananggal?"

"At this point, unknown." He frowned at me. "Why are you dressing?"

"Because you've still got her spell tangled around your fingers and this might be another trap."

"Tala's called Monty in—"

"Yes, but that spell could be activated at any—"

"Then disconnect it."

"I don't know—" I stopped the instinctive denial. It was a simple enough tracker and inactive at that. Detaching the thing really shouldn't be that hard. "Raise your hand."

He did so. I studied the spell, trying to ignore the vein of darkness that ran through its threads and the responding goose bumps that fled across my skin. After several minutes of looking for weak points and possible traps, I began to spell, wrapping my magic around the anchoring thread, ensuring it was kept whole and alive before disconnecting it from Aiden's skin. There was no change in the spell's makeup as I pulled it free; it hung from my fingers by a single thread, an inert ball of twisted evil.

"Okay, it's removed."

His gaze dropped to my fingers, even though he couldn't see the spell. "What are you going to do with it?"

"Nothing."

His gaze jumped back to mine. "Why not?"

"Because it still presents our best means of trapping her."

"Not if this death is the Manananggal's doing. It means she's given up on her quest to kill grooms."

"Not necessarily. She'd be down on strength and probably had to kill to replenish. This"—I lifted my fingers, then remembered he couldn't see the tracker—"is an easy means of quenching her need for revenge."

"What if it activates while you're here alone?"

"If it does, I'll deal with it."

"But—"

I placed a finger against his lips. "I'll be fine. Promise."

He made a low sound deep in his throat, then wrapped a hand around the back of my neck, holding me still as he kissed me soundly.

"I promise to be back as quickly as possible to finish what I started."

"You'd better, Ranger, or I'll have to take matters into my own hands."

He laughed softly, kissed me again, and then gathered his things and left. I glanced down at the spell still hanging from my fingers. I didn't want it in the house; if it activated when I was asleep, then I could be in all sorts of trouble.

I studied the darkness beyond the glass. I could attach it to a tree or something... but that might only send her rampaging through the nearby houses. I couldn't risk anyone else getting hurt.

I sighed. My best bet was to wrap a sensor spell around

it. That way, if it was activated, I'd at least have time to prepare for her arrival.

I carefully placed it on the coffee table, then took a deep breath and began the spell. It didn't take long, as it wasn't a particularly hard spell. I added an audible warning as well as the usual light flash, given I wouldn't see the latter if I was upstairs.

With that done, I did the dishes, then watched a few hours of crap on TV before heading to bed. I wasn't sure what time Aiden came home, as I didn't feel him crawl into bed.

He did, however, keep his promise. It was a glorious way to start the day.

"So, what happened last night? Was it the Manananggal, or something else?"

We were eating a leisurely lunch in front of the open fire. He'd given himself the day off, though he'd spent most of the morning writing up reports.

"Something else, though it was nevertheless pretty traumatic. A kid got hold of a rifle his father had stupidly left loaded and shot his younger brother."

"Is he dead?"

"Yeah." Aiden scrubbed a hand across his eyes. "I'm not sure what's going to happen—it's a tragic situation that won't be made any better by the father being charged. It's the council's decision, thankfully, not mine."

I twined my fingers through his. "Why is it the council's? Aren't there laws regarding the safe storage of guns?"

"Those laws—or rather, the penalties—are somewhat more flexible within the reservation."

"Even with a kid dead?"

"Even with." He was silent for a moment, his expression briefly haunted. Then, with a visible effort, he smiled and said, "Let's talk about something a whole lot happier—like setting a date for you moving in."

"Not without setting a few ground rules first."

He raised his eyebrows. "Like what?"

"Splitting costs, for a start."

My phone rang, the sound slightly muffled thanks to the fact it was buried deep in my purse. I leaned over, dug it out, and looked at the screen; the number wasn't one I knew.

"Ignore it," Aiden said, interpreting my expression correctly. "It's probably a telemarketer of some kind."

"Probably."

I hit ignore and tossed the phone back onto the sofa. "So, splitting—"

"No," he cut in. "Absolutely not."

"Aiden, I won't live with you if you won't let me pay my way. It's not fair and it's not right—"

I cut off the rest as my phone rang again. A quick look said it was the same number. I hit decline again.

"You moving in will hardly add much to current costs, given the solar power and water tanks."

"That's not the point—"

He cut me off with a kiss. A long, slow burn of a kiss.

"As good as your kisses are," I said when I could, "they won't change my mind."

"Maybe I just needed to kiss you."

"And maybe you just wanted to distract me."

Amusement danced in his eyes. "That might also be true."

"Distract me all you want *after* we've laid down the ground rules."

He sighed. It was a somewhat frustrated sound. "Fine. We'll split the cooking, the cleaning, and the washing. We'll even split the driving when practical. But I will not take your money."

"And I'm not taking your charity."

"It's hardly charity."

"I'm not going to set up any sort of life with you on such an unequal financial footing. I pay my way or I'll stay where I am."

He rolled his eyes. "You really are a stubborn wench. Just as well I adore you."

It might not be an admission of love, but it was as close as I was ever likely to get. I leaned into him and kissed him, long and slow.

"I adore you, too," I murmured eventually. "But when it comes to stubborn, werewolves hold all the patents."

He laughed softly and tapped my nose. "Fine. We'll split all the costs. How about we start shifting your things in today?"

"You've a council meeting tonight, and I refuse to spend my first night here mostly alone. That'd hardly be an auspicious start to things." I scooped up the last bit of the chocolate cake we were sharing. "Why the hurry?"

"Trying to counter against a change of mind."

I smiled. "I won't change my mind."

"What about Belle?"

"She's not included in this deal, Ranger."

He laughed. "Won't she miss you?"

"Hell, no. She'll absolutely love having the full run of the apartment."

"So you have lived apart on occasions?"

"Of course we have. We're not joined at the hip, despite appearances to the contrary."

A smile tugged at his lips. "I take it the 'no men' rule goes out the window when you're not living in the same house?"

"It'd be kinda cruel if it didn't."

"And when one or both of you marry? How will that affect your relationship?"

"It won't. Not really."

"Won't her loyalties always be split in two, though?"

I hesitated. "We can't change our relationship, and whoever we marry will have to understand that." I studied him for a second. "Why the sudden bout of questions?"

"You're currently the most important person in my life, and Belle's the most important person in yours." He shrugged. "I was just curious as to how it might affect things."

His use of 'currently' was a knife to the heart—and a reminder that he still didn't see us as permanent, despite his insistence we twine our lives into one.

"Then in all honesty, neither of us really knows how one or both of us getting married and having a family will affect things. As far as we're aware, this is the first time a witch has become the familiar of another. We didn't come with an instruction manual—we're making things up as we go along."

"Does that mean regular type witch–familiar relationships do come with instructions?"

"Volumes of them."

"Huh." He pushed to his feet. "Want a coffee? Or shall we do something more substantial to celebrate your impending relocation?"

A smile tugged my lips. "Coffee will do for now. I've

been drinking so much lately, I'm in danger of becoming a lush."

"Your lushness is the reason I adore you."

My heart did another of those bittersweet twists. "I think we're talking about two definitions—"

My phone rang again. I reached for it and saw it was the same damn number; obviously, they weren't going to quit until I took their damn call.

I hit the answer button and said, "Who the hell is this, and what do you want?"

There was a long pause, then a cultured, all too familiar voice said, "It's your father. I'm ringing to inform you the annulment has been approved."

CHAPTER TWELVE

My heart skipped several beats and then raced so hard it ached. I licked my lips and said, almost in disbelief, "That was a little quick, wasn't it?"

"Clayton is eager to be done with this whole business and get on with his life."

Eager to get out from under my father's watchful eye and get on with his revenge, more likely. "How can it be finalized without my signature?"

"You will of course need to sign the final documents in front of a judge and a witness for it to be official, but that is a mere formality. When that is done, Belle can remove her spell, and everyone can be free of this whole mess."

"A mess that was yours in the making."

"And one I regret. I cannot change the past, however. I can only change the future."

"Not my future."

"Part of our deal was you undergoing another audit, remember. Depending on what the results are, it will probably change your status here in Canberra."

"I don't give a fuck about my status, and neither should

you."

"Like it or not, Elizabeth, you are a Marlowe. That comes with certain responsibilities—"

"Actually, my legal name is Grace. I left the Marlowe name and all the shit it entails behind long ago. Once the annulment is signed, I want nothing more to do with you or that damn name."

There was a long pause. "I understand."

A smile twisted my lips. I knew that tone. Knew it meant that while he did indeed understand, he had no intention of letting the point—or me—go.

"Where and when do we meet?" I said. "I refuse to fly to Canberra, but I'm willing to meet you halfway."

"Not alone, you won't be," Aiden murmured.

I flashed him a quick, tense smile as my father said, "There is a café in Albury called Whitefin. We shall meet there tomorrow at two, if that's convenient."

"A café is hardly the ideal spot to sign legal documents. Besides, I have a business to run."

"I'm sure you could close—"

"I'm sure I can't."

"I see." His annoyance echoed, and it was an incredibly satisfying sensation. "What do you suggest, then?"

"I'm sure you know a magistrate or two in the Albury–Wodonga area. Get one of them to hold a late evening session in his court or office or whatever."

"Fine." His tone suggested it was anything but. "Would six tomorrow evening be suitable?"

"Perfectly." I paused. "What guarantee do I have that Clayton won't retaliate against us the minute Belle removes her spell?"

"He won't. That I promise."

My father might be the ultimate politician, but when he

gave his word, he kept it. The vague sense of foreboding I'd gotten when I'd been talking to Mom stirred again. I might well want to be rid of my father, but I didn't actually want him dead.

"Just be wary of him. He's not in a good frame of mind, and he might well take his anger out on you—"

"Hardly." His tone was contemptuous. "Aside from the fact he hasn't the power, he's well aware such an attack would harm his social standing."

"From what I've heard, he has little enough of *that* left to worry about."

"Then you are misinformed. He still has plenty of allies here in Canberra."

Would those allies protect him no matter what? Would they shield him from the full force of the law if he did succeed in harming either Belle or me? Or would it all be brushed under the proverbial rug and quickly forgotten about? I'd pretty much bet on the latter, especially if the Black Lantern Society decided not to get involved.

But I didn't press the point. He obviously wouldn't listen, no matter what I said.

"Fine. I'll see you tomorrow evening."

With that, I hung up.

And wasn't entirely sure what I felt. I'd been dreaming of an annulment and escaping Clayton for so long; now it was almost within my grasp, some small part of me refused to believe it was actually happening. Of course, a major part of *that* was the conviction that Clayton wasn't about to let Belle or me escape without us paying the price.

But if we survived that—survived him—then we could finally live our lives as we wanted rather than constantly looking over our shoulders, always on the run, always fearful of being discovered.

And maybe that's the reason for your nervousness, came Belle's somewhat amused comment. *Caution has become so ingrained that it's hard to let go.*

Possibly. Definitely.

It'll be fine in the end. I really believe that.

She says with fingers crossed.

And toes, and all things in between. Her amusement faded. *I'll contact Monty and Ashworth and see if they're free tomorrow. I don't think it'll hurt to have backup.*

I very much doubt we'd escape without either of them. I glanced up as a coffee cup appeared in front of my nose and gave Aiden a quick smile of thanks. *I'll see you later tonight.*

You're not staying at Aiden's?

Not tonight—he has some meeting up at the compound.

Then bring home something to eat. I don't feel like cooking.

Will do.

Aiden's shoulder brushed mine as he sat back down. "I know a couple of court officers at Wodonga—I'll ask them to keep an eye on things over the next twenty-four hours."

"My father won't try anything—it's one of the reasons I suggested we meet in a court."

"It's not your father I'm worried about."

"I know." I put my coffee on the table, grabbed his and put it beside mine, then sat astride him. "But I don't want to talk or think about my father, my soon-to-be ex, or even tomorrow night right now."

The lazy swirl of his desire sharpened abruptly, its heady scent filling my nostrils and making my pulse leap. He slid his hand around the back of my neck and pulled me closer.

"More than happy to help you lose an hour or two," he murmured, his breath so warm against my lips.

"If it's only an hour or two, Ranger, I will be severely disappointed."

He chuckled softly, then claimed my lips and helped me forget.

Dusk had settled in by the time we reached the outskirts of Wodonga the next evening. Aiden followed the GPS directions through the myriad of streets and eventually halted in front of an uninspiring, two-story red-brick building.

"Lights are on," Monty commented. "Someone's obviously home."

"I really wish I was," Belle muttered.

"You've more integrity and mental strength in your little finger than either of those two bastards have in their entire beings," Monty said. "You can do this. You can also hold my hand if you want."

She snorted and didn't reply.

"There're several cars with government plates parked across the road," Ashworth noted. "They're obviously here."

"Activate the pendant," Monty said, "so we can check it's working before we go in."

I did so, and then muttered a soft "One, two, three, sound check." He studied the small receiver's screen for a second and then nodded. "Signal's coming through loud and clear. We're ready."

I took a deep breath and released it slowly. "Then let's get this show on the road."

I resolutely climbed out of the truck and strode toward the court's main entrance. The guard stationed outside must have known who we were, because he opened the door without comment.

A second guard waited inside. "This way please, Ms. Grace."

I couldn't help wondering if his use of Grace rather than Marlowe was my father's way of smoothing things over... or whether he was simply trying to lull me into a false sense of security.

It was a thought that had my steps briefly faltering. Aiden's fingers twined through mine, and a thick sense of security rushed through me. I wasn't alone. I could do this.

We followed the guard up the stairs and then down a long corridor. Near the end was a meeting room; the muted pulse of power coming from within it told me my father, Clayton, and at least one other witch waited inside.

The guard opened the door and motioned us to enter. I took a deep breath, then disentangled my fingers from Aiden's and led the way in.

Three men and two women were waiting for us, but it was Clayton who drew my gaze. He made no move and didn't acknowledge me in any way, but his anger burned so fiercely it practically flayed my skin and had beads of sweat breaking out across my back.

Once again, I couldn't help wondering why my father couldn't see just how dangerous he was. It didn't take psychic talents to feel his fury. It wasn't just evident in his aura, but also in the glint of his eyes, in the set of his mouth. In the way he clenched and unclenched his fists and also in his scent, which was a weird mix of ash and fury. A volcano ready to explode, I thought bleakly.

Then his gaze moved past me, and the volcano erupted.

He was up and lunging toward us before my father or the other witch could react. Aiden grabbed me and spun me out of the way. The fist that would have smashed into my face hit his back instead. He growled low and dangerously and swung around, shielding me with his body. No further blows came our way, because we weren't Clayton's target.

Belle was.

But even as he lunged at her, Monty moved. He pulled her to one side, knocked Clayton's fist away with one hand, and threw a punch with the other. The blow smashed into Clayton's face and sent him sprawling backward. Monty took two quick steps and stood over him, his fist still clenched and fire in his eyes.

"You guaranteed Liz's and Belle's safety, Lawrence." Though the words were aimed at my father, his gaze remained on Clayton and his voice was flat and angry. "Allowing this bastard off his leash is hardly keeping your part of the bargain."

"He isn't unleashed. At least not magically." Though his expression and his voice remained coolly urbane, his shock reverberated. "I just didn't expect such a violent—or phys-ical—reaction."

"I did fucking warn you, Father—"

"Language, Elizabeth."

"Aside from the fact I'm an adult, not a teenager, you gave up any right to tell me what to do when you forced me to marry the prick on the floor."

One of the women made a sharp sound of surprise. Obviously, my soon-to-be ex hadn't been entirely honest about the reasons for the annulment, which left me wondering what he *had* said. I mean, how exactly did you explain an annulment after thirteen years of marriage?

Not that it really mattered one way or another, as long as it was all signed, sealed, and made official.

"He will cause no further problems, I assure you," my father said. "Now, please stand back and give him room to rise."

Monty hesitated and then took precisely two steps back and stood beside Ashworth, the two of them providing a physical barrier between Clayton and Belle. Although he'd mostly behaved during our first meeting, this was the first time he'd been in the same room as Belle. Who knew what else he'd do?

My father took a handkerchief out of the top pocket of his jacket then walked over to Clayton and offered it to him. "You will restrain any further urges to violence, will you not, my friend?"

Clayton wasn't so far gone in anger that he didn't recognize a threat, however politely it was said. He accepted the handkerchief with a nod and elegantly dabbed at his bloody and very mashed nose. If it wasn't broken, I'd be very surprised. Monty had certainly put some force behind his blow.

My father helped him rise, then escorted him with one hand under his elbow—and not for support, I suspected—over to the other side of the conference table. Keeping something solid between him and Belle was a damn good idea, but it wouldn't matter in the long run. Once my father had returned him to Canberra and removed his leash, all the fury and hatred so evident in his aura and his eyes were going to boil all over the two of us.

Surviving it seemed to be becoming an ever-distant hope.

I flexed my fingers and firmly pushed the thought—and the fear that came with it—away. Anticipating defeat was the surest way of ensuring it. He hadn't beaten us the first time, and he wasn't going to do it this time.

"I think it's best for everyone's peace of mind if we proceed without further delay." The older of the two women accepted a satchel from the younger woman, then spread a number of documents out on the table. "Mr. Clayton Marlowe, you first, please."

Clayton accepted the offered pen and signed on the lines she indicated. His signature was small and mean—much like the man himself.

It was my turn next. I signed each spot, my heart hammering. I was—so close—to freedom.

My father signed as one witness, and Ira the other.

The older women added a final signature and then the documents were all stamped. One set was handed to Clayton, another handed to me, while the other two were collected by the younger woman and placed back into the satchel. "These will be filed tomorrow, but the annulment is official as of this moment. Is there anything else?"

"There is one private matter that needs to be dealt with," my father said. "If we could have use of this room for a few minutes longer, that would be appreciated."

The older woman nodded. "I will wait for you in the foyer."

My father waited until the two women had left and then said, "Remove the spell on Clayton, Belle."

"Only if you leave the room," I said.

His gaze cut to mine. The dark bruising that accompanied the broken nose I'd given him made the barely restrained anger stand out starkly. "That is hardly wise—"

"Your leash won't break the minute you're out the door, and he's not stupid enough to try anything physical with Monty, Ashworth, and Aiden in the room."

My father's quick glance at his friend suggested he wasn't entirely sure of that. Not now, at least.

"I can't understand why—" He stopped. "You do not wish me to see your magic."

What I didn't want him to witness was the way Belle

and I could combine our magic. Clayton had to be present, but he was too far gone down the revenge trail to even care.

"You're already well aware of my strengths and weaknesses, Father. You spent sixteen years expressing your disappointment with them, remember?"

"It makes no matter where I'm standing. I will still feel the pulse of your magic."

Yes, but he wouldn't see the actual threads of it. Wouldn't know just how deeply Belle's and my magic had converged.

At least, I hoped he wouldn't.

I smiled sweetly. "Maybe I just don't want to be in the same room as you for longer than necessary."

He raised an eyebrow, expression disbelieving, but he nevertheless gave a short, sharp nod and strode from the room.

Clayton didn't say anything. He just watched us with eyes that burned with hate.

Dead. We were dead if he ever caught either of us unawares...

I met Belle's gaze. *Can you actually remember the spell you used that night?*

It was done on the fly, but I think so. I'm still not sure it's the wisest thing to do.

We have no choice, given it was part of the agreement. If we don't go through with it, my father is just as likely to rip up the annulment papers and enforce the marriage. Or turn a blind eye to whatever Clayton does next.

If your instincts are right, the latter will happen anyway. She took a deep breath and then said, "If this is going to work, then Clayton—"

"That's *Mr.* Marlowe to you, girl," Clayton ground out.

"You need some lessons in respect, and I'm more than happy—"

"Threatening the one person who can remove the erectile dysfunction spell isn't the wisest of moves," Monty said, voice deceptively mild given the anger he was radiating. "And if you harm one hair on her glorious head, I'll—"

"What?" Clayton retorted. "We both know you're in that backwater because you haven't power enough for Canberra."

"While that may be true enough," Ashworth said before Monty could, "all either of us has to do is talk to the Black Lantern investigators. You're already in enough trouble with them, Clayton. Don't make it any worse for yourself."

It was just as well expressions couldn't kill, because otherwise both Monty and Ashworth would be dead right now.

"Just get on with it," he growled. "I want this done and over with so I can move on to the next phase of my plans."

"I hope that wasn't a threat," Aiden said. "Because if you meant anything else, I'll arrest you now."

"You hold no power here, Ranger."

"I wouldn't bet on that."

"Enough, all of you." Belle's tone showed none of the uncertainty I could feel in her as she stepped up beside Monty. "Clayton, I can't do anything with you glowering at me like that. Turn around."

He continued to glower, but did at least obey. Belle took a deep breath—calming nerves more than centering energy, I knew—then added, "When I originally did this spell, he instinctively retaliated. That might happen again."

"Monty and I will shield you, lass," Ashworth said.

"And if all else fails, I'll shoot him," Aiden said. "It's amazing how distracting a bullet in the knee can be."

Clayton cast Aiden one of his glares even as he snapped, "Can we just get on with this? It's late, and we've a long drive home."

Monty briefly gripped Belle's hand and then stepped back beside Ashworth. As the two of them raised a protection barrier, I silently said, *How do you want to do this?*

I don't know. She crossed her arms and stared at Clayton for several seconds. *The spell is so deeply ingrained I can barely even see it.*

For the first time, I actually looked at the spell that had saved me and incapacitated him. It was set low near the base of his spine and had been thrust deep into his body, which was probably one reason why it had lasted as long as it had. Most spells sat on the skin rather than under it, and were therefore easy to examine and unpick. It was only those designed to kill that went internal—and few witches dared perform such spells, thanks to the threefold rule. Only a threat of grave harm could override that rule, and that's undoubtedly why Belle had never suffered any blowback from her dysfunction spell.

The spell was a thick combination of both our magic and the wild, the latter still pulsing with power. It was no doubt a reason the spell had lasted so long—and also why my father had spent so long looking for me. It was proof that the daughter he'd long thought useless actually wasn't.

I can see the wild magic, I said eventually. *If I pull its threads apart, you should be able to see and unlock the rest of the spell.*

Worth a shot. I may have to pull on your magic to do so, though, as that's how the spell was created.

Take what you need.

Right. She took another deep breath. *Let's do this. You first.*

I crossed my arms and studied the gentle pulse of wild magic, following its long, twisting thread. When I found the beginning, I reached out magically and carefully pulled it free from the threads of magic it was fueling. It pulsed in response and quickly unspooled from the main spell, but it didn't disintegrate, as I'd half expected. Instead, it traveled back up the magical line and became part of me again. It felt weird... and yet somehow right.

But with its light gone, the rest of the spell was finally revealed. It was hard to tell Belle's magic from mine; the connection between us really had been deep when she'd performed the spell.

Can we just take a second to admire the beauty of that spell? came Belle's comment. *Because, damn, it's good.*

A smile twitched my lips. *I don't think Clayton would agree.*

Clayton can go fuck himself. Are you sure we can't leave a parting gift behind? Her mental tones were somewhat wistful. *After all, we only promised to remove this spell—we never said anything about not replacing it.*

I wish we could, but with my father outside...

Belle sighed. *Fine. Let's undo the damn spell and unleash future hell.*

With that, she deepened our connection then pulled my magic into hers and began the process of picking the spell apart. It was an even tougher process than I'd first presumed, because not only had the spell been embedded deep, but some of its threads had latched around the two main arteries that ran the length of his penis. Their removal was tricky—especially given he had his back to us.

By the time the last traces of the spell had been removed, Belle was shaking with fatigue. She took a deep breath and then said, "It's done."

Clayton turned around. "Life stirs where none has existed for thirteen years."

I didn't want to think about life stirring. Not now. Not ever. Not when it came to him, anyway.

"Thank you for keeping to the deal." Though his tone was genuine enough, there was something in his eyes that said she was a fool. That if the circumstances had been reversed, he wouldn't have.

The door opened, and my father stepped in. "*That* was an interesting experience. Perhaps I should study the use of magic from behind closed doors more often."

His gaze briefly fell on me, and I knew then that he was now aware just how deep the connection between Belle and me was—and what it meant for us magically.

"Clayton," he continued, "let's go. Elizabeth, I'll be in contact to arrange the audit."

"Fine." My voice was surprisingly even given the tumultuous state of my stomach. "But after that, don't bother. I don't want to see you; I don't want to hear from you."

A cool smile touched his lips, but he didn't actually reply. He simply gave me a somewhat mocking bow and then followed Clayton from the room.

Relief hit so hard my legs went to water. I would have collapsed had Aiden not caught me. "It's okay," he murmured. "It's over—done."

He was a good enough judge of people and situations to know that it wasn't, but I didn't say anything. I simply enjoyed his embrace while I could.

"Well," Monty said into the silence. "That went way better than I thought it would."

"Aye," Ashworth agreed, his tone dry. "None of us are dead."

"Clayton's furious, not insane," Monty retorted. "He

won't break the threefold rule."

"That rule doesn't apply to physical attack," Belle said quietly. "And that's what's still coming."

"Then we need to get you somewhere safe." Monty paused. "Both of you, I mean."

"Of course you did." My voice was dry. I pulled free from Aiden and turned around. "And we have a plan for that."

"No, we really don't," Belle said. "Not unless it's absolutely necessary."

"I think it will be."

"And I think you'd better enlighten the rest of us," Monty said.

I waved a hand. "Later. For now, can we get the hell out of here? Clayton's stink lingers, and my stomach is threatening to revolt."

Ashworth's gaze sharpened. "I've got a good nose for cologne, lassie, and he wasn't wearing any."

I hesitated, but he deserved the truth. Or at least part of it. Neither he nor Monty knew about the second wellspring and had no idea Katie's spirit controlled it, and I really wanted to keep it that way. The fewer people who knew what Gabe had done, the better—especially when it came to people like my father, who cared for nothing except power and its uses.

"It appears the wild magic is sharpening some of my senses."

Ashworth frowned. "Why would it be doing that? It's a force—a form of magical energy from deep within the earth. It can kill, but it can't alter."

"I know, and I don't understand why it's happening. It just is."

Which was totally the truth, and yet his expression

suggested he knew there was more I wasn't saying.

"Once the current problem has been dealt with, I might take a trip up to Canberra," he commented. "The Society has an archive of old magics—there might be something on wild magic there."

"They have?" Monty's eyebrows rose. "I don't suppose you need a research assistant, do you?"

"No, laddie, I do not."

"You're reservation witch," Belle said, voice dry. "You can't be flitting about willy-nilly."

"Even a reservation witch gets holidays."

"Not when they've only been in the job a few months."

"There is such a thing as pro-rata," he commented, amusement crinkling the corners of his eyes. "Truth is, you just want to keep me close."

A smile touched her lips. "Well, you are handy when it comes to psychos wanting to punch me out."

"If you've finished flirting with each other," Aiden said, his voice dry, "how about we get on the road? I've an early start tomorrow."

"It's all right for you," Monty grumbled as he led the way out the door. "You've caught your girl. Mine's still playing hard to get."

"Not hard," Belle drawled. "Impossible."

"Impossible isn't in my vocabulary."

"Then look it up. You'll see a picture of me."

Their by-play continued as we headed down the stairs and walked across to the truck. To my relief, both government cars had gone. For some reason, I'd half expected Clayton to do something crazy—like try to run us over or even shoot us. But perhaps he wanted to check the spell had indeed been fully removed before he got down to the business of revenge.

I had to find a way to protect Belle. Had to.

I didn't say much on the way home, and I didn't stay at Aiden's, as much as I wanted to. Belle's exhaustion pulsed through me, its force so sharp and strong my own bones were aching.

I made us both a strength potion, but shoved such a big dose of sleeping herbs into hers that she barely even made it to bed. I tugged the blankets over her, then walked across to the bookcase and studied the old books secured behind glass doors. While the twenty or so leather-bound volumes we had stored here were only a tiny portion of the books Belle had inherited from her grandmother, I had a vague memory of seeing a spell that could protect the recipient from physical assault. I had no idea if it had been in one of these volumes or those stored offsite, but if I could find it, then maybe I could prevent Clayton doing to her what he'd tried to do to me.

I opened the door and ran a finger across the spines, hoping instinct or even that distant memory would kick in. Neither did, so I pulled the most logical three out and headed into the living area. After making myself a large hot chocolate and liberally dosing it with Bailey's Irish Cream, I settled down for a long night of reading.

It was close to dawn before I found it, though it wasn't in any of the books, but rather amongst a number of handwritten notes tucked in the back of the rather oddly titled—and also unfinished—*Spells from Uncertain Times*. Nell had obviously died before she'd been able to finish the book.

I carefully unfolded the brittle piece of paper and studied the spell. It required the recipient's hair or skin, as well as something he or she held dear, and would only work if there were a deep connection between witch and recipient—which was rather odd.

It wasn't until I reached the end of the spell that I realized why—it required the blood of the practitioner to fuel it.

Blood magic.

Dark magic.

Which explained the title. Blood magic had been in heavy use during the Dark Ages, but had thankfully petered out since then. Few these days used it—and those who did were hunted down and killed.

While many of Nell's other books mentioned counters for dark spells, none—as far as I was aware—detailed an actual blood spell. So why this one? Did that mean it was safer? That it didn't stain the soul as deeply or as darkly as the others did?

I scrubbed a hand across my eyes, uncertain what to do. There'd been no other workable spell that would protect her from physical assault, but dare I risk blood magic?

My gaze swept the note again. At the very bottom of the page, in writing so small I had to hold it closer to the lamp to read it, was a note; *I foresee a need for this in the distant future, but be wary of its use, dear witchling. The spell lies in the gray zone; it will not draw the ire of the council but it will make you more susceptible to the darker forces of this world.*

I swallowed heavily. Being more susceptible to darkness was not something I needed or wanted in a reservation that still had several years of being invaded by those same forces ahead of it.

But if it could protect Belle from what was coming...

I grabbed a pen and quickly jotted down the instructions, then carefully refolded the note and tucked it safely back in the book. I returned all three to the bookcase, then collected the candles and other magic paraphernalia I needed from the reading room. I collected some hair from her brush, then walked over to her dressing table. There were many beautiful necklaces and rings that she no doubt loved, but the spell had called for an item the recipient held dear, and to me that meant something they didn't want to lose.

Nothing here fit that bill.

But I knew something that did.

I opened the top drawer and reached past her underpants to the small stack of ribbon-wrapped letters sitting there. They'd all come from Belle's first lover—a much older French chef with a poet's heart who not only taught us both to cook, but who'd fallen madly, passionately, in lust with the then-eighteen-year-old Belle. Their affair had burned bright for seventeen months and had ended equably, but during that time Miguel had sent her numerous poems and letters detailing his admiration and desire for her. She'd kept every single one of them.

They were all yellowed with age and smelled faintly of the rose petals that had once accompanied each one. I carefully undid the red ribbon, then opened the top note. It was obviously the letter he'd written after they'd made love for the first time, and detailed exactly what he intended to do the next time. The intimacy of it had my cheeks burning and my pulse racing.

I grabbed my phone and took a photo so that Belle would always have his words if not the actual note, then quickly did the ribbon back up and tucked the letters back into their hiding spot.

One would have to be enough.

After placing the candles around the bed and ensuring there was nothing close by to catch alight, I carefully lit each one and then sat within their semicircle. I lit the final candle, placed it in front of me, then tugged her hair from her brush and put it and the letter beside the candle and my copied instructions. I took a deep breath to center my energy and still my nerves, and then began the incantation. It was long and intricate, and the forming threads were clouded and heavy. By the time I neared the end, my pulse raced and I was shaking with fatigue.

I blinked the sweat out of my eyes, then slid the tip of my athame into the folded letter and held it over the candle, watching it burn as I whispered the spell's penultimate line. As the paper blackened and burned, and tiny sparks of red spun into the air, the spell's threads began to pulse with power.

It was working. Just one more thing to do... and it was possibly the hardest.

My hand shook as I pressed the tip of my athame to my finger. I briefly closed my eyes, gathering courage, and then pierced my skin and let the blood drip onto the candle. Something fractured deep within, and uneasiness stirred. I ignored it and spoke the final few words. The pulsing threads settled like a blanket over Belle's sleeping form and slipped under her skin. She stirred, murmuring a soft protest, but didn't wake.

I closed my eyes and took a deep, shuddering breath. It was done. All I could do now was pray that it lasted long enough to counter Clayton's arrival.

Belle clattered down the stairs midway through the breakfast rush. "Why the hell didn't you wake—" She stopped and studied me through narrowed eyes. "Why do you look like utter crap?"

"I didn't get much sleep last night. It's nothing serious."

In truth, I hadn't gotten any. It had been close to six by the time I'd finished cleaning up the spell stuff and sprayed the room so that it didn't smell like burned hair, and I'd figured it was pointless going to sleep for less than an hour. I'd come down, made myself breakfast and several coffees strong enough to stand a spoon in, and then started the day's prep work.

"When you say things like that, I know it's time to worry." She hesitated, her face paling slightly. "You've done something—something you're desperately trying to hide from me."

Meaning, for whatever reason, she wasn't immediately aware of the spell's presence, which was something of a relief. How long that would last, I had no idea, as the strength of our connection made it difficult to keep secrets long-term. She'd kill me if she ever did discover the risk I'd taken to protect her.

I quickly piped cream onto the apple pie I'd plated up and pushed it across the counter for Penny to collect and deliver. "I placed a protection spell on you last night, that's all."

She frowned. "You did? Then why can't I feel it?"

"Because it's embedded, just like the spell we lifted from Clayton."

"No protection spell we know can do that."

"This was one I found in your gran's books. I didn't tell you about it because I didn't think we'd ever use it."

Her confusion deepened. "Why ever not?"

"Because it called for an item close to the recipient's heart to be sacrificed."

Her eyes went wide. "Not Miguel's letters...?"

"Only one—and I took a picture of it before I burned it."

I caught her hand and added softly, "I'm really, *really* sorry, but believe me when I say it was utterly necessary."

"I do. It's just..." She stopped and blinked rapidly.

"I know." I squeezed her hand and then released her. "But if Clayton attempts to rape you, the spell should prevent it."

She absorbed this in silence for a few seconds. "And what about you?"

My smile felt thin—humorless. "I have the wild magic."

"Which won't help if you're unconscious."

I shrugged again. "It's acted before to protect me without direction. There's a good chance it'll do so again."

"The problem with that theory is that Clayton now knows you can use it. It's more than possible he's researching means of circumventing it even as we speak."

"If Ashworth and Monty are having trouble uncovering information about wild magic, I don't think Clayton will have much more success."

"Except for the fact he has a hell of a lot more contacts."

"I'm thinking positively here. Don't spoil the illusion."

She snorted softly. "Delusion, more likely."

"Whatever works."

She shook her head, then nudged me to one side. "You're making a goddamn mess of that cappuccino. I'll take over—you do the cakes."

I smiled, switched positions with her, and fervently hoped the matter of the spell was now forgotten.

The rest of the day passed uneventfully. Once we'd closed and cleaned up, I called Aiden.

"Hey, gorgeous," he said. "I was just about to ring you."

Alarm slipped through me, even though there was little in his voice to suggest anything was wrong. "Why?"

"Ciara's invited us to dinner."

"Why?" I repeated.

He laughed softly. "Because she likes you. And because I told her you'd finally agreed to move in. It's a celebration, of sorts."

More likely a cross-examination. I wearily scrubbed a hand across my eyes. It was an unfair thought. Ciara wasn't his mother, and though she'd been somewhat standoffish at the start, she'd slowly accepted my growing presence in Aiden's life.

But this invitation was still unexpected.

"I'd love to accept, but I had a really shitty night last night, and I'm dead on my feet."

"Dreams again?" Concern vibrated through his voice and warmed me deep inside. "Or something else?"

"I was working on a spell that would protect Belle." She was within earshot, so I fudged the truth. "It took all damn night."

"Was it successful?"

"I think so. We won't really know for sure until Clayton tries something."

He grunted. "Get some sleep then. I'll tell Ciara we'll make it next week."

"Thanks." I paused, torn between the need to sleep and the call of desire. "I can sleep as easily at your place as mine. That's if you don't mind a snoring companion."

"I'll take you any way I can get you. Be there in an hour."

He didn't only pick me up, but carried me upstairs when I all but fell asleep in the middle of dinner. He stripped me off, tucked me in, and kissed me, soft and lingering.

I protested sleepily when he pulled away, and he chuckled softly and dropped another kiss on my forehead.

"Plenty of time for that in the morning, love. You need to sleep, and I've got reports to write up."

Love. He'd called me love. I couldn't help but wonder if he even realized it.

"Promise?"

"Promise." He sealed the deal with another kiss, but this time it was fierce—demanding—and full of hunger. He broke away with a groan. "Sleep."

"Like I can after that sort of enticement."

He chuckled softly but didn't kiss me again. I closed my eyes and listened to his retreating steps. I was asleep before he reached the base of the stairs.

Nothing happened on the Clayton front, and no more deaths were reported over the next few days, which suggested that the ghoul might have moved on. I certainly hoped so—I was over the whole dramatic confrontational final battle thing that always seemed to happen whenever a new evil stepped into the reservation.

The café was also quiet, which at least allowed us to do a stock take and to catch up on baking cakes and slices. But each day that went by uneventfully had tension rising within. The longer Clayton had to plan, the more dangerous he'd be.

What made the situation worse was the fact that we were relying on other people—on Ashworth's connections with the Black Lantern Society, and on my mother actually keeping her word—to get the heads-up we needed if we were to have any chance of surviving Clayton. Belle and I had spent nearly thirteen years depending on no one but each other, and while it felt good to have people in our lives that we could count on, there was a part of me—undoubtedly a very stupid part—that would have preferred it to remain just the two of us.

Still, there was one good point about the continuing silence from Canberra—it allowed me to spend extra time with Aiden, even though I hadn't officially moved in.

A hot chocolate appeared in front of my nose. I flashed him a smile as he reclaimed his position next to me on the sofa. It was close to midnight, but we both had tomorrow off so had made the best of it by catching up on some new release movies.

"What do you want to do tomorrow?" he asked.

"Shop? We're almost out of food."

He wrinkled his nose. "Shopping is boring."

"Shopping is necessary if we want to eat. Besides, living together on a more permanent basis will involve boring moments. Life's full of them."

"Not when one has you in their life."

I snorted and would have nudged him if not for the fact it would have spilled the rather full cups of hot chocolate. "Then what do you want—"

I stopped as bells chimed, a sound that was accompanied by a wash of rainbow light. Then magic stirred, and my gut clenched.

It wasn't any old magic.

It was *dark* magic.

"What's wrong?"

My gaze met Aiden's. "I placed an alarm around the Manananggal's tracking spell—it just activated. She's on her way."

He swore softly and pushed to his feet. "What do we need to do?"

I thrust a hand through my hair. "We need to call Monty, but I'm not sure he'll get here before her."

He frowned. "Can't you cage her until he does get here? You've done it with other demons."

"Her awareness of my presence makes it more difficult."

"Or it may act as an enticement—remember, she's tried to kill you twice now."

"True."

I twisted around and studied the now alive tracking spell sitting on a bookshelf. An idea stirred... probably a bad idea, but right now we were out of options. She was closing in fast, if the quickening pulse of the tracker was anything to go by.

"I know that look," Aiden said. "I'm not going to like what you're about to suggest."

A smile tugged my lips. "Possibly not."

He made a low growly sound. "What do you want me to do?"

"I want you to grab the salt and run a line across the bottom of the stairs. Then I want you to go upstairs and run a line along all the window sills up there."

"While you're doing what?"

"I'll be creating two circles in the middle of your living room—one to protect me, the other to snare her. When she's caught, you're going to shoot her fucking brains out."

"I'm liking the sound of that last part; the rest, however —" He stopped, then kissed me fiercely. "I know I keep saying this, but please be careful."

"I've never left a good hot chocolate unfinished, Ranger. I'm not about to start now."

He laughed softly, then kissed my forehead and headed toward the pantry. I followed him across to grab a butcher knife from the wooden block near the stove. Then, with a deep breath that did little to settle the uncertainty churning within, I sat cross-legged in the middle of the living room and carefully placed the Manananggal's spell in front of me. The knife I tucked behind me; it was a last means of protection, and one I hoped I didn't have to use.

But for this trap to have any hope of working, I had to appear weak. Vulnerable.

After removing the alarm spell from the tracker, I closed my eyes, centered my energy, and set to work. I started on the outer ring first, creating my cage, keeping the threads tightly woven and pushing as much strength into them as I could. Hopefully, it would hold long enough for Aiden to shoot her.

The tracking spell's threads pulsed with greater intensity. She was close, so damn close. My heart hammered so hard, I swear it was going to tear out of my chest. I sucked in a deep breath and tried to calm down. Panic wasn't going to help me; it would only help the bitch who, even now, was swooping down from storm-held skies.

I began the protection spell. I didn't have my spell stones with me, but Ashworth had taught me how to create one without using anything as an anchor. It wasn't the strongest of spells—at least, it wasn't for me, thanks to the lack of practice—but it didn't need to be.

Once the circle had shimmered into existence, there was nothing I could do but wait.

Seconds slipped into minutes. My breath was a harsh rasp that filled the silence; though Aiden was perched midway up the stairs, he was barely visible in the darkness and ghostly quiet. I felt alone, even if I wasn't.

This time...

I ignored the intuition. One problem at a time.

An odd scratching sound had my gaze jumping back to

the front door. A shadow passed across the wall of glass. A shadow that was winged and half formed.

The Manananggal.

I swallowed heavily and cast a warning glance to Aiden. He raised his gun in readiness, something I sensed more than saw.

Again the shadow passed across the glass. She knew I was in here. Knew I was waiting for her.

Tension curled through me, and I flexed my fingers. It didn't help.

Her shadow appeared again, but this time she paused. Her eyes were ruby orbs that glowed with hunger and anger. Bile rose, and I swallowed heavily. If she didn't damn well hurry up, she might just be met by the contents of my stomach rather than magic.

She pressed a clawed hand against the door; the lock tumbled, and the door clicked open. Magic. I hadn't even felt it.

Her gaze swept the room, no doubt searching for traps. I hadn't yet activated my cage, but I couldn't help wondering if she'd sense it anyway. Some of the more powerful witches certainly could.

For several seconds, she didn't move. She simply hovered midair, the long, slow sweeps of her wings making her entrails slap lightly against the glass on either side of the door.

Eventually, she moved in. The force of her energy stung my skin and had the hairs at the nape of my neck rising. And her scent... rotten meat smelled sweet by comparison. She was *putrid*.

I switched to breathing through my mouth, but it didn't help any. The smell coated my throat and made my stomach churn harder.

She paused again, her gaze coming to rest on the salt lining the base of the stairs. "That little line of white does not deter me."

Her voice was so harsh it hurt my ears. "Then cross it if you wish."

"I do not wish." She studied me, her eyes little more than narrow red slits. "You seek to trap."

"No, I seek to kill."

Her smile flashed, revealing rows of needle-sharp teeth. "So do I."

And with that, she attacked. Not physically, but magically. In little more than a heartbeat, she'd peeled back my protection spell to the point of collapse. I threw out a hand, pushing more energy into it. The threads stretched to breaking point but somehow held.

The force of her attack increased. The threads of my magic were pulsing, thinning in stress, but I fought the instinctive need to shore it up. I needed her to think she was winning. Needed her to come closer... just one more meter. That's all I needed.

I closed my eyes, silently prayed that luck was on my side, and then let my protection shield fall. She laughed harshly and darted forward. I grabbed the knife, pushed backward, and activated the cage. It swept up and around her, surrounding her in an instant. She hit the fabric of its walls and screamed, tearing at the threads with her claws even as her magic began to pick and pull at them.

"Now, Aiden!"

He fired. Bullets ripped into her body but somehow bounced off her head. What the hell...?

I narrowed my gaze and saw the shimmer of magic around her skull. She was shielded, which likely meant the only way to kill her while separated like this was to get through that spell.

But how?

Holy water, Belle said. *It counters evil.*

I've never heard of it countering a protection spell, I replied, even as I scrambled for my purse.

You don't need it to—weaken her, and you'll weaken her protective magic.

I wasn't sure the solitary vial I kept in my purse for emergencies would be enough to do that, but it wasn't as if I had any other options or ideas. I unzipped the purse's inner pocket and pulled the holy water free. The Manananggal was now ripping long threads of my magic free; it felt like she was ripping into me. My body shuddered and shook with every blow.

I screwed the top off the vial and then said, "Aiden, fire when this water hits her."

"Will do."

I spun and ran back. My cage was flickering, failing, the threads of the spell barely clinging together. She screamed when she saw me and lashed out. Her claws cut through the magic and hooked the edge of my dress. She screamed again and dragged me closer; her tongue flicked out, snake-like and needle sharp. I jerked my face back but felt a sting as one forked tip slid across my cheek. As warmth tricked to my chin, I raised the vial and threw the holy water at her face.

It hit her eyes, her mouth and her tongue; the response was instantaneous. Her skin began to bubble and steam, and her eyes exploded, splashing blood and God knows what else across my face. Even as I gagged and fell back, several shots echoed, hitting the Manananggal, spraying blood and gore and brains across the nearby wall.

Her screaming stopped, and she collapsed to the floor, lifeless and silent except for the bubbling hiss of the holy water still reacting against her skin.

I drew in a deep breath and dropped to my knees. Fuck, that was close...

That, Belle said heavily, *has become an unsettling theme when it comes to demonic events around here. You okay?*

Yeah. I wiped a hand across my cheek; my fingers came away smeared with red. The cut wasn't gushing, so at least that was something. I raised the small vial and saw there was a little bit of holy water left; just enough to sterilize the cut.

Aiden knelt in front of me and caught my chin, raising it to inspect the wound. "Do we need to sterilize that?"

"Undoubtedly." I gave him the small vial. "Pour the rest of this over it."

I tilted my head to make it easier. He carefully dribbled the water over the wound; it stung like blazes for several seconds before easing off.

"Is that it?" He quickly scanned the rest of me. "Your dress is shredded, but I can't smell any blood."

"Because there isn't any." I glanced down. "Shame about the dress though. I really liked it."

"Better the dress than you." He caught my hands, then rose and tugged me up with him. "Do you want to head up to bed? I'll deal with this mess."

"It might be wise to call in Monty. He can make sure it's safe to move her body."

"She's not likely to resurrect... is she?"

"I doubt it." I hesitated and glanced at the Mananang-gal. There were few supernatural creatures that could survive having their face eaten away by holy water, let alone having their skull shot apart, but this particular one could live without half its damn body. "I don't suppose you have a couple of wooden stakes hanging about, do you?"

His eyebrows rose. "No, but I could get them easily enough. Will any old wood do, or do you need something specific?"

"Ash is preferable, if there's a tree nearby."

"There is. Won't be long."

As Aiden headed out, I grabbed my phone and called Monty.

"What's happened?" he said without preamble.

"The Manananggal made a surprise visit to Aiden's. She's now dead, but I was wondering if you could come out and supervise her removal."

"Dead? Damn. Missed the fun again. How'd you kill her?"

"A mix of holy water and bullets."

"And you're sure she's dead?"

"She ain't moving, but we're going to stake her with ash, just in case."

"Good idea. I'll be there in ten."

My eyebrows rose. "You're already in Argyle?"

"Close to. Belle rang and demanded I get my butt over to Aiden's because you were about to be attacked. She just didn't mention by what."

Meaning he must have been in the area anyway, because even if he'd broken all land speed records, he couldn't have gotten to Argyle from Castle Rock in such a short amount of time.

"I'll see you soon," he added, and hung up.

Aiden returned with several branches of ash. Once they were cleaned and sharpened, he said, "How many stakes do we actually need?"

"If she's a distant relative of the vampire, then one

should be enough. But I'd use them all, just to be safe."

He nodded and did the grisly deed, shoving one stake into her heart and the rest into her chest. I watched through narrowed eyes, but there was no reaction and there surely would have been if there'd been any life left in her.

Relief stirred, its force so strong my knees threatened to collapse. Aiden caught me and tugged me close.

"Why don't you go up to bed," he said softly. "It's going to take me a while to deal with this mess."

"Monty's only a few minutes away. Wait for him to get here, just in case you need magical help." I rose on to my toes and quickly kissed him. "This is not how I'd hoped the night would end."

"Me neither." His quick smile was rueful. "But there's always the morning."

"There'd better be, or I may just scream."

I kissed him again, this time with all the frustrated hunger that still burned within, then headed upstairs for a shower.

I didn't hear Monty arrive. I had no idea what time Aiden slipped into bed and gathered me in his arms.

But the morning, when it finally arrived, was glorious.

It was late the following afternoon when the phone rang, and it was another unknown number. I hit the answer button and said, somewhat tentatively, "Lizzie Grace speaking."

"Elizabeth, it's your mother."

My heart skipped a beat and then started to race. "What can I do for you, Mother?"

"It's your father. He's been shot."

CHAPTER THIRTEEN

"Is he alive?" I might not want my father in my life, but I'd never wanted him dead. Despite everything, he was still my parent.

"Yes. Lawrence set a new perimeter alarm spell around his office, and while the thief managed to slip past the other spells, he missed that one."

Which suggested the thief might have been familiar with the placement of the other spells, but not the new one. It also meant the new spell had probably given my father enough time to throw himself sideways but not to raise a retaliatory or protective spell. "Was the shooter caught?"

"No. But it wasn't Clayton, if that's what you're thinking. He was across the other side of town, at an official gathering."

I snorted. "It's not hard to hire a killer, Mother. Not if you have the right connections."

"I'm sure I wouldn't know." It was somewhat stiffly said. "And I'm sure Clayton wouldn't know, either."

She was severely underestimating Clayton's slip into madness, but I didn't bother saying so. Like my father, she'd known him for too long—she still saw the man she'd known rather than the one he'd become.

"How did the shooter escape?"

It was odd that he had, especially given that, despite them being two of the strongest witches in Canberra, they'd always had security guards on the front and back gates—and those guards were generally of mixed blood, meaning they were at least sensitive to magic even if they couldn't perform it.

"Via a spell, as far as we can ascertain."

I frowned. "The guards would have sensed a concealment spell."

"He wasn't concealed. It was something else."

"What?"

She hesitated. "At this moment, we're not sure."

My frown deepened. "Why not? Surely a spell strong enough to allow the shooter to slip past the security net would have left some sort of signature behind."

"It should have. It didn't."

"Meaning we're dealing with a blueblood." A very powerful blueblood. Like Clayton.

"Possibly," she said. "The High Council has placed their top investigators on the case."

"Father couldn't tell you what sort of spell it was?"

"No. As I said, he'd been shot."

"But he's obviously not dead."

"He underwent emergency surgery and is currently sedated. It'll be a few days before anyone can speak to him."

Meaning the gunshot wound really had been serious. Guilt stirred; I should have felt a little more concern...

Why? came Belle's comment, *especially after what he did to you?*

He's still my father—

263

So? A blood relationship doesn't automatically trigger love or respect. It has to be earned, and he certainly hasn't.

While that was totally true, it didn't in any way ease that wash of guilt. "When did the shooting occur?"

"A day after their meeting with you."

The edge of accusation in her voice had anger stirring. "If you think I had anything to do—"

"No, no, of course not," she said hastily. "But the investigators do want to speak to—"

"Why?"

"It's routine—they're interviewing anyone who'd had contact with him in the preceding twenty-four hours."

"Then I hope they're intending to speak to Clayton," I retorted. "I know you think otherwise, but I'd bet everything I own on the fact he's behind this."

"I believe they intend to. The trouble is, he's currently unavailable."

My heart did several more skips. "Unavailable? Or gone?"

"That is another unknown."

"When did this happen?"

"Only a few hours ago."

"You promised to ring me—"

"Which is exactly what I'm doing." Her voice was sharp. "I was with your father all day yesterday; I wasn't aware Clayton had disappeared until one of the investigators rang for an update on your father's condition."

"Has a locator spell been initiated?"

"Yes, with no success—though that in itself is not surprising."

Not when most powerful witches were well able to counter such spells. "Did he fly out? Did the investigators check flight records?"

"They checked. He didn't. And Rafael remains at Clayton's residence."

Clayton didn't hold a driver's license; Rafael had been his chauffer for as long as I could remember. "It's easy enough to hire another driver."

"I believe all local companies were checked. He hasn't approached any of them."

Which still left the non-local. I thrust a hand through my hair and tried to keep a grip on rising panic—but it was damn hard given Canberra was little more than six hundred and sixty kilometers away. That was only a seven-hour drive if you didn't stop.

It was very possible Clayton was already in the reservation.

"Have they put a warrant out on him?"

"Of course not." Her voice remained sharp. "There's currently no evidence of his involvement—nothing other than your psychic certainty, anyway, and I'm afraid no court will process a warrant based on a precognitive dream."

That, unfortunately, was very true. "I know you don't place much faith in psychic talents—"

"With good reason, given few practitioners have your strength."

She hadn't ever considered mine a strength, and I had to wonder what had changed her mind. Was she now aware of my affinity with the wild magic? Was that what this was all about?

"It still might be worthwhile to find a psychometry-registered psychic," I said. "They could do a location search."

"Perhaps." Meaning I shouldn't hold my breath waiting for that to happen. "However, I'm more than willing to send something of his down to you, if it would be at all useful."

Surprise rippled through me—at both the offer *and* the fact that she had access to his house. "It would, but it'd have to be something that he wore regularly."

"Would a watch do?"

"That would be perfect."

"I'll arrange for it to be delivered posthaste."

"Thank you."

"I don't want to lose another daughter, Elizabeth, no matter how strained our relationship is. I might not believe Clayton capable of violence, but I will do what I can to aid you."

If she really wanted to aid me, she could have called in the full force of the High Witch Council. She certainly had the clout to do it. But I guess that no matter how much respect Clayton might have lost recently, he would always be given the benefit of the doubt because of his long term status as a powerful, influential witch. Few would act against him without definite proof.

"Thank you," I repeated.

"I'll let you know what your father says when he wakes."

It was on the tip of my tongue to say, "don't bother," if only because it'd probably be all over by the time that happened. But she was at least being civil, and I could do no less. "That would be appreciated."

She hesitated. "Your brother would like to contact you—"

"Why?"

"You're the only sibling he has left—does he really need another reason?"

"Think back, Mother—were we ever close?"

"Well, no, but things change—"

"Things like the possibility of my being able to use wild magic, perhaps?"

There was a long pause. "Your father did mention it, Elizabeth, but it's not—"

"Like hell it isn't. The answer is no. Goodnight, Mother."

I hung up and took a deep, frustrated breath. It was always about the power with my family. Always.

A whiskey on ice appeared in front of my nose, and I took it with a grateful sigh. "You know, for years I dreamed of having the sort of power that would make me acceptable to my family. Now that the possibility is there, I'm realizing just how goddamn stupid that dream was. I don't want them in my life. I don't even like them."

Belle plopped down on the chair opposite. "They'll never change. You know this."

I did, but it had never stopped the dreams of the inner child.

But meeting my father—and talking to my mother—as an adult certainly had.

"Families sometimes aren't the ones you're born into, but rather the ones you make," Belle said. "I think we've gotten ourselves a pretty damn fine one here."

I lightly clinked my glass against hers. "They're not the problem at the moment. Clayton is."

"If he disappeared yesterday, then it's likely he's already in the reservation."

"Yes, and that means we have to put plan B into action."

"I'm *not* staying at Émigré. I don't trust her not to take an uninvited bite or two."

"She won't—she gave her word to the council, remember."

Belle snorted. "Like you can trust the word of a vampire."

"In this case, I think we can—if only because she owes us a favor and wants it put behind her."

"So she can nibble on us later," Belle said gloomily.

A smile twitched my lips. "Possibly. Doesn't alter the fact that it's far safer than here. As I said before, I doubt even Clayton is mad enough to tackle a vampire's abode."

"After what happened in Wodonga, I wouldn't bet on that."

Neither would I, actually. "Please, Belle, you've more chance being safe there than here."

"And what if he decides to attack us *here* during the day?"

"He won't, because there'll be too many witnesses."

"Given he doesn't appear to be thinking logically, witnesses aren't a watertight guarantee of safety."

"I know, but I still don't think he will."

She sighed and drank her whiskey. "Fine. But if she decides to dine on me, I won't be happy."

"She wants to dine on me. You, she wants to fuck."

"That does not make me feel any better." She waved a hand. "Just do it."

I grinned and made the call.

"Lizzie Grace," Roger said in an effusive manner. "To what do we owe this honor?"

"You're in a rather good mood tonight—is there any particular reason?"

"It's the radiance that comes from the mistress feeding."

"Belle will be extremely happy to hear that."

"And why would that be so?"

"Remember the favor I'm owed? I'm calling it in."

"Indeed? I shall hand you over to her." There was a

pause, and then Maelle said, "And what is it you wish of me?"

"You know that man I mentioned?"

"Indeed."

"Well, he's either in the reservation or on his way."

"And you wish me to hunt him down? Because I cannot take life in this place unless personally threatened—it would jeopardize my position here."

"No, I'd actually like you to keep Belle safe at Émigré."

"Is that all?"

"It's not a simple task, Maelle. The man we're talking about is a blueblood witch of high power—and he'll go after Belle in order to get to me."

"He wouldn't dare attack my lair."

"If he was in his right mind, I'd agree. He's not. You'll need full defenses."

"Full defense might well alert the other witches in this reservation. I prefer to avoid that if necessary."

A statement that was yet another confirmation she *was* capable of darker magic.

Sometime in the future, we'd be confronted by it.

Fear knifed through me, even if it was pretty pointless worrying about a future battle when I still had to survive the current one.

"As long as you keep her safe, I really don't care what you do or don't use."

"And when am I to expect her?"

"Is tonight too soon?"

"Yes, it fucking is," Belle muttered, her expression a mix of resignation and trepidation.

"That will be fine. Roger is preparing a room as we speak." She paused, and then continued with evident amusement, "Please assure her that it will be a private bedchamber. No sharing of any kind required."

"She's positively ecstatic to hear that."

"As she should be—there are not many who stay here who can claim that."

People stay there? Belle said. *Why on earth would anyone want to do that?*

Perhaps she's referring to her feeders.

None of the feeders who were killed lived within Émigré's walls. If they had, there's every chance they'd still be alive.

I sipped the whiskey. *I don't think she's referring to her regular feeders.*

Then who? Belle said, even as Maelle added, "What time shall I expect her?"

Eleven. I'm not getting there any earlier than damn necessary.

I repeated the time to Maelle.

"Excellent," she said. "Roger will take her through to the accommodation wing."

"Thanks, Maelle."

"It is entirely my pleasure."

"I'm not liking the sound of that last comment," Belle muttered, as I hung up. "And wing? How can there be an accommodation wing on a building that's basically square?"

"Either she's purchased the buildings on either side or she means the basement. I suspect the former, given the escape route from her aerie."

She took another drink. "It's one thing for me to go into hiding, but what are you going to do? You can't stay at Aiden's—you're both far too vulnerable there."

"I know." I lightly swirled the whiskey around in my

glass. "But I think I'll be safe enough here, as long as you're elsewhere."

"'Think' isn't a reassuring term, you know. And if he can't find me, he may just concentrate all his viciousness on you—and trust me, you don't have to be a telepath to know he intends to take what we denied him thirteen years ago."

The memory of his weight on me as his cold hands tore at me rose. I shuddered and gulped down the whiskey, but it did little to burn the memories away. "I don't think he'll attack me directly. Not until he has a means of ensuring my compliance—either via you or maybe even Aiden."

"Aiden should be safe enough at the compound, but he won't be there twenty-four seven. He'll insist on continuing to work."

"Of course I will." The bell above the door chimed merrily as he stepped through. "Why is this suddenly a problem?"

I rose and met him halfway across the room. After a long kiss hello, I said, "It makes it easier for Clayton to snare you."

He tucked a stray strand of hair behind my ear, his fingers warm against my skin. "Clayton doesn't scare me."

"He should."

"Over the last few months, I've had to deal with all manner of powerfully evil supernatural entities." His voice was dry, his eyes warm. "A witch hell-bent on revenge seems mild by comparison."

"You won't think that if he gets his mitts on you."

"I'm more worried about him getting his mitts on you and Belle. What are we doing to counter that?"

"Belle's going into hiding."

"Rather reluctantly," Belle said. "You staying for coffee, Ranger?"

"Love to, but I'm on my way to another council meeting."

"Then I'll put it in Liz's travel cup. Just make sure you return it, otherwise she'll get grumpy."

He grinned. "I can handle her grumpy."

"Just as well, considering you're going to be living together."

I moved back to the table and sat down. Aiden followed me across. "Why is she going into hiding rather than staying here? I was under the impression neither he nor your father were able to break through all the protections here."

"Only because they didn't know about the wild magic," I replied. "That's now changed."

"They attacked the place twice—if they'd been able to do something about the wild magic, wouldn't they have done it the second time?"

"They wouldn't have had time to do the research then, but Clayton now has."

"I was under the impression wild magic couldn't be countered."

"It generally can't be controlled, but we've always been able to contain and protect it."

He accepted the coffee Belle handed him with a nod of thanks. "Which means it's no safer here for you—and yet I take it you're not intending to hide?"

"No, because I also believe that he'll only come after me as a last resort—and if he can't get Belle, he'll go after you. Which is why I'd like you to stay at the compound for the next few nights."

"I'd rather stay here and protect you."

"That's not really wise—"

"Why not? Between my gun and your magic, I'm

thinking we stand a very good chance of taking the bastard down."

"You're overestimating my magic."

"You're underestimating it."

"Actually," Belle said, "he does have a point. Even Clayton can't out-spell the speed of a bullet."

It'd also make me feel a whole lot better if you weren't alone here.

"Fine." I gulped down some whiskey. "What time is the meeting?"

"Ten minutes—why?"

"Give me your charm—I want to weave through another spell that'll warn you of an incoming magical attack."

He immediately handed it to me. The multiple threads of protection magic I'd already woven through the basic copper and leather necklace pulsed, sending a ripple of rainbow energy spiraling through the café. It might not stand up against a full-on assault from a witch as powerful as Clayton for very long, but it *would* stand.

I quickly threaded the warning spell through the outer protection layers, activated it, and then handed it back. "It'll begin to pulse if there's an imminent threat—the stronger the pulse, the closer the threat."

"Good." He leaned forward and kissed me. "Be back soon."

"All our measures so far have centered on prevention," Belle said once he'd left. "What we haven't discussed is how we're actually going to deal with the bastard once he does attack."

"That's because what we do depends entirely on what he does." I picked up my glass and finished the whiskey. "Given he's undoubtedly behind the shooting of my father, it's very possible he's also decided to get his revenge on us the old-fashioned way—especially given the shooter wasn't caught."

"You don't believe that. You can't. Not after seeing his demeanor in Wodonga."

"Maybe, but I didn't actually think he'd resort to shooting my father, either."

Belle was silent for a moment, then her gaze met mine and she said softly, "If it came down to it, could you kill him?"

"Without a moment's hesitation." Especially if it came down to a choice of his life or that of anyone I cared about.

"Taking his life won't be the same as taking the life of a demon. It'll have deeper ramifications."

I knew she meant personal ramifications more than rule of law. "Then I'll go to a psych and deal with them. I will *not* allow him to take any more of my life or my time, Belle. He's already taken far too much from both of us."

"Amen to that." She clicked her glass against my empty one. "Hopefully, it won't come down to that choice."

"Hopefully."

But even as I said it, I knew the chances were low. There was only one way this was going to end, and that was with one of us dead.

Aiden had left for work the next morning by the time Belle returned, which was probably just as well, as I wasn't in the mood to answer any questions about where she'd been. Not when my dreams had been filled with warnings of looming death and destruction. Of fire and smoke and distant, insubstantial glimpses of charcoaled wall struts that were impossible to identify and yet left me terrified.

"Well," I said, as she walked in. "How was it?"

She shuddered. "The Addams Family has nothing on her inner sanctum, let me tell you."

I smiled and slid a cappuccino across to her. "Meaning she has all manner of 'Things' crawling around the place?"

"Well, I didn't spot any creepy crawly hands, but there were certainly plenty of weird noises—cracking whips and clinking chains—all accompanied by a chorus of groans, moans, and shrieks." She took a quick drink and licked the froth from her lips. "I swear she's running an underground BDSM den of some kind."

"Anything is possible with Maelle, though it'd be hard to keep something like that secret given the power and reach of the gossip brigade."

"Unless she's not catering to locals but rather outsiders. It wouldn't be hard to conceal the comings and goings of her patrons, given this whole reservation survives on tourism."

True. And a BDSM den certainly seemed a more appropriate business than a dance club for someone with Maelle's dark energy. "Were there any problems?"

She shook her head. "I didn't even see Maelle. Roger escorted me to my room—which thankfully had its own en suite, so I didn't have to leave said room—and reappeared once I was awake and showered to escort me out."

"Was the room located underground?"

"We certainly accessed the area from the basement, but I couldn't be certain where we went from there. There was some sort of weird veil that confused the senses."

Unease prickled down my spine. "Magic?"

She nodded. "And powerful enough to disorientate. I honestly couldn't have said whether I was in the same building or not. I certainly couldn't hear the music, which was weird given I could hear all the other stuff."

It sounded like some sort of transport spell—but was something like that even possible? And if it *was*, then why wasn't Canberra using it? Surely it'd be easier to magically change locations rather than hopping on a plane or driving for hours to get somewhere. "You okay with going back?"

"I'd rather not, but if it has that effect on me, then it's likely to have the same effect on Clayton—if he gets that far, that is." She grimaced. "I just wish the room had better soundproofing."

"Earplugs might solve that problem."

"That and a knockout potion." She scrubbed a hand across her eyes. "If I fall asleep in the middle of service today, at least you'll know why."

Thankfully, we weren't all that busy, no doubt due in part to the bitter storm that hit right before lunchtime. Belle headed upstairs around one for a nana nap while Penny and I looked after the few brave souls who came in despite the torrential downpour.

My phone rang just as we'd closed for the day; the tone told me it was my mother. I answered it with more than a little trepidation.

"Your father is awake," she said, without preamble. "He's given a description of his assailant to both the police and the council's investigators."

"I take it he didn't know the man?"

"It was a woman. And no, although he did say the veil of power around her felt familiar."

"How familiar?"

She hesitated. "He said he didn't have time to fully examine the threads and couldn't guess at their origin."

Couldn't? Or wouldn't? I rather suspected the latter. "I take it a warrant has been issued?"

"Yes. She boarded a Melbourne-bound plane late last night."

My heart began to beat a whole lot faster. "Did the cops intercept her at Tullamarine?"

"No, because the plane had already landed by the time the warrant had been issued. A check of security cams indicated an unknown gentleman in a black Mercedes picked her up. The Mercedes was found abandoned just outside Sunbury. It had been stolen the night before."

Meaning she—and whoever had picked her up—not only had this all planned out, but could already be in the reservation.

"Was the veil dad mentioned how this woman slipped into the house?"

"We believe so. It was designed to counter known spells, as far as your father could ascertain."

If he could ascertain that, he really should have been able to ascertain origin. And perhaps he had; perhaps it was a simple matter of neither he nor my mother wanting to admit that I'd been right when it came to Clayton.

"What's being done to find her?"

"The council is sending a team that includes one of their top tracers down to Melbourne. They should be in the reservation within the next twenty-four hours."

"Which might be too damn late."

"If Clayton is behind this," she said, her tone a little stiff, "then there's time. He was never one to act irrationally or without meticulous planning."

There'd been nothing meticulous about his actions on our wedding night, but that had at least played in our favor. If he'd been more controlled, he might well have sensed Belle's assault on his defenses and countered them. If *that* had happened, we might never have escaped.

But he wouldn't make the same mistake again—and he certainly wouldn't underestimate either of us again.

"The investigators will be in contact with you when they arrive at the reservation," my mother continued. "I've given them your address and phone number."

"Fine. Thanks."

"They have one of Clayton's watches in their possession, and I've directed them to give it to you. They've been informed of your psychic capabilities."

If the investigators got here quickly enough, and *if* I was able to find Clayton through the damn watch, then maybe we could stop him before everything escalated.

Maybe.

"Who's in charge of the investigators?" I asked.

"Samuel Kang—I believe you went to school with him."

I frowned. "The name doesn't ring a bell."

"He said he remembers you."

"That's hardly surprising, considering there were no other Marlowe witches with a human familiar. Doesn't mean we actually knew each other."

"Indeed." She paused. "How's Belle?"

"Fine." *And more powerful than you imagine,* I wanted to snipe, but she and my father already had plans to have me audited. I didn't want my link with Belle or Belle herself to be included in all that.

"Good." She paused again. "If you do encounter Clayton and are forced to defend yourself, keep to his left if possible."

I frowned. "Why?"

"He had an unfortunate accident a few months ago and has little sight in his left eye."

"How does that help? He only needs one good eye." And sight certainly wasn't necessary when it came to spells.

"Yes, but he now has difficulty tracking moving objects, judging distances, and perceiving depth. It gives you more of a chance—perhaps not magically but definitely physically."

"If it comes down to a physical fight between the two of us, I'm still going to be in trouble." I might have had youth and speed, but he was taller and stronger.

"Perhaps," she said. "But in all likelihood, it's doubtful it'll come down to such a base confrontation. Samuel and his people will undoubtedly take care of this whole messy situation before then."

I liked the positivity in her voice. I just didn't believe that would be the case.

"I hope so." I hesitated, torn once again between the childish need to reach out and the adult desire to keep my family at arm's length. "I'll update you if anything happens."

"That would be appreciated. We'll talk later, Elizabeth."

"Samuel Kang," Belle mused, once I'd hung up. "Wasn't there a Kang in Monty's homeroom?"

"There were Kangs in every homeroom," I replied, voice dry. "There are only three royal lines, even if there are lots of branches of each."

"Yes, but I'm sure this one was called Samuel." She glanced at the door as it opened and Monty appeared. "Was there a Samuel Kang in your homeroom?"

"Yes, why?"

She shrugged. "He's apparently in charge of the team the High Council is sending here. Just wondered what he was like."

"He's not as fabulous as me, if that's what you're asking."

She gave him the 'don't be stupid' look, which only made him laugh. "In all honesty, I didn't have much to do with him. He was the studious type."

"Which is probably why he ended up working for the High Council," I said, "and you ended up in the dusty bowels of cataloguing."

"Possibly," he said, "but being ensconced in said dusty bowels has at least had one payoff—I think I've found a book that might tell us more about the wild magic and your connection to it. I've put in a request for its retrieval."

I raised my eyebrows. "How did you find it?"

"It was referenced on some old data cards being transferred to the main database. They catalogue out-of-date or superseded reference manuals."

"Will you have to fly up to Canberra to view it?"

He shook his head. "It's an obsolete manual, so there's no restrictions on loaning or viewing. Jamie will sign it out for me and then express post it down."

Jamie was his professor friend, if I remembered correctly. "Did he say how detailed the book was?"

"No, but it's titled *Earth Magic: its Uses and Dangers*, so that suggests a fair bit of detail."

Belle frowned. "Earth magic isn't wild magic, though."

"Actually, it is. Earth became wild after a few cataclysmic events in the eleventh century."

"And you know this how?" she said.

"Because I have a good memory for that sort of rubbish," he said. "And because I sometimes *did* pay attention at school. When's the High Council's team getting here?"

"Sometime in the next twenty-four hours."

Concern flitted through his expression. "Why are they taking so long? Why didn't the council move the minute Clayton disappeared?"

"Probably because it wasn't until my father was shot that they believed Clayton was actually a threat."

Monty blinked. "When did that happen?"

"A few days ago. He's out of surgery and recovering, though."

"Fuck." He scrubbed a hand through his hair. "Despite what happened in Wodonga, I didn't think Clayton would resort to a physical attack."

"No one did, which is no doubt why he resorted to hiring a hit man—or woman, as it apparently was." My voice was grim. "It does mean that you and Aiden could both be in danger."

He frowned. "Aiden, I understand, given he's your current partner, but why me? It's not like I had anything to do with your family when this whole crooked deal went down."

"No," Belle said, "but you've stood up to him twice now, and while I certainly appreciated the punch that broke the bastard's nose, I doubt he did."

"There's not much I can do to counter a bullet."

"The ghoul was protected against them," I said. "So there obviously *is* a spell out there capable of doing just that."

"No doubt, but it's not one I currently know."

"Then go over to the ranger station when you're finished here and put on the bulletproof vest Aiden's pulling out of storage."

"Do you really think that's necessary? I mean, they're not exactly hard to spot, and a good enough shooter would have no trouble with a head shot."

"Some protection is better than no protection," Belle said. "And as annoying as I find you, I'd hate to see you dead."

"It warms my cockles to hear you say that."

She rolled her eyes. "Just go over and grab that vest—and don't get shot between here and there or I will be displeased."

"That makes two of us." He glanced at me. "What are we planning to do about Clayton?"

I grimaced. "There's not much we can do at this point. There's a seeker on Samuel's team, and Mom's sending down one of Clayton's watches. I'm hoping that between the seeker and my psychometry skills, we can track Clayton down before he attempts anything."

"And the shooter? Do we know where she is?"

"She flew into Melbourne this morning. Her current whereabouts are unknown."

"Is Aiden checking hotel registrations?"

"He probably will when I mention it, but I can't see it being of much use. There's a hell of a lot of hotels and private guest accommodation within the reservation. It's a needle in a haystack."

"Needles can sometimes be found." He hesitated. "I know Aiden is already staying here, but if you need additional spell power, I'm more than happy to bunk down for a few days."

I reached out and squeezed his arm. "Thanks, but I'd rather not make it easy for the bastard by having all his targets neatly collected in the one spot."

He hesitated and then nodded. "I'll head over to the ranger station now. Ring me as soon as you hear or see anything."

"I will."

"You won't," Belle said the minute he was out the door. "And for the same reason you won't ring Ashworth or Eli—you don't want them caught in the crossfire."

"It's more because of what I saw in my dreams last night." Visions of blood and broken body bits rose once again, and I shuddered. "People are going to die, Belle. I just don't want it to be anyone I care about."

"In the end," she said, voice resolute, "it's not about what we do, but rather what he does."

"I know." And that's what made this whole thing so nerve-wracking. Until he made his move, there was nothing more we could really do—nothing other than take what precautions we could and hope like hell my worst fears didn't eventuate.

We spent the rest of the evening making cakes and doing prep for the following day. Aiden arrived around eight, and the three of us sat around drinking coffee and chatting about everything and anything other than the situation that was no doubt forefront in all of our minds.

At eleven, Belle sighed and rose. "I'd better head over."

"We'll escort you," I said, rising with her.

She frowned. "Why? It's not far to Émigré—"

"That's where you're staying?" Aiden cut in, surprise evident. "Why?"

"For the very reason you're surprised," I replied. "It's a location few would think to look."

"But there's no accommodation—"

"Maelle lives there," Belle said. "I'm using one of her rooms to bunk in."

His gaze ran between the two of us. "There's something more to this than what you're saying, isn't there?"

He'd always been able to see through my lies and avoidances, but this secret wasn't mine to share. Still, a little bit of the truth wouldn't go astray. "Maelle arranged to have Émigré shielded after the Soucouyant firebombed it. If anyone with ill intent crosses her boundaries, she'll know about it."

His gaze searched mine; seeing the truth, knowing there was more. But all he did was rise and take his keys out of his pocket. "I'll drive you over, Belle, and pick you up in the morning."

She frowned. "I'm fine to catch a cab—"

"Not if that bastard's out there and watching, you're not."

"He can hit your truck as easily as he can a cab, Ranger."

"Yes, but my senses and reflexes are sharper than the average cab driver's. Besides, keeping you safe is one less thing Liz has to worry about."

"Ah," she said, amusement twitching her lips. "I knew there was an ulterior motive. Give me a couple of minutes to gather my things, then we can head off."

As she went upstairs, I said, "Have you got your bullet-proof vest in the truck?"

"I have." He caught my hand and tugged me into his arms. "I'll even put it on when I escort Belle to the club, though I really don't think it'll be necessary."

"It's always better to be overcautious than under."

I rested my cheek against his chest and listened to the steady thumping of his heart. It was a calming sound in a world about to go crazy.

"I'll remind you of that the next time you snipe at me for insisting on more caution when you're dealing with a demon." His tone was amused.

A smile tugged at my lips. "You know it won't make much difference."

"This is sadly true." He brushed a kiss across the top of my head. "Given all the near misses you've experienced over the last few months, I think I'm destined to become gray before my time."

"And no one will ever know, given all the silver you already have."

He laughed, kissed me again, and then followed Belle out the back door. As his truck roared to life, I made myself another coffee and headed upstairs. But for some reason, I just couldn't sit. I drank my coffee as I paced, my gaze on the storm-clad night beyond the glass sliding doors.

Watching.

Waiting.

Not just for Aiden to arrive back safely, but also something else. Something very big and very deadly.

Last night's dream was about to come true...

I swore, shoved my coffee onto the table, then snagged my jacket off the chair and clattered down the stairs. After grabbing my phone and keys from the under the counter, I strode across to the front door.

As I opened it, there was a huge *whoomph* followed by a massive fireball that lit up the sky.

For several, seemingly overlong seconds, shock held me immobile. I could only stare at the orange glow that was even now being smothered by thick black smoke.

Then shock gave way to the realization of what I was seeing and where it was coming from.

A building had just exploded into flame—and that building was Émigré.

CHAPTER FOURTEEN

Belle! I screamed mentally. *Are you all right?*

No answer came. The line between us was dead... but was she? I had no idea, and that was perhaps the scariest thing of all.

I bolted out the door and ran, as fast as I could, into the night and the storm. I didn't bother locking the café's door or grabbing our SUV—which probably would have been quicker in the long run, given the distance.

Except... it wasn't. Power flowed through me, power that came from within and without. The wild magic, enhancing my speed and endurance, giving me werewolf-like speed, just as Katie had said.

The wind lashed at me and the rain pummeled, but I didn't feel any of it. All I felt was fear. It churned my gut and made my heart feel like it was about to break.

Belle had to be all right. She had to be...

Wild magic stirred around me; it filled me with energy and hastened my steps even as it sharpened my fear. Aiden. Oh *God*, Aiden. It shouldn't have taken him this long to simply drop Belle off. He should have been back long before Émigré had erupted into flame.

He must have escorted her inside.

Fuck, fuck, *fuck.*

The word pounded through my brain, its rhythm as swift as my footsteps. Alarms bit through the night. Building alarms. Fire alarms. Emergency services.

I'd get there before the rangers, the ambulances, and the fire brigade, but would it do any good? Would the burned bodies I'd vaguely glimpsed in my dreams belong to the two people I cared most about in the entire world?

I hoped not.

Hoped that I had read Clayton—and his need for revenge—so very wrong.

I skidded around the corner, my arms flailing as I fought for balance. The wild magic spun around me, its force burning my skin, urging me on, urging me to hurry.

Up ahead, flames leapt high and black smoke billowed. The air was thick with the stench of burning wood, material, and flesh, and my stomach churned at an even faster rate. Shadows moved through the smoke—some staggering, some supporting others, all of them trying to get away from the heat and the flames. My gaze swept them, desperate to find someone I knew. No one. There was no one familiar.

The closer I got, the fiercer the heat became. I threw up a hand in an effort to see against the glare and the smoke. Dear *God*, the whole front of the building had been blown apart. All that was left was fragmented skeletons of what had once been walls and roof beams... and yet the rear half of the building looked relatively intact. If there was any chance of survival, then perhaps it was there...

Energy wound around my fingers, then Katie said urgently, *This way.*

She led me into a lane that ran along one side of a smaller building. All its windows were shattered and its security alarm was ringing, but the explosion that had torn apart the front of Émigré had done little more than blacken the paint here. But the pungent black smoke cut visibility and made breathing even more difficult. I pulled my sweater over my nose in an effort to filter out some of the muck and wished I could do the same when it came to the thick waves of emotion that rolled from the building—from all those who'd been injured or were close to death.

Dozens; there were dozens of them.

I swallowed heavily and tried to ignore the psychic wash. I couldn't save everyone... and it was very possible I might not be able to save the two people I loved most in the world.

The lane came out into a small parking area behind Émigré. Though bits of wood, concrete, and metal lay scattered all over the area, the flames and destruction hadn't yet reached the back of the building or the loading bay. A metal grate barred entry into the latter; beyond it, at the top of the stairs, was a double-width door. Entry into the back of Émigré.

Given the state of the building and that door, there was a very good chance that Belle, Aiden, and others might still be alive... but only if they'd been in *this* portion of the building rather than the front.

I gathered the wild magic, blasted the metal shutter apart, and then raced up the steps and strode toward the door. The wild magic stirred around me even as Katie silently urged me to hurry.

"Do you know what lies behind the door?" I asked.

A hallway leading into the rear storage areas.

"How close to the destruction zone and the fire is it?"

Close enough.

"And Aiden?"

I warily pressed a hand against the door. It was warm to the touch, and there were thin threads of smoke leaching out from underneath it, but neither were an indication that the hall beyond was ablaze. I once again used the wild magic to punch the door open. Smoke billowed out, its stench a mix of wood, burning plastics, and who knew what else. The hallway beyond was dark, filled with the crackle of distant flames and the groaning of a building on the verge of collapse.

He's trapped in the basement, Katie said. *The roof has fallen onto the main stairs, and a beam blocks the secondary exit door that leads into this hall. You must hurry.*

I knew that, but I nevertheless stalled. My heart raced a million miles an hour, and my fear was so thick it squeezed my throat and made breathing even more difficult.

It was stupid to go in there. Absolutely stupid. But if I didn't—if I did the sensible thing and waited for emergency services to get here and do their job—there was every chance that no one in the basement would survive. It wasn't only precognitive ability telling me that; it was also evident in the growing pulse of Katie's fear.

My heart skipped several beats and then kicked up a gear. "What about Belle? Is she with him?"

She's not in the basement. Nor is she outside or amongst those who lie in the rubble.

Her words only made the sick churning in my gut intensify. Either she'd escaped through that weird doorway she'd mentioned with Roger and Maelle, or she was now Clayton's prisoner. While I'd definitely prefer the former rather than the latter option, it didn't explain why I couldn't sense her presence. As far as I knew, the only thing that could break the connection between us was death, and I had to believe she wasn't yet dead. Surely, *surely*, I would have known if she was.

"And Maelle and Roger? Have you seen them?"

No.

Meaning it was possible Belle *was* with them. Maybe they were all safe in the accommodation quarters, wherever they were. It was a hope I clung to even as instinct said it was unlikely.

I cautiously stepped into the hallway. Between the smoke and the lack of lights, it was almost impossible to see, even with my enhanced eyesight. I wish I'd thought to bring a flashlight or even my damn phone, but clear and rational thinking hadn't exactly been a priority... The thought had barely crossed my mind when the threads of wild magic came to life, giving the turbulent, smoke-filled air an eerie bluish-white glow. I picked my way through the rubble that was strewn everywhere, heading for barely visible stairs.

"The beam that blocks the basement's exit—can you move it?"

I can't interact directly with physical items.

"Why? You have before."

Smaller items, yes, but I can only affect larger items— including both humans and the supernatural—through or with you. That may change, but for now, I remain restricted.

Her frustration sang through her mental tone, but that was absolutely understandable. If not for those restrictions, she could have rescued Aiden herself.

I paused at a distant *whoomph*. The walls around me shuddered, and dust rained down, thick and choking. My gaze jerked upward; the ceiling had cracked, and spiderlike veins were now crawling along its length. Another explosion, however minor, might just bring the lot down on top of me. I swallowed heavily and forced my feet on.

Up ahead, gleaming dully in the wild magic's ghostly light, was the railing that lined one side of the stairs that led into the basement. The smoke and dust became a wall thick enough to carve, and the air burned. My eyes stung, my skin was on fire, and my throat felt raw. Breathing through the mask of my sweater wasn't really doing much to keep the muck and the smoke out of every breath. And with every step, I drew closer to the destruction zone... and the possibility of death.

I briefly closed my eyes, fighting the panic, fighting to keep moving. I *had* to keep moving. I had no other choice. Not if I wanted to save Aiden and uncover where the hell Belle was.

Though I knew. Deep down inside, I knew.

I gripped the railing, then hesitated, eyeing the debris that covered the steps. The walls shuddered as another explosion ripped through the front of the building and a thick chunk of plaster came down, hitting the third step and then shattering into a myriad of pieces. I was running out of time...

I headed down the stairs, gripping the metal railing with one hand and brushing away the bits of wood and plaster still dangling from the ceiling with the other. The air was even hotter here, and sweat broke out across my body, stinging my eyes and dripping down my spine. Even my palm felt slick against the hot metal railing.

I paused again on the bottom step and studied the darkness ahead. Plaster had fallen in several places, and the faint glow of fire was now visible through the upper-level flooring, but this section of the basement was certainly far more intact than the hall above. How long that would last was another matter entirely.

I pushed on. Up ahead, lit by the faint glow cast by the wild magic, was a large pile of plaster and wood. But that wasn't what was stopping them getting out—rather, it was the ceiling. It had partially collapsed, crushing one side of the doorframe. Even if we moved the pile of debris, there was no way we were going to get that door open—not without getting the ceiling's weight off it.

I swallowed heavily and then called out, "Aiden? You there?"

"Lizzie?" came the immediate and somewhat incredulous reply. "What the fuck are you doing here?"

"What the fuck do you think I'm doing? Rescuing your ass."

"You shouldn't be here—"

"On that, we agree. But here I am anyway. Step back—I'm going to open the door."

"The SES boys are bringing in props to support the wall—"

"Aiden, half the building is gone and the rest is on the verge of collapse. We can't afford to wait for them."

As if to emphasize this point, another explosion ripped through the air and shook the walls. Large cracks appeared even as the broken ceiling dropped another couple of inches.

Aiden swore. "I had no idea it was that bad. Do what you have to."

"Get well back, just in case this doesn't go to plan."

It will, came Katie's comment.

I wished I shared her certainty. I took a deep breath and then reached out for the wild magic. A storm of power that was both familiar and yet alien flooded through me, seeming to stretch me, making me more even as it made me less. It had been damned scary the last time I'd done it, but this—this was something else. This suggested *I* could be something else.

But now was *not* the time to worry about it.

I flung one hand out, directing part of its power at the wall, forming a column of sheer energy that pulsed between the floor and the broken ceiling beam, forcing its weight up and off the door. With my other hand, I made a sweeping motion. The rubble that blocked the door rose in the air, flung itself past me, and then settled on either side of the shaking walls behind, leaving a path wide enough to walk through. I redirected that energy back to the column, reinforcing it.

Pain began to pulse in the back of my head. I might be using wild magic to hold up the wall, but it was costing me personally.

"Aiden," I growled, "force the door open and get everyone out."

There were several thumps that echoed through the wall and tore through me via the wild magic, then the door burst open and Aiden appeared. He took one look at me, then turned and growled, "Everyone out—fast!"

Men and women streamed through the door—and there were far more than I'd expected. I pressed my back against the wall to give them room to pass; they stank of fear and smoke and blood; some were burned, some were cut and bleeding, but most looked unharmed. The main stairs into the basement might have collapsed, but that same collapse might also have protected them from subsequent explosions.

With what sounded like a gunshot, the plaster above me cracked and fell. I thrust a hand up, knocking the huge chunk away with wild magic. Pain lanced through my head, and moisture dropped over my eyelashes and slipped down my cheeks. I couldn't hold for much longer...

"Hurry" was all I said.

Six more people came out, then Aiden was beside me. "Fuck, Lizzie, you're bleeding—"

I was? "It doesn't matter—go. Get everyone out of here—"

"Not without you—"

"I'm currently the only thing stopping this section of hall collapsing, so get your ass out of here. I'll be right behind you."

He made a low sound deep in his throat, then swung around, wrapped an arm around a limping young man, and disappeared into the smoke and dust haze that now filled the hall.

I waited, one arm still outstretched, feeding the wild magic into the column, keeping it strong. My limbs shook, and the ache in my head was now fierce enough that my vision was blurring.

Why?

I wasn't really doing anything here that I hadn't done before...

Magic is never without cost came the comment. It wasn't Katie—it was too masculine in tone. Gabe, speaking through her. *You may be one with the wild magic, and will therefore avoid the price most pay for its use, but you are still flesh and blood rather than energy. Using it in such a manner will always come at a personal cost.*

Like eyes bleeding?

Yes. They will heal, but every time you use the wild magic in this manner, the worse the bleeding will become and the longer it will take you to recover.

Not something I wanted to hear... but right now, it didn't really matter.

Aiden and the others had climbed the stairs and were now in the hall leading to the parking area. It was time for me to release the wall and get the hell out of here.

You will have to run came Katie's comment. *Fast.*

I took a deep breath, then clenched my fingers and unleashed the wild magic. The thick column of blue-white light flickered and then broke apart, once again becoming tiny fragments of blue-white light. Without support, the wall immediately dropped. As the doorframe took its weight and began to splinter further, I spun and ran back along the hall. Threads of wild magic spun ahead of me, providing enough light to not only see through the gloom but to also see the ever-widening fissures appearing in the walls and the ceiling.

With a soft *whoomph,* the basement wall collapsed. A heartbeat later, a thick cloud of dust flowed over me, cutting what little visibility there was, throwing me into a deep, dangerous darkness.

Tiny filaments of wild magic encircled my wrist, and Katie's energy—her being—flowed into me. My senses expanded—sharpened—and while the fog of dust and smoke remained as thick as ever, I could at least see shadows now. It was enough to keep running, to avoid tripping over anything. The stairs came into view. I was almost safe...

But that thought had barely even crossed my mind when what sounded like a freight train started up behind me.

The ceiling and walls were collapsing.

I swore, grabbed the railing, and bolted up the stairs two at a time.

Faster, faster, Katie urged, panic in her tone.

I tried to obey, but my strength was slipping away and I had nothing left in the tank. It was all I could do to remain upright.

As chunks of plaster rained all around me, a figure appeared out of the gloom at the top of the stairs. Though little more than a white-covered silhouette, scent told me it was Aiden. He grabbed me—lifted me—in one smooth motion, and then raced up the remaining stairs and pounded down the hallway. A huge cloud of dust and debris chased us as, section by section, the building began to collapse.

Aiden burst into the loading bay, jumped down the stairs, and then ran into the parking area where more than two dozen people had gathered.

With a sound that vaguely resembled the groan of a dying beast, the center of the building collapsed inward, leaving only the outer walls still standing.

We were safe. Against all the odds, we were safe. The shaking started, and I blinked fiercely against the tears stinging my eyes. It wasn't over yet. Not by a long shot.

Aiden put me down, then gently caught my chin with his fingertips and lifted my face. "It looks like you've burst a blood vessel in your eyes."

"It was the stress of using the wild magic to prop the wall. I'll be fine." The sudden sharpening of sirens had me glancing around; several ambulances and an SES truck were entering the parking area. "What's happened to Belle?"

"Roger escorted her into a secure area. After that, I don't know." He frowned. "Can't you contact her?"

"No, the line between us is dead."

"I'm sure she's fine, Liz."

But his words fell flat. She might be alive, but it was very doubtful that she was fine. Not if Clayton had her.

I took a deep, steadying breath. "You need to concentrate on the mess here. I'll head back home—" I held up a hand to silence his protest. "I'm fine. I just need to make myself a potion and grab some rest."

"At least have your eyes looked at—"

"They can't do anything for an eye bleed like this, Aiden. The only thing that can heal it is time." I rose on my toes and brushed a kiss across his lips. "Do what you have to here, and don't worry about me."

He lightly cupped my cheek, his touch warm and his gaze worried. "Just promise me you won't do anything stupid."

"I won't."

Which didn't mean I wouldn't do anything at all, and he was well aware of that. He shook his head, kissed me lightly, and then let me go.

I walked past the ambulances and SES vehicles, my head pounding in time with my footsteps and my body feeling like it had been run over by a truck. Which in many respects, it had—one driven by the wild magic.

The café's door remained wide open. I stepped in, and then realized the place wasn't empty.

And the person standing in the middle of the café was the one person I really didn't want to confront right now.

Maelle.

She was deeply, furiously angry.

Even worse than her anger were the lightning-like cracks of her magic. Dark magic. It struck at my skin and, for a second or two, seemed to freeze my pulse and my heart. But there was no snapback from the magic protecting this place, so no matter what it felt like, neither the magic nor her anger was aimed specifically at me.

Which *didn't* make me feel any safer.

I drew in a deep, steadying breath, then turned to face her. Her chestnut hair—usually swept up onto the top of her head—was in disarray, covered in plaster dust and ash. Her face was black and her clothes—what looked to be a deep red riding habit from the Regency era—were all but shredded, revealing multiple cuts and suggesting her escape had not come lightly.

But it was her gaze that held me—scared me. Her eyes were usually a gray so pale there was only the slightest variation between her irises and the white. But here—now—they were black. All black. Ghoulish black.

She might not currently mean me harm but it wouldn't take much to change that. One show of weakness and that would be the end of it. The end of me.

Like I needed another fucking problem right now.

I gripped the anger that rose with that thought and stepped closer. She'd hear my pulse and know the truth, but I nevertheless had to outwardly remain strong.

For Belle's sake, if not my own.

"How the hell did Clayton get into Émigré, Maelle, let alone cause such damage? You had a multitude of magics protecting the place."

"He didn't set the bomb. I believe a woman did."

Her voice was calm and collected, at total odds with the fierceness of her eyes and the utter darkness of her aura.

But if she was right—if it was a woman who'd caused this catastrophe—then it was more than likely the shooter who'd flown in and disappeared. "How did she get the thing in? It wouldn't have been a small thing, given the damage it caused."

"My people had to break up a fight that happened outside the entrance. I believe now it was a diversion, as it happened a few minutes after Belle and your ranger entered the building."

"What happened to Belle?" I paused and looked around. "And where's Roger?"

"Roger has been forced into a period of stasis."

I frowned. "Meaning what?"

"He was so badly injured that he's been forced into a period of inactivity in order for his body to heal and recover." She paused, and though she didn't move—didn't even blink—it suddenly felt as if death had swept into the room.

The surrounding magic flickered but didn't fully activate. For the moment, she wasn't a direct threat.

For the moment.

I flexed my fingers and tried to remain calm.

"And Belle?"

"Was taken."

Even though I already knew that, her confirmation hit like a blow to my gut. I sucked in air and tried to restrain the urge to scream and rant and rage. It wouldn't help the situation; it wouldn't even make me feel any better.

"How? From what she said, your accommodation center isn't directly under Émigré and was even better protected than the night club."

"All of which is true, and I can only presume she used one of my customers to get inside information. There's no other way she could have gotten in and out with such ease." Her dark gaze glimmered. "I want revenge."

She wanted Clayton's death. And she wanted it done slowly, wanted him pulled apart piece by tiny piece, wanted him screaming in agony as she bathed in his innards and consumed his blood...

I shuddered and shut the insights down. "You can't. You promised the council to take no life within the reservation."

"My promise was conditional on not being attacked. I did warn that I would retaliate to protect me and mine." She paused. "I will, however, take him beyond the reservation's boundaries before I kill him."

And make sure he suffered in the meantime. I briefly closed my eyes. Clayton had to pay for the damage he'd done and the lives he'd taken, but allowing Maelle to take her revenge was little more than condoning his murder.

And yet, did I really have any other choice? I rather suspected that if I didn't play by her rules, she'd simply bind me and find him without my help.

The only reason she was even here was the fact that she'd given her word to keep Belle safe—and she had to see that through *before* she made any move on Clayton.

The front door opened before I could reply, and the bell chimed merrily; it was a jarring sound in the uneasy, threatening atmosphere.

Monty stepped into the room and closed the door. "What the fuck happened over at Émigré? Is Belle—"

He stopped abruptly, his eyes going wide. "Jesus fucking Christ, you're a *vampire*." His gaze came to me, and understanding swept his expression. "And you knew."

"Yes, but I was sworn to secrecy."

"Does the council know?"

"Yes, but not the rangers." I returned my gaze to Maelle. "Were you able to unleash any sort of tracking spell when he hit Roger?"

"No. He took Roger out when my attention was diverted by the first explosion. The second took out my aerie. Only my magic and my escape tunnel saved me."

"A vampire capable of dark magic," Monty muttered. "Just what we need."

"In this case, it just might be," I said. "I'm not sure the four of us will be able—"

"There is no need for the other two witches," Maelle said in a voice that suggested she wanted no arguments. "There's no need for even this one. You and I will track down your ex, and then *I* will take him."

"Maelle, he's obviously aware what you're capable—"

"He's barely tasted a fraction of what I can do," she cut in softly. "I underestimated him once. I will not make the same mistake again."

Dark wisps of evil spun around her, speaking not only of the strength of her magic but the utter darkness of it. The heretic witch we'd dealt with a few months ago had been squeaky clean in comparison.

I shivered—and I knew I wasn't the only one. Monty's fear ran across my senses like sand.

"Even so," he said, his voice showing little sign of his deep unease, "as reservation witch, I at least need to be present to—"

"No," she cut in again, "you don't. And you won't."

"That really isn't wise, given you'll need witnesses for whatever action the council might—"

"They fully understood what they let into the reservation. They will take no action against me, as long as I hold to my promise." Her gaze returned to mine, and my stomach flip-flopped. "Contact Clayton. Arrange a meeting."

I got out my phone. I didn't dare do otherwise, even though I doubted Clayton would be using the same phone or phone number. He might have firmly stepped into insanity's grasp, but even he'd be aware he could very easily be tracked through his phone.

The call rang out. I shoved it away and said, "He'll ring me when he's got his trap set."

"Then I will wait here until he does."

Like I needed *that* on top of everything else. I thrust a hand through my tangled hair and glanced at Monty. "You want a drink?"

"A coffee would be great."

"Maelle?"

"I daresay you don't stock what I need right now." Her gaze fell onto Monty. "And I dare not take from the unwilling."

"And I'm *very* unwilling." He took a long detour around her and followed me to the counter.

I made his coffee, then, after taking a couple of painkillers, mixed up a very large revitalization potion. I was going to need all the strength I could get to make it through this night.

One hour crawled by, then two. I didn't change clothes and I didn't grab a shower. I just paced, as did Monty. Maelle didn't twitch; I doubt she even breathed. She simply stood in the middle of the café, her arms crossed and her aura a shimmering curtain of angry purple-black.

It was close to three in the morning when my phone finally rang. I tugged it out of my pocket and glanced at the screen. It wasn't a number I knew, but I knew who it was anyway.

"Wait," Monty said urgently and got out his phone. "Put it on speaker, and I'll record the conversation. It'll work as evidence for the High Witch Council."

"He won't live to be judged by the witch council," Maelle noted softly.

"While that may be true," Monty said, "We nevertheless need to protect our asses, given they will want answers as to what happened to him."

He quickly hit the record button and then gave me a nod. I pressed the answer button but didn't get the chance to say anything.

A scream ripped down the line, a scream that was high-pitched and filled with pain. A fist grabbed my heart and squeezed tight, making it difficult to breathe, to think.

Belle.

It was Belle.

CHAPTER FIFTEEN

Her scream cut off as abruptly as it had started, but the ensuing silence was worse. The fist around my heart squeezed tighter, and for a moment, everything went black. My spell hadn't protected her... not fully.

"If you kill her," I said, my voice flat but full of repressed violence, "any hold you have on me will die. I *will* kill you."

Clayton's chuckle rolled down the line. It was a low, deep, and utterly confident sound. "You both know you will do no such thing, because the death of your familiar will rip out your heart and kill your mind. You will be little more than a flesh shell—one that will be mine to do with as I wish."

And what he wished was what he'd always wished—me bearing him children.

I swallowed heavily as the memories of rough hands rose but couldn't prevent the shudder that ran through me. I said, as evenly as I could, "You vowed not to take any retaliatory action, Clayton, and this—"

His sharp snort cut me off. "I said what I had to say to

appease your father. The leash has been removed from me, Elizabeth, but I'm afraid you'll not be so lucky. I want you here within the hour, otherwise your familiar's suffering will continue."

Fear surged anew, but once again I ruthlessly thrust it down. What he wanted—what he *needed*—was me reacting blindly. If we were to have any hope of survival, I had to remain rational and aware.

"Where do you want to meet, Clayton?"

He gave me an address and then said, "No one is to accompany you. The perimeter is monitored—the minute I see—or feel—the presence of anyone else—be they witch *or* ranger—I'll kill her. If I sense any of your tricks—if I so much as sense a glimmer of wild magic—I'll kill her."

As if to emphasize this point, Belle screamed again. I closed my eyes against the sting of tears and fury. If there was one good thing about our psychic lines being down, it was the fact that the backwash of her pain and terror wasn't immobilizing me. But it also meant she couldn't reach out and grab my energy to keep hers going.

She might not last the hour... not if that scream was anything to go by. I pushed the ugly thought aside and hung up. Clayton would keep her alive until I was at least in that house with him, if for no other reason than the fact he'd want to drink in my reaction when she died.

"According to Google, that house is a short-term rental." Monty glanced at Maelle. "That means you can enter without invitation, doesn't it?"

"Indeed it does."

"And Clayton's magic?" I asked. "Will you be able to get past it without activating it?"

Her smile held no humor and far too many teeth. The vampire was anticipating her kill. "But of course. You will keep him occupied, I will save your familiar, and then you will walk away and leave him to me."

"I'm not sure it'll be that easy, Maelle—"

"Just as I underestimated him, he underestimates you. This reservation's power is with you, young woman. Remember that."

I could hardly forget, given my body and head still ached from my efforts at Émigré. I glanced at Monty. "Have you any idea what the range of the recording device Ruby and Jenna gave us is?"

"I believe about half a kilometer in an open area. Reception will depend on whether he's using a jammer again, though."

"Fingers crossed that he isn't."

Not that it really mattered if he did, because the council would undoubtedly send Ruby and Jenna back down here to mentally wheedle out the full details from all of us. Of course, if they did *that*, then Maelle was in trouble. Clayton might have gone rogue, but he was still one of them; they wouldn't appreciate any sort of vigilante action, especially from a vampire capable of dark magic. Her actions would out her, but I had no doubt she was aware of that and didn't particularly care.

I returned my gaze to her. "You'll have to remain silent if you don't want your presence recorded."

"My presence will not remain a secret for long, and we're both aware of that," she said, "But I do not need to converse. I just need to bathe in his blood and dine on his agony."

"Thanks for those images," Monty muttered.

Maelle's smile flashed. It remained altogether too toothy. I swallowed heavily and headed to the reading room to grab my gear. Monty trailed in after me. "I really don't like the idea of you going in alone."

"It's not like we have any other choice. You heard him, Monty—he'll kill her the minute he senses another witch."

"I know but—" He stopped and thrust a hand through his hair. "All this time we've been going on about how we're all one big family, and how we'll all back you up, no matter what he did. It's all been for naught. In the end, it'll just be you and him."

"Me, him, and one motherfucking scary vampire."

The smile that touched his lips was fleeting. "True, but even so, I don't like it."

"I'm not exactly thrilled either." I reached for my backpack and then walked across to the storage boxes hidden behind the bookcase. "But it was always destined to end with just the two of us, Monty. I might have spent close to thirteen years hoping it would be otherwise, but fate isn't often circumvented."

"Unfortunately, in this case." His voice held a frustrated edge. "The first thing he'll do is take your phone and that pack from you."

"Undoubtedly, but he also might think it strange if I don't come armed." I opened the nearest storage units, retrieved the opal pendant, and slung it over my neck. Then I picked up the small box of holy water and held it out. "Use these on whatever wounds Belle has."

He accepted them with a nod. "Have you got any regular weaponry? Like a gun?"

I shook my head. "I wouldn't know how to use it even if I did."

"Maybe you should call Aiden—"

"He's got a bombed building and multiple casualties up at Émigré to deal with. He can't help us."

"He could give us a damn gun."

"And what good would that do—can you use one?"

"Anyone can pull a damn trigger, Liz."

"*You're* not going to be close enough to do so."

"I know, but that doesn't assuage my need to shoot the bastard multiple times and then dance all over his bleeding body."

Despite the fear that sat like a weight deep in my stomach, a smile twitched my lips. "Who knew you had such a bloodthirsty streak."

"Anyone who's ever gone after someone I cared about certainly knows." He glanced at his watch. "We'd better get going."

I slung the pack over my shoulder and walked out. Maelle hadn't moved. If not for the shifting, churning curtain of her aura, she could have been a statue.

Perhaps she was conserving her energy. Or perhaps she was pushing what energy she could spare across to Roger. I doubted she'd be able to make another thrall very easily, no matter how strong a dark witch she was.

I walked behind the counter to grab my keys. "We'll have to take both vehicles—you'll need to get Belle out of there the minute Maelle rescues her."

"And leave you? No way—"

I swung around and said fiercely, "I can survive whatever he throws at me, but I won't survive Belle dying. Do as I say, Monty."

He threw up his hands. "Okay, okay."

"Good. Maelle, you coming?"

She didn't answer. She just turned and flowed toward me; death shone in her eyes, and her anticipation—her hunger—was so fierce it burned across my skin and left me breathless.

But as long as she played her part—as long as she saved Belle—then I could live with the outcome. Whatever it was.

It took us twenty-five minutes to reach the acreage outside Argyle. As I turned down the long dirt road that led up to the property situated on the top of the hill, my phone rang. It was Monty, not Clayton.

"I'll stop here on the main road," he said. "It should be close enough to pick up the pendant's signal, but far enough away that he won't sense me."

"Okay. Keep safe."

His laugh was short and sharp. "I'm not the one walking into a madman's trap."

"Maybe not, but given he *is* mad, don't drop your guard. Especially when Maelle gets Belle out."

"I know, I know. Just... be careful, and come back alive."

"That's the plan," I said, and hung up.

"I'll also depart your company here," Maelle said. "It will take me at least ten minutes to construct the invisibility net, and probably another five to get through his barriers." Her gaze came to mine, her eyes flat. Lifeless. "Can you last that long?"

"Yes."

"Good."

She opened the door and disappeared into the scrub lining the side of the road. I undid my seat belt and leaned across to close the door. As I did, tiny moonlit threads encircled my wrist, pulsing with life, strength, and awareness.

Katie.

You are not alone, she said. *We are with you.*

"Which is the last thing I need—he's already warned me against using the wild magic."

I shoved the SUV back into gear and lightly pressed the accelerator, all but crawling forward. The longer I took to get up to the farmhouse, the less time I'd have to survive him.

He may sense a major wave of wild magic, but he will not sense this link.

"And how will that help?" Up ahead, lights glowed, a welcoming warmth that belied the darkness waiting within.

If you allow it, Gabe can come through and share his magical knowledge.

"Come through? As in, his spirit will leave the clearing and start sharing my body space?"

A mix of doubt and trepidation filled my voice. Allowing spirits to share body space generally didn't work out that well for those who weren't strong spirit talkers. Gabe wouldn't intentionally harm me—and he certainly wouldn't attempt to oust my spirit and claim my body as his own—but there were certainly many other dangers. I didn't have my link with Belle to fall back on, and such a merger took a serious toll on the body's strength—a dangerous thing when mine was already way down.

It's only a partial merger—he can never fully leave the clearing. He is irrevocably bound to the wellspring.

Meaning what he intended was something along the lines of what I did with Belle when I needed her to see through my eyes. "Even with Gabe's knowledge, I'm not sure it'll help counter Clayton's power—"

You have more magical strength than you know, came Gabe's comment. *It may not have lived up to your parents' expectations, but do you really think someone such as Clayton would have wanted the marriage if you were truly underpowered?*

"If that's true, why didn't it show up when I was tested?"

I crawled around a corner and brought the SUV to a

brief stop. The trees on either side of the road had fallen away, and the house on the hill was fully visible. It was a long ranch house style brick building with wraparound verandas and not a skerrick of shrubbery or trees around it to hinder a view that probably went for kilometers on a clear day. Even at night, it was the perfect spot for such a confrontation.

I suspect the presence of the wild magic in your DNA may have stymied your natural magic, Gabe said, *but with puberty, those restraints began to fade. It would also explain why the spell that saved you from Clayton was infused with wild magic.*

It made as much sense as any theory I'd come up with.

You only need to use your magic and Gabe's knowledge to block whatever Clayton intends for however long it takes Maelle to rescue Belle came Katie's comment. *After that, you can deploy the wild magic.*

But not to kill—and not just because that would have Maelle's need for revenge twist onto me. A death-based act of revenge would irrevocably stain the wild magic.

"Fine," I said. "What do I do?"

Nothing more than what you do when you wish to share sensory awareness with Belle. Gabe can see and react through you, but it will be your magic rather than his or the wild magic.

I hoped she wasn't overestimating my magic. This could all go to hell in a handbasket very quickly if she was.

After a deep breath that did little to calm the inner churning, I reached psychically through the wild magic's connection for Gabe's spirit. His energy flowed down the link and then fused with mine—not so deeply that his spirit shared body space, but deep enough that he could use his skill and direct my magic while seeing through my eyes.

It felt weird. Felt like I was present in my body and yet standing apart.

You're in control, Gabe said, his words echoing loudly through my brain, *I will only intervene as necessary.*

I hoped it wouldn't be necessary, but that was a futile hope, and we all knew it. Things would get nasty, especially once Belle was freed, and it was very possible none of us was going to be magically strong enough. Maybe I should have asked Aiden for a goddamn gun... My gaze went to my backpack and, after a slight hesitation, I drew out my silver knife and tucked it into the back of my jeans. A last resort if all else failed.

I continued on into the ranch house's long driveway, but the inner weirdness had my hands slipping on the steering wheel, briefly sending the SUV in the wrong direction before I readjusted.

Up ahead, the front door opened. No one stepped out. My heart pounded so damn fast, it felt like one long scream. I flexed my fingers and tried to remain calm. I wasn't alone. I had help. I could do this.

I *had* to do this.

I stopped the SUV, but didn't immediately kill the engine or get out. No one appeared to be moving within the house, and I had no sense of either Belle or Clayton. But his magic was very evident. It cloaked the entire building, layered with every sort of protection and retaliation spell imaginable. I could get in—the exception was so plainly visible it was obvious he wanted me to see it—but I had to wonder if getting out was going to be possible.

I squeezed the pendant lightly to turn on the recorder, then grabbed the backpack and climbed out of the SUV. My legs wobbled briefly, and it was only my grip on the door that kept me upright. The weird, almost out-of-body sensation of sharing brain space with Gabe was disconcerting, to say the least. I swallowed heavily and forced my feet forward, concentrating intently on every step, rather than the magic that flickered angry snakes toward me. His magic was strong, fierce, furious, and it stung my skin as it probed both the backpack and me. My breath caught in my throat, but I clenched my fingers and resisted the urge to react.

"Lose the pack," Clayton said, his voice coming from somewhere to the left of the door. "And your phone."

But not the knife. And not the pendant. For whatever reason, he hadn't sensed the presence of either on my person. I obediently dropped the pack on the top step and then placed my phone beside it.

"Excellent," he said. "Please proceed inside."

I took a deep breath and then stepped through the thick cloak of his magic. I might as well have stepped through a wall of white heat. His magic tore at me, a wave of tiny claws that ripped into my skin, seeking to contain, to bind. My magic rose in response, and the charm at my neck burned to life. The wave briefly abated, then surged anew. Panic rose; I couldn't do this. Couldn't fight him—

Yes, Gabe cut in calmly, *you can.*

My hand rose unbidden, and words sprang to my lips. Power shimmered from my fingertips, and a shield flared around me. The tiny claws of magic were torn from my skin, and Clayton's magic rolled back several inches. It wasn't much of a gap, but it gave me breathing space. I pushed through his spell and stepped into the house.

Clayton stood in the middle of the large living room, looking very much the utter gentleman in his expensive black suit and shiny shoes. Only his eyes gave the game away—the savage had well and truly risen. "Your magic is stronger than expected—what an absolute delight."

The last thing I *ever* wanted was to delight him in *any* way. "Where's Belle?"

He motioned to his left. "Here, awaiting your arrival, as promised."

I scanned the space between us. I couldn't see any sort of snare—magical or otherwise—but the confident amusement in his expression had every inner alarm going off.

I stepped to the side rather than into the room and finally saw her. There was duct tape over her mouth; her wrists and ankles had been similarly bound to a kitchen chair. There were multiple wounds across her torso and arms, but they didn't appear to be caused by a blade or fist, but rather magic. She didn't look as if she'd been sexually assaulted, and that had me blinking back tears of relief. The blood spell had been worth the price I might yet pay...

Though her aura was filled with pain, there was only fury in her gaze—and much of it was aimed at me. I wished I could tell her there was a plan; wished I could tell her it would be all right.

Wished I actually *believed* that.

What I couldn't see was any form of magical restraint... until my gaze hit her shoulder. What looked to be the black metal grip of a knife poked out of her shoulder.

What's that?

A dark restraint spell came Gabe's grim reply. *One that not only contains her telepathy skills but also her magic. Any spell she attempts is turned threefold back onto her. It also appears to be some kind of conduit for his magic.*

That doesn't sound good.

It isn't. It means his magic is amplified without him having to push much magic strength into it.

Well, fuck. But I guess he'd had thirteen years to plan his revenge, so it was no surprise he was so well prepared.

I forced my gaze back to him. "What have you done to her?"

"Not as much as I might have wished," he replied evenly. "Your magic is greater than I presumed, which gives me great hope for the viability of our children."

A shudder I couldn't control ran through me, but the images that usually came with the thought of him touching me didn't rise. Perhaps Gabe was busy in the background...

"You're delusional, Clayton," I bit back. "You never managed to fuck me when we were married, and you certainly won't now."

My reply was met with a short, sharp laugh. Anyone listening would presume my barb hadn't hit him where it hurt, but they'd be utterly wrong.

Maelle approaches came Katie's comment. *Keep his attention on you.*

I flexed my fingers and hoped like hell Maelle hurried. There was a storm rising in the middle of the living room, and I wasn't really sure I could withstand its force for long.

"You forget, I have your familiar." His voice was low, vicious. The veneer of civility had been stripped away by that one remark. "You will entertain me however I wish, or she will pay the price."

"And how long do you think that will last, Clayton? How long do you think it'll be before the council and my parents rain hell down on your sorry ass?"

"They have to find me first."

"And you think they won't? Your DNA was registered at birth, right along with every other witch born. How long do you really think it'll take seekers to find you?"

He smirked. "Except my DNA isn't in the registers. When you have the pull and the power, it is amazing what you can do. Strip."

My gut was churning so hard that for a moment, I thought I'd misunderstood his order. "What?"

"You heard." He motioned up and down. "Remove your clothes. I want to see the full bloom of your body."

Bile rose and magic stirred, bright sparks that danced across my fingertips. It only made the gleam in his eyes fiercer.

He appears to be warded against both your natural magic and the wild came Gabe's comment. *I also suspect he actually wants you to attack him that way.*

Why would he want that?

Magic shimmers around him. The spell is not one I'm familiar with, but it has old bones. Perhaps he found some means of both protecting himself against the wild magic and using it against the user.

If that sort of protection were possible, surely my mother would have used it before she tackled the wellspring that almost killed her. To Clayton, I added, "It'll be a cold day in hell before I ever—"

He clicked his fingers before I finished. Power rose and energy spun through the air, striking Belle with such force that her body jumped and shook. As a muffled scream was wrenched from her lips, I yelled, "Enough!"

He obeyed. Belle's head dropped, her nostrils flaring as she sucked down air, her whole body shaking.

You'll pay, you bastard, you'll pay... The promise ran through my mind, a song that could not be sung. Not yet.

He raised an eyebrow. "Strip, or the next one will burn off her fingertips."

I hissed, but there was little I could do right now but obey. I slowly stripped off my jacket. I could feel Belle's gaze on me, could feel her demand that I do anything but obey, but I ignored it. Until Maelle got here, I couldn't react. Not when she was at his mercy.

You do have one option, Gabe commented. *The knife.*

Using it means getting far too close to the bastard. It wasn't practical to throw it, given it wasn't designed for that sort of thing and I certainly wasn't trained for it. *Besides, wouldn't he guard against something like that?*

Sane witches would, but I suspect that word doesn't currently apply.

Which doesn't mean he hasn't.

No. Gabe paused. *I cannot see a thread that indicates protection against non-magical retaliation, but that doesn't mean it's not in the deeper layers.*

Which isn't comforting. Not in the least. *How far away is Maelle?*

She's weaving an entry into his barrier, but it will take a few minutes if he is to remain unaware.

Meaning I had no real choice. Bile surged, closing my throat and briefly making breathing difficult. Though I could think of nothing better than puking all over his shiny black shoes, I was too far away even for that. I swallowed heavily, then tugged at my sweater's left sleeve. As I pulled my arm free, I took one step forward. I repeated the process and then threw the sweater at him with as much force as I could muster.

He laughed and casually knocked it aside. I'd half hoped it'd hit him and perhaps indicate whether his protections ran to real-world items.

"These delaying tactics only increase the anticipation, dear Elizabeth. Are you sure that's what you want?"

"What I want is you on your knees bleeding from multiple wounds, begging for your life."

He tsked. "So bloodthirsty for one so young."

"I'm not fucking sixteen anymore, Clayton. I'm twenty-nine." I took several more steps, then carefully tugged my T-shirt free from my jeans, making sure the knife didn't move in the process. I pulled the shirt off and once again tossed it at him. This time it hit his chest and fell to his feet. I hoped it meant he *wasn't* guarded, but until I used the knife, I wouldn't know for sure.

I licked my lips, my heart racing, and sweat trickling down my spine. Five steps. Five more steps and he'd be within reach... and I'd be within his.

But for this to have *any* chance of working, I'd have to let him touch me.

I shuddered even as the memory of rough fingers against tender skin rose. Just for a moment I froze, unable to force my feet any closer. Then determination surged, a thick wave of strength that quickly washed away uncertainty. It didn't come from Gabe or even the wild magic that burned unseen around my wrist, but rather from deep within.

I wasn't that frightened sixteen-year-old anymore. I was a strong, capable woman who'd faced down rogue mages and the darkest of demons.

He might be stronger than me, both physically and magically, but he was also overconfident. He didn't think I was a threat—not in any way. That gave me an advantage—a brief but very important advantage.

As did the fact he was blind in the left eye.

I took a step forward and to the left. Three more, and I could knife him.

His eyes skimmed my breasts, and heat stirred in his eyes. "The bra." His voice was husky. Urgent. "Remove the bra."

I reached back and undid my bra. As I tossed it onto the

floor, Katie said, *Maelle's entered the house. Keep his attention.*

I took a deep breath and another step forward. I was now within stabbing range. For several seconds, he watched the rise and fall of my breasts with almost avid fascination. Then he reached out and, with one cold cruel hand, grabbed a breast and squeezed. Hard. I gasped in pain and fought the urge to reach for the knife. To slice away the offending fingers and then cut the satisfied smile from his lips. But I couldn't, not as long as Belle remained trapped by his power. Out of the corner of my eye, I caught a brief shimmer of movement; a heartbeat later, the duct tape binding her ankles had been sliced away.

Maelle. Relief surged, but the danger was far from over. If I did anything—if I even twitched the wrong way—he'd sense her.

His grip moved to my other breast, and I hissed in pain. He laughed, the sound sharp and familiar. The same sound had haunted my dreams for nigh on thirteen years now.

"Enjoy it while you can," I growled. "Because one day your attention and your control will slip, and then I will kill you."

"Oh, you can try, young woman, but we both know that you have neither the magic nor the strength to defeat me." He tugged on a nipple; tears stung my eyes, and I blinked them back fiercely. I wouldn't give him the satisfaction.

He laughed again. "Take off your jeans."

Belle made a long, long sound that was part muffled scream, part growl.

"It's okay, Belle," I said, holding Clayton's gaze. "Everything will be okay. Just *trust* me."

Her quick flick of understanding rolled around me. She

might not know what I planned, but at least she now knew there *was* a plan.

I took another of those deep breaths. All but one of Belle's restraints had been removed. Maelle would have her out of here any second now... but the minute she moved, the game would be up and all hell would break loose.

I had to time my assault to perfection...

I kicked off one boot. Saw the last piece of tape fall away. Kicked off my other boot. Saw a shimmer fall around Belle, cloaking her from sight. I undid the top button of my jeans. Clayton took a sharp breath, his attention on my fingers as they caught the zipper tab. I reached back with my free hand and gripped the hilt of my knife.

The chair shifted, scraping across the wooden floor, the sound sharp in the silence.

Clayton's head snapped around. "What the fuck—?"

I yanked the knife free and lunged forward; his magic burned across my hand but didn't react to the knife. A heartbeat later, it was buried deep in his gut.

He howled in fury and backhanded me so hard that I was flung back across the room. I hit the wall with a grunt of pain and slithered to the floor. Felt the fury of his approach through the floorboards and threw myself sideways. Magic seared my side, wrenching a scream from my lips. A hand grabbed me, drew me upward. I kicked him in the nuts with every ounce of strength I had. He grunted and released me with a suddenness that had me staggering backward.

His magic rose again, and I flung out a hand. Words poured from my lips, a spell I didn't know. Power swirled around me, forming a shield that met Clayton's magic and pushed it away.

He screamed and charged, punching and slapping and cursing. I ducked and backed away, but the room wasn't large enough and I wasn't fast enough. One blow got through, skimming my chin, sending me flying. I tumbled over the chair and hit the ground hard enough to see stars. Heard the thunder of his approach, smelled his utter fury, felt the rise of magic so fierce it blistered my skin. Words sprang from my lips, and magic rose. Clayton batted it aside easily.

This was the end.

Something snapped inside—the last of the inner restraints, perhaps. Wild magic surged, but it wasn't the reservation's; it was mine. It flooded my body with strength and power and then leapt from my fingers in a fierce white wave. It met Clayton's magic—caught it, held it. Held *him*. I pushed slowly to my feet. My limbs trembled, blood poured from my chin, and there were blisters and welts across my chest and stomach. I didn't feel any of it. All I felt was the power.

And it felt *so* good.

He cursed, long and loud, as he fought against my restraints, trying to attack, trying to move. Every movement tore at me, and deep in my brain the ache began, a slow beat that would soon be followed by blood if I didn't end this.

"You will eventually escape the magic that binds you, Clayton, but by then, it'll be far too late."

His gaze snapped to mine. For the very first time, a smidge of uncertainty was evident in his expression.

"Meaning you intend to kill me? And risk internment for a very long time?" He snorted. "You didn't have the courage thirteen years ago. I doubt you have it now."

"I have no intention of killing you." I grabbed the hilt of my knife and slowly withdrew it from his flesh. As a dark stain began to spread across the silk of his suit jacket, he hissed and his hands twitched. Whether he meant to grab at his stomach or me was a moot point—he was too tightly bound to do either. "But that doesn't mean you'll live to see the rise of dawn."

"The wound won't kill me," he growled. "You'd better run, dear Elizabeth, because I'm through playing games—"

"Oh, so am I." I stepped away from him. "There's one very vital thing you forgot—the wellspring in this reservation lay unprotected for over a year, and that allowed all manner of dark entities to come seeking its power. I'd wish you luck against them, Clayton, but in truth, I hope they tear you apart piece by tiny piece."

His sneer remained, despite the strengthening swirl of unease in his aura and the growing smell of his fear. "They won't get through my protections—"

"They already have. You're going to die wishing you'd never ever laid a goddamn hand on me and Belle."

And with that, I grabbed my clothes and walked out.

His rage and threats chased me out the door. I picked up the backpack and my phone, but as I walked down the steps, awareness stirred.

Maelle had returned.

Her anger—and her hunger—was so deep, so fierce, that it stained the night and burned across my skin. I didn't stop. I'd made a bargain with the devil herself, and I dared not go back on it. And, in reality, I didn't want to. He deserved the slow dance of death he was about to get. I only wished the souls of all those he'd killed could be here to witness it.

Her magic surged, and Clayton abruptly fell silent. I climbed into the SUV, started the engine, then turned around and left.

I didn't look back.

EPILOGUE

Everything that happened after that was somewhat hazy. I had no memory of reaching Monty, no memory of ambulances or doctors, and only the vaguest recollection of anxious faces staring down at me.

Consciousness was a long time returning; I stirred, aware first of a soft, slow beeping, a rhythm that not only matched the beat of my heart, but that of another.

Belle.

She was here, in the same hospital room, in the bed next to mine.

"And alive, just like you," she said softly. "But I'm going to fucking kill you when I'm feeling up to it. You scared the hell out of me, woman."

"Not as much as I scared the hell out of me." I opened my eyes and studied her. There were healing wounds on her arms and a thick bandage around her shoulder where the black knife thingie had been. The blankets were tucked up over her breasts, so I couldn't see the state of the wounds on her torso, but given her thoughts were free of pain, they were obviously on the mend.

And lord, it felt so good to have the background buzz of her thoughts in mine again.

"How long have we been here?" I added.

She grimaced. "Five fucking days. My shoulder was a mess, and you were unconscious and unresponsive to any and all treatment, and they had no idea why."

I did. It was the cost of tearing open the last of the restraints and allowing the full force of my inner wild magic free. There would be further consequences, of that I was sure. "Has there been any blowback from Canberra?"

"Not as yet." She wrinkled her nose. "Aiden and Monty have been handling all their enquiries, but they'll want to interview us eventually."

"Did Monty give them the recordings?"

"Yes. From what he said, they were rather shocked."

I snorted. "I'm not sure why. We did warn them he'd lost the plot."

"I think they were rather shocked at just how far he'd fallen, though." She hesitated, and then added softly, "Apparently, there's been no sign of either Maelle or Roger. They're sifting through Émigré's remains, looking for them."

"Monty knows she's not dead."

"So does Aiden. The council finally told him about her, though I suspect only because he demanded the truth from them."

I wrinkled my nose. I daresay that meant he and I were going to have another one of *those* conversations about honesty.

"Have they found Clayton's body?"

"Yes, although to actually define his remains as a body would apparently be something of a stretch."

"Maelle did say she was going to bathe in his blood and dine on his agony." I did my best to ignore the vague pinpricks of guilt. No matter how much they might suggest I should have at least ensured him a quick, clean death, there was no way in truth I could have ever swayed Maelle from her chosen means of revenge. "Was he found within the reservation or outside of it?"

"Out. They've declared it a 'death by unknown supernatural entity.'"

"Is Maelle on the suspect list?"

"From what Monty said, not officially—there's no evidence linking her to his murder. The High Council's investigators will probably want to talk to her if she does reappear though." Belle paused. "Do you think she will?"

"Oh, yes. She still very much wants to taste the power in my blood." Probably even more so after this whole episode.

Belle grunted. "The investigators also want you to clarify several of the statements you made on the tape."

I shrugged. It wasn't like I could do anything to stop them. I'd done what I'd done to save Belle, and now I'd have to live with the consequences. "After which, my father will no doubt send in his auditing team. The next few months are going to be filled with a never-ending procession of nosy Canberra witches."

"And probably an endless stream of possible suitors for his suddenly not so worthless daughter."

"Probably," I replied gloomily.

She laughed. "There *is* a bright side of all this that you're forgetting."

I raised an eyebrow. "And what might that be?"

Her sudden smile was filled with deep and utter joy. "We're free, Lizzie. We don't have to run anymore. We don't have to hide. For the first time in close to thirteen years, we can be who we really are. We can stop, and relax, and *live*."

I smiled and reached out for her. She leaned over and twined her fingers through mine. I didn't say anything. I didn't need to. She knew my thoughts, just as I knew hers.

For the first time in a long time, the world was our oyster.

And damned if we weren't both going to make the most of it.

ABOUT THE AUTHOR

Keri Arthur, author of the New York Times bestselling Riley Jenson Guardian series, has now written more than forty-eight novels. She's won a Romance Writers of Australia RBY Award for Speculative Fiction, and two Australian Romance Writers Awards for Scifi, Fantasy or Futuristic Romance. She was also given a Romantic Times Career Achievement Award for urban fantasy. Keri's something of a wanna-be photographer, so when she's not at her computer writing the next book, she can be found somewhere in the Australian countryside taking random photos.

for more information:
www.keriarthur.com
kez@keriarthur.com

ALSO BY KERI ARTHUR

The Witch King's Crown

Blackbird Rising (Feb 2020)

Blackbird Broken (Oct 2020)

Blackbird Crowned (June 2021)

Lizzie Grace series

Blood Kissed (May 2017)

Hell's Bell (Feb 2018)

Hunter Hunted (Aug 2018)

Demon's Dance (Feb 2019)

Wicked Wings (Oct 2019)

Deadly Vows (Jun 2020)

Magic Misled (Feb 2021)

Kingdoms of Earth & Air

Unlit (May 2018)

Cursed (Nov 2018)

Burn (June 2019)

The Outcast series

City of Light (Jan 2016)

Winter Halo (Nov 2016)

The Black Tide (Dec 2017)

Souls of Fire series

Fireborn (July 2014)

Wicked Embers (July 2015)

Flameout (July 2016)

Ashes Reborn (Sept 2017)

Dark Angels series

Darkness Unbound (Sept 27th 2011)

Darkness Rising (Oct 26th 2011)

Darkness Devours (July 5th 2012)

Darkness Hunts (Nov 6th 2012)

Darkness Unmasked (June 4 2013)

Darkness Splintered (Nov 2013)

Darkness Falls (Dec 2014)

Riley Jenson Guardian Series

Full Moon Rising (Dec 2006)

Kissing Sin (Jan 2007)

Tempting Evil (Feb 2007)

Dangerous Games (March 2007)

Embraced by Darkness (July 2007)

The Darkest Kiss (April 2008)

Deadly Desire (March 2009)

Bound to Shadows (Oct 2009)

Moon Sworn (May 2010)

Lifemate Connections (March 2007)

<u>Anthology Short Stories</u>

The Mammoth Book of Vampire Romance (2008)

Wolfbane and Mistletoe--2008

Hotter than Hell--2008

CPSIA information can be obtained
at www.ICGtesting.com
Printed in the USA
LVHW040103230620
658752LV00001B/157

9 780648 497394